The
Maximum
Contribution

by
Rick Robinson

The Maximum Contribution

By

Rick Robinson
copyright ©2008 Rick Robinson

To order additional copies of this book or for book publishing information, or to contact the author:

Publisher Page
P.O. Box 52
Terra Alta, WV 26764
www.publisherpage.com

Tel/Fax: 800-570-5951
Email: mybook@headlinebooks.com
www.headlinebooks.com

Publisher Page is an imprint of Headline Books, Inc.

ISBN 0-929915-69-0
ISBN-13: 978-0-929915-69-2

Library of Congress Control Number: 2007932125

Cover photos: Capitol by Christopher Allison, United States
Red Shoe by Nikolay Suslov, Russia

PRINTED IN THE UNITED STATES OF AMERICA

To Linda

So it is that Conservatism, throughout history, has regarded man neither as a potential pawn of other men, nor as a part of a general collectivity in which the sacredness and the separate identity of individual human beings are ignored. Throughout history, true Conservatism has been at war equally with autocrats and with "democratic" Jacobins. The true Conservative was sympathetic with the plight of the hapless peasant under the tyranny of the French monarchy. And he was equally revolted at the attempt to solve that problem by a mob tyranny that paraded under the banner of egalitarianism. The conscience of a Conservative is pricked by anyone who would debase the dignity of the individual human being. Today, therefore, he is at odds with dictators who rule by terror, and equally with those gentler collectivists who ask our permission to play God with the human race.

Senator Barry Goldwater, 1960
Conscience of a Conservative

It's not personal, Sonny. It's strictly business.

Michael Corleone, 1972
The Godfather

PROLOGUE

"Did you read the AP story in the *Times*?" Lawson demanded as he burst through the door of the office.

Frank Alley, the man behind the mahogany desk, jumped slightly in his chair. He did a little dance to keep his morning dose of hot caffeine from spilling over the edge.

"What story? What the hell are you talking about?"

Lawson flopped the front page down on the desk. "Right there." He pointed to the lengthy news article on the bottom fold of the *Washington Times*. "Read this."

Alley picked up the article and read. The look on his face went from an emotionless stare to a scowl that reddened the wrinkles protruding on his forehead. He leaned forward in his chair as he read. After each paragraph, he'd let another expletive escape under his breath. By the time he finished the article, no expletives were left for Alley to spit. "This is not good," Alley said. "This is not good at all."

"No shit. Why do you think I brought it in here?"

"Who is this guy?" Alley tapped the article.

Lawson leaned close. "A former Jackson aide. That's all I know."

"Shit! Well, you better find out more." Alley slapped the paper against the desk. "He'll be convinced this guy—this Richard Thompson—was the second gunman on the grassy knoll in Dallas. He'll flip out."

"Any chance he is?"

"Is what?"

"The second gunman." Lawson moved back. "He's running for Jackson's seat. Is there any chance he knows what's going on?"

"For God's sake." Alley rolled his eyes. "Don't you lose it on me too. Larry's just psychotic enough to pull this off, but I don't think I could take two of him. Jackson was a believer and would never leak anything he learned. Anything he knew about us—and that was a suitcase load, my friend—went to the grave with him."

Lawson stopped walking and turned to face Alley. "What about the dyke from Dayton?"

"Naw, she's too scared."

Lawson paced. "Did I tell you last week he asked me to start carrying a gun?"

"Yeah, he did the same with me." Alley grunted. "He wants all of us to."

Lawson paused by the desk. He was a lobbyist in D.C.—and lobbyists couldn't legally carry a gun. "Why the hell would I need to carry a gun?"

"Look, he's nuts," Alley said. "Remember the secretary I hired for him last month? You know, Debbie, the one with the big tits and bad perfume."

"Yeah," Lawson said. "I've not seen her around this week. Where's she been?"

"He fired her for forwarding a call from a salesperson he thought was trying to prod him for information on the deal." Alley shook his head.

"I don't know if I can last until the closing." Exasperation edged Lawson's voice.

"Once the deal goes down and we get our cut, we're done with Larry, his rants and his personal paranoias." Alley filled his lungs with air and slowly exhaled. "So, you haven't gotten a phone call from him yet either?"

"Not yet," Lawson said, "but you know he will be reading this article in the car any minute now."

"Yeah, he will. Bobby will have his hands full of more than driving this morning. And you damn sure better be ready for his superior tone on the call when it comes."

"What do you mean *I'd* better be ready? This one is in your department, Kemo Sabe. You talk him off the ledge."

"We have worked too damned hard to have this blow up now. I'll deal with Larry, but you get on the horn and find out everything you can about this Thompson guy. I want Larry to think we're ahead of the curve on this one. He'll want us to pull out all the stops. I'll get a PAC check from one of our accounts, but see if you can get a couple more from some of your other clients. And the girl, don't forget to drop a check in the basket from the girl. If this guy doesn't cave quickly, he'll want to use her."

"So then, I guess that means we'll be making a visit to the Sultry Club."

"I hope so." Alley smirked. "God, I certainly hope so."

Both men jumped with an unsure movement when Alley's phone rang. Putting it on speaker on the first ring, Alley suddenly sounded nervous. His jovial thoughts of visiting a strip club were instantly replaced with speaking to his boss, Lawrence Carpenter. "Good morning, Mr. Carpenter. I assume you are calling about this morning's *Washington Times*?"

Carpenter cut to the chase, "Of course, I'm calling about this morning's article, you nitwit. What are you doing about it? Have you ordered another sweep of the office?"

"Not yet, but Virgil has already started doing a backgrounder on Richard Thompson and the race in Kentucky's Fourth District."

"And?" asked Carpenter.

"Not much in yet," Lawson chimed in. "But he appears to be clean and one of those true believer types. Peller Marks is running the campaign, Michael Griffith on site. Polling is being done in-house at PM. We're trying to get their numbers through our trade group, but conventional wisdom is that he'll win. It's a Republican lean district to begin with and the Democratic opponent isn't very well funded and he is making a lot of mistakes early. The 527 Committees aren't too hot on the Democrat, so they may save their money for next fall and not play much. I've got a call in to the AP reporter to see what she thinks, but if we're going to move, I think we need to assume that Thompson is the front-runner."

"How quick can we get money into him?" queried Carpenter.

"We're one step ahead of you," Alley replied while quickly scanning internet hits looking for any additional information on Richard Thompson as he spoke. "I'm cutting a PAC check and Virgil is going to book a flight today.

Did you know that the Greater Cincinnati Airport is in Kentucky?"

Carpenter ignored the inane question. "I want you to go with Virgil and take a couple of personal checks with you."

"I was going to Florida to work on the deal."

"Cancel. This is far too important. I think this guy knows about the deal and is trying to queer it for all of us."

"Do you really think so?" Alley asked sincerely remembering his statement to Lawson on the same question.

"Of course I do, you dimwit. I wouldn't say it if I didn't think it. Why else would this guy bring up a stupid issue like Section 936 other than to do this to me? No, this whole damned story is timed too perfectly. He knows what we did to Jackson. I don't know how yet. Jackson may not have told him before he died, but he knows. Put a tail on that stupid bitch you hired as my secretary. Maybe she's the one. I don't care. Just do whatever you have to do to get this little piss-ant to shut up until after his election. And don't forget to sweep the offices for bugs again."

"His web site says he's got a fund raiser coming up later in the week," said Alley looking at the schedule on Thompson's campaign web site. "I'll invite myself."

"You do that. And take a check from the girl. We may need her."

"Yes, sir. Do you want me to contact Elmer Fudd?"

"Negative. I'll do it myself. I want to make sure he realizes that he and his rebel amigos have just as much to lose here as we do."

"Check."

"And don't call him Elmer Fudd to his face again," Carpenter warned. "We don't need him living under the burden of self-doubt." He paused. "No, we need him living under the mistaken impression that he's important."

CHAPTER 1

Bat Out of Hell sounded a lot more imposing when Meat Loaf was screaming out his tribute to teenage angst from the leather cockpit of a Mazda Miata.

But the Miata was three kids ago. The child seat didn't fit well on the passenger side, and, anyway, a candidate for public office couldn't be seen driving around Kentucky's Fourth Congressional District in a foreign made car. Yet, even though the "British Racing Green" Miata convertible had given way to a sensible Republican green, American made, Ford mini-van, Richard Thompson still started out every campaign trip by popping in his favorite Meat Loaf CD.

The music Thompson played from his house, down the winding hills and valleys of the Double A Highway to Ashland on the far east end of the District, was always the same. Meat Loaf's *Bat Out of Hell* woke him up in the morning and took him to Tollesboro. After a cup of coffee at Himes' General Store, John Prine *Live* got play time until he reached Ashland. On the return trip, it was a dual CD set of Warren Zevon and two cigars that got him home.

He had been making the trip at least twice a week for the past month or so, sometimes leaving the house as early as 4:30 a.m. in order to make a breakfast meeting with the Ashland Rotary or some such group. It wasn't an easy trip. The Double A Highway was one of the more treacherous roads in Kentucky. Though mostly a straight two-lane roadway, the hills and valleys of the terrain hid side roads from which slow moving cars and tractors pulling beds of freshly cut tobacco often pulled out in front of oncoming, fast moving traffic. Traveling the road in the misty dark of early morning or pitch black of late night offered the additional excitement of an occasional deer jumping onto the road and freezing in the headlights of Thompson's oncoming mini-van.

After spending weeks traveling it almost daily, Thompson became personally aware of why the newspapers routinely featured stories of people severely injured or killed on the Double A. Your senses could easily be lulled by the peaceful confines of the rural surroundings, and your foot on the gas pedal could become as heavy as your eyelids. Last week a county police officer had pulled him over in Mason County for speeding. Luckily, Thompson had gotten the endorsement from the county Fraternal Order of Police two days before. The officer had remembered having a couple of beers with him at the F.O.P. Lodge and let Thompson go with just a warning and an admonition to slow down a bit. Even with the mini-van on cruise control to slow him down in the radar of Mason County's finest, it was still a treacherous drive.

As the election drew closer, however, Thompson had more opportunities to take his eyes off the road to view the beautiful rural scenery lining the Double A Highway. These days, he had volunteers driving him around. He could spend his hours on the road listening to his music and watching as the tobacco fields passed by outside his window in a 55 m.p.h. blur of green and brown. It was almost as if he could see the burley leaves growing bigger and wider with the miles from each successive trip. And even though he still occasionally pumped imaginary brakes on the passenger side of the car in a vain attempt to assist the driver in avoiding a tractor or white tail playing chicken with his vehicle, the scenery of the trips, coupled with "his music," frequently lulled Richard Thompson into a serene sense of peace just before he jumped into the hectic stops of the day's campaign schedule.

While Thompson appreciated that the young kids driving him around had offered him a new perspective of life along the Double A (and, more importantly, kept his name off the District Court speeding dockets), he still longed for the days of his first campaign trips when he drove the road by himself. It wasn't that he disliked the kids behind the wheel. He liked them, especially the new kid, Josh. In fact, driving for a rising star in politics was how he had gotten his first job in Washington years earlier and he wanted to give these kids the same shot. Thompson was just getting tired of constantly explaining to them who Meat Loaf, John Prine, and Warren Zevon were.

But today, thank God, the driver was different.

Michael Griffith was now in town until election day and was driving his old fraternity brother and college roommate on today's campaign trip. Thompson and Griffith had been nearly inseparable since their days as roomies at the Phi Delta Theta house at Eastern Kentucky University in Richmond. Thompson looked forward to the opportunity for adult conversation and was more than excited to bring Griffith up to date on the campaign field activities.

"After all these years, you still listen to that crap," Griffith said as Thompson turned up the volume on *Paradise* by the Dashboard Light.

"Yup," was Thompson's simple reply.

"I had to listen to Meat Loaf every day we roomed together in college, and now I've got to hear him on the road, too?"

"Yup," repeated Thompson, who was now smiling a wide grin.

"Boy," mused Griffith, "What in the hell do you think the voters of Kentucky would say if they knew that their next Congressman knew all the words to every song on this CD?"

"I don't know—do you think that we ought to play *Two Out of Three Ain't Bad* as the background music for our next campaign ad?" Thompson teased.

Griffith mustered up his best announcer voice and mocked a campaign ad. "When you cast your vote in next month's special election for United States Congress remember, you *want* him, you *need* him, but there ain't no way you ever will *elect* him. Well don't feel sad, 'cause two out of three ain't bad. I'm Meat Loaf and I approve this message. Naw…doesn't work."

The pair laughed out loud like they were still in the living room of the frat house.

"And to think I'm paying you good money for this kind of abuse," said Thompson.

"You haven't seen abuse yet. Wait until you see what I have planned for your opponent. He sleeps with the fishes."

CHAPTER 2

Richard Thompson and Michael Griffith were the perfect pair for politics.

Thompson was the consummate candidate. He knew the policy behind nearly every bill passed by the United States Congress over the past century. He was great in a crowd, always said the right thing to the right person at the right time, and was once described on the campaign trail by a national reporter as a Bill Gates look-alike. Thompson never really liked the description and even tried to comb his sandy brown hair differently to avoid the resemblance. But deep down inside, he knew that from the top of his wire-rimmed glasses to the tip of his black wing-tipped shoes, it was a pretty accurate description.

Richard Thompson went through life with a soundtrack playing in his head. Whether it was Meat Loaf, John Prine, Warren Zevon or some obscure barroom performer from Key West, Thompson was constantly humming a tune to fit the current situation in his life. His good-natured irritation with his friend was further fueled by the fact that Thompson still hummed a tune written by one of those barroom performers in Key West some twenty years ago, comparing Thompson's good-guy image to those of The Lone Ranger and The Cisco Kid.

"Good Lord. If you're going to be constantly humming a song, at least hum the ones written about someone else!" Griffith once told Thompson.

Thompson had waited a full two minutes before he started humming it again.

Michael Griffith was, at least superficially, the exact opposite of Richard Thompson. His jeans, snake-skin cowboy boots and rumpled shirts stood in stark contrast to Thompson's perfectly cut suits and French cuffed shirts. He was taller than Thompson and didn't have to worry about how reporters described his hair. When his dark locks began receding several years ago, Griffith began shaving his head on a daily basis. The slick head, dark eye brows and furrowed forehead gave him a look which often scared the living hell out of campaign volunteers and produced a similarly intimidated reaction from opponents.

Many years ago, Griffith won a race while refusing to shave his beard during the last month of the campaign. And so, as each successive year's election day neared, his superstitions would get the best of him and he would shave his head, but refuse to shave his beard. By the time election eve rolled around, Griffith would look less like a Washington power player and more like Yul Brynner in a spaghetti western.

Scrappy looks aside, Mike Griffith was admired by friends and feared by foes as one of the best political campaign consultants in the business. His reputation came for good reason. He could shut himself into a room with nothing more than some simple demographic research, past election results, a pad of paper, a calculator and a bottle or two of Maker's Mark and emerge days later with a winning campaign plan for the worst of candidates.

But having him on your team wasn't without its baggage. Michael Griffith was more than a little gruff. He could be an outright pit bull chomping at the tail ends of his opponents and at times be even tougher on his own candidates. Thompson often teased Griffith about how his frank nature had gotten him fired by more than one client who was more concerned about having his political ego stroked than winning.

Politicians are known for the books they read and re-read for guidance. These are the books which define their true beings and guide them when they look for focus. Lee Atwater, who ran the 1988 White House victory for George H.W. Bush, was known to re-read Machiavelli's *The Prince* annually and carried a worn-out Cliff's Notes version with him on the trail during campaign crunch time. James Carville was said to have based a large part of President Clinton's two campaigns for the White House on Sun-tzu's *Art of War.*

As they drove up and down the hills of the Double A Highway, the briefcases on the back seat of the mini-van held the secrets to Michael Griffith's and Richard Thompson's inner beings. Griffith had scripts to *The Godfather I, II and III* in his brief case, with dog-eared pages and yellow highlights marking passages which embodied Griffith's political rules of battle. Thompson kept a highlighted copy of Barry Goldwater's 1960's manifesto on right-wing thought, *Conscience of a Conservative,* in his.

It was the differences between the highlighted lines in their respective favorite books that Griffith admired in Thompson. Michael Griffith wanted to win and knew how to win, but Richard Thompson **believed**. He believed in the democratic experiment. "That small-town hick actually believes he can make a difference in the lives of people," Griffith would tell folks as he stood at the back of the room watching Thompson work a crowd.

Griffith was a big fan of the trilogy of movies produced by Francis Ford Coppola based on the novel by Mario Puzzo about the Corleone Family. Actually, "big fan" wouldn't be a fair characterization of Griffith's feelings about *The Godfather.* It bordered on obsession. Even though he had each movie on video (and, later on DVD), every time they were shown on late-night commercial television, he stayed up and watched to the end. He had an autographed photo of James Caan as Sonny Corleone on his desk and one of Al Pacino as Michael Corleone on his wall. When his cell phone rang, it played the Godfather theme.

Griffith had concluded that the Corleone Family members were the ultimate political consultants in America. They were smart and powerful. They refused to lose. They made decisions which literally meant life and death. "If Michael Corleone had an office in D.C.," he said once, "he'd be the King of K Street instead of the Godfather. And just as many people would want him dead."

Loyalty was the foundation for Griffith's Godfather Rules of Battle. In the first Godfather movie, the importance of loyalty is stressed. Guests come to the Corleone wedding reception to pay their respects to Vito Corleone (or to ask a favor, "for no Sicilian can deny a favor to a friend on the day of his daughter's wedding"). One person who wanted to see the Godfather on this important day was Luca Brasi, the Corleone family's chief muscle man. He stood in line outside Vito Corleone's study, memorizing the words he would say to his Don when they met. He could have asked for any favor and it would have been granted. Instead he simply pledged to Vito Corleone his "ever-ending loyalty."

Griffith knew that a candidate in today's political marketplace can purchase any expertise under the sun. Consultants, staff, pollsters—all are bought and sold as quickly and often as baseball cards on e-Bay. Today, candidates even pay people to do things that volunteers did in the old days, like stuff and stamp direct mail. What a candidate cannot purchase is **loyalty**. It must be earned and it must be unconditional. Like Luca Brasi, Griffith knew that his loyalty was his number one asset in politics. Through the highs and lows, Michael Griffith learned to stand by his candidates.

When Thompson had run for city council in Ludlow, Kentucky, Griffith had come to town and run the campaign as if it were New Hampshire in March of a Presidential year. The two of them, along with Ann, had knocked on the doors of literally every voter in the small Kentucky river town. They had used designs from old winning Griffith-run campaigns for the yard signs and they had printed recycled Griffith campaign literature on their home PC. By the time election day rolled around, Richard Thompson knew literally everyone who voted in the election and they knew Richard Thompson. He became the top vote getter for council, surpassing some old guard councilmen who had served for decades. The entire endeavor cost less than a couple of hundred bucks and Thompson had paid for the whole effort out of his own pocket.

But, for Michael Griffith, this trip to Kentucky was very, very different.

This was a race for a seat in the United States Congress.

This was the big leagues. And they both knew it.

When Representative Garrett Jackson had died of a heart attack early in his 9th term in Congress, Thompson had been far from the favorite to be chosen by the Republicans as their candidate in the special election to fill the remaining year and six months of Jackson's term.

The Democrats chose their candidate quickly. By picking William Pope, the D's thought that they had their ideal candidate to capture a seat that had been held by the R's for decades. Pope was a moderate businessman, with the backing of some country-club, Chamber-types, who had been knocking around the fringes of local politics for years. He had written a lot of checks to candidates and had even spent some time on the party's state executive committee. But he had never before put his name on the ballot. Now, the aging community leader was at the end of his business career and, as many in his station of life do, he was looking to start a career in politics. Believing that Pope was all flash and no substance, Griffith was drooling to run a campaign against him.

"Billy Boy sleeps with the fishes" quickly became Griffith's mantra upon learning of Pope's nomination. "His depth on the issues is about as thin as his support in the party. He's one of those liberals Senator Goldwater spoke about as being too broadminded to take his own side in a quarrel."

But before he could figuratively send Pope to sleep with the fishes, Griffith would first have to get his underdog, small town city councilman friend the Republican nomination.

The G.O.P.'s nomination was up for grabs. Thompson and two others were seeking the Republican nomination—a state senator and another local lawyer. Griffith used his 1998 Iowa Caucus experience to line up support from the Republican chairmen and vice chairs from the 22 counties which make up Kentucky's Fourth Congressional District. He'd go into a county with no fanfare and spend a couple of hours at the local greasy spoon and (where it wasn't a dry county) at the honky tonks, learning all he could about the local scene.

Griffith would also go to the folks supporting the opponent and befriend them. Being somewhat of a big-time political star, it wasn't hard to get in to see these people. No one could turn down someone who regularly appears on *Cross Fire*.

A candidate, with less faith in his consultant, might have felt uneasy at his consultant spending time with the enemy. When Griffith had used this tactic while working for other candidates, he had eased their jitters by explaining to them what Michael Corleone once said to ease Frankie "Five Angels" Pantangeli's concerns about his close relationship with rival Hyman Roth: "My father taught me many things here — he taught me in this room. He taught me — keep your friends close but your enemies closer." Obviously, Griffith didn't need to assure his old college roommate about his loyalty, but he had repeated the rule to Thompson several times anyway.

And so it went that, by the time Richard Thompson would finally pay a visit to the county party officials, both Griffith and Thompson knew the pulse of the county — who was supporting whom for county sheriff, when the tobacco crop would be in this year, and who the locals were sleeping with.

"It doesn't matter if you're in Atlanta, Georgia or the thriving metropolis of Augusta, Kentucky," Griffith said to Thompson. "If you're in the South and you tell the cook at the 'Sweet n' Eat' that you love her green beans, she'll tell you everything going on in the town."

When the Republican chairs of the 22 counties in the Fourth Congressional District met as a nominating committee, Thompson was a slam dunk. His support was so strong that the other two candidates declined their nominations and Richard Thompson became the Republican candidate for the United States Congress by acclamation on the motion of one of his opponents.

The moment Griffith delivered the nomination; he looked over and winked at his old pal. Now, it was Thompson's turn to go to work. He, Ann and the kids went to the podium and waved to the crowd like they were always meant to be there. After congratulating his opponents for conducting a clean and spirited race, and thanking those who had supported him, Thompson did that thing that he had always been able to do so well. He went about owning the room.

"When I worked in Washington for Congressman Jackson, Ann and I had the opportunity to go to the White House one evening and watch President Ronald Reagan return from one of his trips to Europe. You remember the scenes of his arrivals, throngs of screaming supporters waving flags. We had a friend who worked for the President, so we went down to the White House quite often to watch arrivals. This one night, though, was different.

"It was very early in the morning—about 2:00 am. There was no traffic around the White House and no throng of reporters shouting questions or supporters waving flags. There were just a couple of us standing there in the dark of the south lawn waiting for the helicopters to approach. First, you hear them. The thumping sounds of rotor blades cut through the silence of the night. Then, you see lights from three helicopters coming down the Potomac River and making a north turn around the Washington Monument. Until that moment, you don't know which helicopter the President is in. But then, as they make the turn, two choppers break away and Marine One, carrying the leader of the free world, slowly approaches the South Grounds.

"The chopper lands on a dime, the door pops open, and a lone United States Marine emerges and snaps a salute to guard the door. And then…wow…I remember like it was yesterday, President Reagan steps to the door and returns the salute."

Thompson was *on* today. With Ann at his side, he was making eye contact around the room as he continued to weave his story. In return, there wasn't one eye in the room that was not following his every move.

"Then, the most remarkable thing happened. President and Mrs. Reagan looked to the rope line, walked toward Ann and me, and the President stuck out his hand. And at that moment, I met a man who I believe was the greatest president of our lifetime."

The applause wasn't forced like you see at some political speeches. It was real. These folks were hanging on Thompson's every word and he was clearly in "the zone."

"I remember that night and I still get chills down my spine."

He paused and took a deep reflective breath.

"I look at Washington today and I get a chill down my spine, but not the chills which excite me. It's no longer Reagan's shining city on the hill." His voice rose in intensity. "It's a city that needs the homegrown values of a kid from Ludlow, Kentucky."

The room roared. They stood up and shouted.

Thompson looked at Griffith and made eye contact. The same eye contact that Griffith had seen Thompson give so often to others was finally directed at him. No words needed to be said. Griffith allowed himself a simple moment to take in Thompson's private gaze, winked back and then slowly, quietly made his way out the back door.

Griffith knew what happened from here: personal background, strong positions from "The List" and the "warm and fuzzy" closer. It was time to step outside. The race was far from over. It had just begun.

But as he stepped outside the meeting hall to take a smoke, he heard another round of applause.

I pledge my ever ending loyalty.

CHAPTER 3

"Right after we cross the Lewis County line, make a left at the flashing yellow light by the gas station," Thompson told Griffith as they approached their first campaign stop of the day.

"You sure that kid Josh was able to get everyone in the press out here to the boonies?" Griffith asked.

"A little touchy that I have a college student handling our press? You forget how old you were when the NRCC gave you your first shot. Don't worry, he'll be loyal," Thompson replied.

Thompson and Ann had hired Josh Barkman to be the "kid" of the campaign and had great confidence in his skills and commitment. Deep inside, however, Thompson wondered if he and Griffith had ever looked as young as this kid.

"Kid. God I'm starting to sound like my Dad," Thompson thought to himself.

Still, Thompson could remember being 21 and thinking how cool he looked in khakis, penny loafers, a light blue button down and a navy blue blazer. But, for the life of him, Thompson couldn't quite remember looking as baby-faced as his young, frizzy blond-haired press secretary, political director and general campaign go-fer.

"I know I can teach him to be loyal. But this is a special, six months into a presidential term, with one in Ohio to follow in about a month. Every talking head in the country will be watching this race as a test for what will happen up in Dayton," said Griffith. "You're supposed to win, you know."

"So?" replied Thompson.

"So? Pal, the national news will be calling this race and the margin referendum on the President. I mean, think of it, we've got national publications and dailies coming to Tollesboro freakin' Kentucky to cover your special for Congress."

"Okay, I'm still not getting it."

"They aren't here for you, Rick. They just don't have anything better to do than look for a train wreck. One wrong step by a green press secretary and the media could try to make this a race just to rub the President's nose in it. For God's sake, they're covering this race on the Sunday morning talking heads shows." Griffith paused. "Besides that, we don't know him. I'm not sure if we should let him in The Family yet. Remember, we can't let anyone outside The Family know what we're thinking."

"That's why you're here buddy," Thompson said with a sarcastic scowl. "You're doing a great job pumping me up right before I meet the voters." Thompson leaned forward and turned up Meat Loaf. "You'll teach him about the 'Family Business.' Now, let me get my game face on."

Throughout the Godfather trilogy, the nefarious activities of the many crime organizations are referred to as The Family Businesses. Treating politics like The Family Business was a Rule of Battle which Griffith placed second only to loyalty in importance when describing how to run campaigns.

When Michael Corleone announced to the family he would kill the man who had attempted to assassinate his father, he was teased by his brother Sonny that this was business and he was taking it personal. Michael's response assured Sonny it wasn't personal, "It's strictly business."

Griffith believed that campaigns, like the Corleone crime operations, had to be run like a business. Too many strategy decisions in campaigns are made on the basis of emotions. Griffith's goal in each campaign was to take emotion out of politics and make decisions with the same steely-eyed determination Michael Corleone had used in killing a rival crime figure and his Irish Cop bodyguard.

The last mile or so into Lewis County, neither of them spoke as Thompson collected his thoughts and put on his game face. He was glad that Griffith always spoke his mind; he just wished sometimes that Griffith would pick better times to do so.

All right, put Griffith out of your mind. His name's not on the fucking ballot. These are your folks. These are the folks who are going to send you and Ann to Washington. Come on, boy, it's show time!

The car came to a stop on the gravel outside Thompson's unofficial eastern Kentucky headquarters, Himes' General Store. The store itself was right out of a Norman Rockwell painting, an old white wood-frame building that was once used as a car garage. The three aisles created by metal shelving units contained the staples of life for the good folks of Tollesboro, Kentucky. The floors had crevices worn in the wood from where decades of customers had walked up and down those aisles buying everything from groceries to guns. One of the coolers along the back wall had gallons of milk on the top shelf and Styrofoam cups filled with dirt and fishing worms on the bottom one. The store also had a lunch-counter and a couple of booths where you could sip a freshly-brewed cup of coffee. Those booths were a comfortable place for Thompson and the store owner, Jeff Himes, to talk about their two favorite topics, politics and baseball.

Jeff's wife Suzanne, Jeff and forty-some of their customers from Tollesboro were waiting at the front door when Thompson stepped out of the car. "How all y'all doin'," shouted Thompson as he stepped from the car and gave Suzanne a hug. A true Southerner knew that "all y'all" was the plural of "y'all."

"You didn't bring Ann and the kids," scolded Suzanne.

"And let them be at the mercy of these ugly press folks? Why, you've got to be kidding," joked Thompson pointing at the row of reporters standing in the haze of cigarette smoke over by the lunch counter watching the festivities.

"Mornin,' boys and girls!" he said as he waved to the road weary press corps who had somehow found their way up and down the hills of the Double A Highway to the store. "You wanted to see the Fourth Congressional District. This is it. Welcome to America!" Then,

Thompson started slowly making his way through the crowd of locals—one firm, eye-contacted handshake at a time.

As Thompson worked the crowd, Griffith made his way over to the reporters and young Josh. "He's just kidding around, guys. Did you have any problem finding this place?"

"No, sir, they got perfect directions," Josh interjected, feeling the lack of confidence in Griffith's tone.

Two handguns and a rifle sitting on the check-out counter caught the eye of one of the reporters. "Jesus Christ, are they making them check their guns at the door?" he gasped, looking for the nearest exit.

"Naw," said the lady behind the lunch counter. "It's the damned Brady Bill. Folks buy their guns and we gotta keep 'em here for three days 'til the government says folks can take 'em home. F.B.I. oughta call me. I could tell them who in this town oughta have a gun and who shouldn't," she laughed.

"I bet you make the best green beans in all Lewis County," said Griffith to the woman.

As she winked in confirmation to Griffith, Jeff and Suzanne hushed the crowd and told them stories of how they had first gotten to know Thompson years ago when he had worked for Congressman Jackson. They explained how Thompson had helped them out of a jam, and how he had stayed in touch after he had come back home to Kentucky. "He's our kind of folk and we need him representing us up in Washington," Jeff said.

The crowd applauded that polite applause you hear from people who know they are expected to applaud.

"I grew up about 70 miles down river from here in a little town called Ludlow," said Thompson as he started his talk.

"Never heard of it," shouted an old man in the back.

Thompson snapped back immediately, "Don't worry, Pops. No one in Ludlow has ever heard of Tollesboro either!"

Everyone laughed, including the old man.

"But I'll tell you this—both little towns have a lot in common. They both are towns where things like democracy, liberty, and freedom still mean something, where hard work is a virtue that we instill into our kids. These are places where the churches are filled on Sundays and Wednesdays."

"You know, you and I are not going to agree on every issue I vote on in Congress, so I'll make you no other promise than this: when I'm making up my mind on how to vote, I'll do so using those same values we learned here in our homes in Ludlow and Tollesboro, Kentucky."

Thompson was looking into the eyes of the folks in the crowd with a gaze of sincerity that captured more than their interest. He was earning their respect. Several of the heads in the crowd nodded approval as he spoke.

"He's good," whispered Vicki Prichard from the Associated Press.

"Good, hell! Hold on to your ass, Vic, he's just getting started," grinned Griffith as he fumbled in his shirt pocket for his pack of cigarettes. "God, I love places where they encourage people to smoke."

"You're in 'baccy country, hun, smoke 'em if ya got 'em" whispered the old lady behind the counter as she pulled a lighter from the pocket of her stained apron and fired one up herself. "I like that boy. He don't talk down to us. He'll do good fer us in Warshington."

Thompson gave a shortened version of his normal stump speech. He didn't need more. Jeff and Suzanne had hand picked the attendees to make sure the faces were friendly. Still, even if these folks were friendlies when he started, they were warriors when he finished. They came in because Jeff had asked them to come and look happy. They were leaving as part of the Thompson Team.

Thompson was pumped. When he finished his speech, he walked through the crowd again shaking hands. He gave Jeff and Suzanne each a big hug and whispered something in their ears.

"Don't worry, Rick," Jeff said with a smile. "We're going to win this thing like the Reds in '90, wire-to-wire, baby!"

"Okay, troops, want to go outside and ask Mr. Thompson some questions?" asked Josh as Thompson led the crowd from the wood floors of the general store to the gravel of the street. Thompson took off his sport coat and tossed it to Josh. "Who's first?" he said as he loosened up his tie and started to roll up his sleeves in the hot summer sun.

"Why here? Why did you want us to come to Tollesboro, Kentucky, to meet you for an interview?" asked the reporter from the *Washington Post.*

"Because I wanted to bring you folks to one of the places in America that still doesn't have cell phone coverage," laughed Thompson to snickers from the press crew.

"Seriously, these folks are why I'm running for Congress. Where I'm from, up in Northern Kentucky, we're doing all right economically. Unemployment is down, we're near statistical full employment and growth continues in double digit annual numbers. But as you drive along to our next stop you'll see the only two factories in this county. Both are shut down. You know that hellish road you just drove down? I know some folks in this county who drive that road every day for a job in Northern Kentucky, Cincinnati or West Virginia. We've got to work to bring jobs back to places like Lewis County, Kentucky."

"How do you intend to do that?" Vicki Prichard asked.

"Tax incentives," snapped Thompson. "Encourage some company to come in and open one of those factories by offering them job training credits and, if they keep the factory open for ten years, give the investors zero capital gains."

"Any idea how you're going to pay for that?" was the cute AP reporter's follow up.

"We've got to put the entire United States Tax Code on the table. We've got provisions in the Code that have been around so long, we no longer know why they are there. Give me the tax ax and I'll find money by cutting tax provisions that have long since lost their relevance."

"For instance?" she asked.

"Section 936 is a good example of a provision that needs to go. We're giving tax credits to American companies to create jobs in the Caribbean Basin. Think of that. The American government is doing in Puerto Rico what we say we don't have the money to do in Lewis County, Kentucky. It doesn't make sense to me."

"What makes you think you can kill one of Washington's sacred cows? There are a lot of big companies, especially drug companies, which would throw all their influence against such a change."

"I care about the folks here in Lewis County, not the lobbyists inside The Beltway." He paused. "Somebody's got to do it. Might as well be me."

"You talked about a lot of issues in there, Mr. Thompson. How would you describe your political philosophy?" asked another reporter.

"Let the government help those who can't help themselves, and get the hell out of the way for the rest of us," said Thompson.

"So where does that put you?" was the follow up.

Thompson smiled. "Guys, I may be the last person in the Republican Party who is willing to call himself a Barry Goldwater Republican."

"Using Federal tax incentives for jobs doesn't sound much like a Goldwater platform to me," the gal from the AP challenged.

After a pause Thompson added, "Well, because I grew up like these folks, I probably got a little mean streak of populism in me too."

"A Goldwater Populist…that's certainly a unique political characterization," said the reporter.

"In the words of the late Senator, 'think of me as a choice, not an echo,'" replied Thompson. "I'll live with being called unique."

Griffith finished his cigarette and tossed it to the ground. "Stop's over, gang. We'll see you at the Republican Women's Club meeting tonight in Ashland," he said as he stomped it out with his cowboy boots.

"Great stop, Boss," said Josh with the enthusiasm of a young volunteer kissing up to one who would hopefully be his future employer. "I'll give them the normal stuff off your web site," he added. Josh had spent many hours and a significant amount of campaign funds in developing www.richardthompsonforcongress.com.

"Thanks, Josh," said Griffith. "We'll see you in Ashland. What time are we due at the radio station?"

"4:30. I'll see you there. I'm going over to Huntington first to check on our TV buys. For all the cash we're going to be dropping on those bastards over the next couple of weeks, I should be able to get some coverage of tonight's stop."

Thompson had barely shut the door to the mini-van when Griffith started in on him.

"Section 936 of the United States Tax Code…936 of the Code…where in the hell did that come from?"

"What's wrong?" asked Thompson who was startled by Griffith's anger.

"Jesus, Rick, we talked about this. I know you're a wonk at heart, but fight the urge to be a geek on the trail. On the campaign trail you've got to be relevant. People on the trail don't give a happy horse shit about Section 936 of the Code."

"Lighten up, Griff," Thompson replied. "I didn't talk about it in the store. One of the D.C. reporters asked how I'd pay for my jobs bill and I told her."

"Bullshit," barked Griffith. "You replied to that girl like you've just been waiting for a moment like this to play this issue."

"Maybe I have been. Remember—let your candidate talk about the issues for which he feels passionate."

"Yeah, but Section 9 thirty-whatever of the United States Tax Code was never an issue we discussed—ever."

"Come on, Griff, you don't think I'd let you take all my issues to use for your other candidates. I was saving one or two for me. They'll love this on my blog. Where'd you hide my John Prine *Live* ?"

"Man, I don't give a happy damn about your CDs or your blog," said Griffith as he rolled down the window. "You've got me so riled up, the vein in my neck is about to pop. I need a smoke."

Griffith had no clue his wasn't the only blood pressure to be elevated by Thompson's quick press conference at Himes' General Store. Tomorrow morning, when the newspapers hit the stands in D.C., there would be three men in business suits boiling over about Thompson's tax theories. The difference would be they couldn't care less about how many votes Thompson's words would garner, or fail to garner, in Kentucky's Fourth Congressional District.

CHAPTER 4

There is one thing which you can count on.

Summers suck in Washington, D.C.

If you think you've traveled to places that are hot and humid, spend a few summer months in the nation's capital and your opinion of those other places will quickly change. The temperatures in Washington regularly top 90 degrees and the humidity there rarely falls below the same number. When Richard Thompson first went to Washington he lived under the mistaken impression that 100% humidity meant it was raining. It doesn't. It just means that it's July in Washington.

In the heat of mid-day, the blacktop on the streets is so hot and mushy that a person's shoes can leave noticeable footprints as they walk across the street. And, don't even try to cross that same street in high heels. High heels will sink into the blacktop on a woman's first step off the curb. It's so bad most women in town wear tennis shoes with their dark business suits to avoid the sinking heel syndrome. Of course, they don't really care too much about how the tennis shoes look because, if there's no good reason to leave the office and go outside, they don't. It's so damned hot that you get covered in sweat with just a five-minute walk down the street.

To make matters worse, the summer heat intensifies the smells of D.C. The blacktop on the street smells. The dumpsters in the alley smell. The cabbies who refuse to roll up their windows and turn on their air conditioning smell. The only mitigating factor is that, by the end of one of these hot summer days, you'll probably smell too.

If the summer heat in D.C. isn't enough to shut down the city, there are the tourists.

Everywhere.

Tens of thousands of them.

Everywhere.

Every age, color, nationality.

Everywhere.

Mini-vans filled with kids are constantly circling the busy city streets looking for precious parking places. Gaggles of families are standing on the Mall trying to locate "The" Smithsonian and not realizing there are nearly 20 separate museums which make up the system. There are so many lines at so many security systems at so many doorways that a large part of the family vacation is spent standing in line to go through metal detectors.

On Capitol Hill, the same cattle call is taking place. Tourists are dropping by the offices of those they voted for (or not) in order to get passes to the galleries in the House and Senate. If they are lucky, a staffer or intern will escort them over to the Rotunda for a quick tour. In the summer, Congressional staffers go from being under-paid personal aides to overpaid tour guides.

But, don't be fooled by the endless lines of tired, smelly tourists. Even at the height of the summer vacation season, Washington, D.C. is a business town. It is the business side of Washington, D.C. which tourists ought to be glad they never see.

Business in D.C. smells just as bad as the city itself in summer, but the lines are not nearly as long.

The three branches of the United States government being centered within blocks of each other has spawned a cottage industry of lobby firms, trade associations, embassies, do-gooder corps and corporate government affairs headquarters.

The heads of D.C. corporate offices are high up in most business organizational charts. While most Harvard Business School graduates don't understand what happens in Washington, they do know what happens in the nation's capital can impact their bottom lines. So, their boards are afraid to be without the advice and counsel of someone who knows the town and they pay big bucks for someone who knows it well. They pay big bucks for small offices overlooking K Street. They pay big bucks for salaries. They pay big bucks for expense accounts. They even pay big bucks for the cars and drivers which tote the lobbyists around town to their high-powered lunches, meetings and receptions.

Spending time driving around D.C., one would think the city boasts more black Lincoln Town Cars per capita than any other place in the world.

Moms and dads on the Tour Mobile are constantly turning their heads sideways as they pass the dark Lincolns on Constitution Avenue, trying to peek inside the tinted windows and wondering out loud to their children what important person is sitting in the back seat reviewing the morning paper under the car's custom installed reading light. Unfortunately, they would shudder at the dark topics often being discussed behind the black glass of those Lincolns.

This was one of those mornings.

As one particular black Lincoln Town Car made its way across the Roosevelt Bridge from Roslyn, a tall grey haired man, his black pin-striped Armani suit jacket hung neatly on the side hook, sipped his Starbucks coffee and read the *Washington Times* story on the bottom fold about a special election in Kentucky. He kept lightly kicking the back of the seat in front of him, mumbling inaudible vulgarities, as he read each line.

Stumping on a Sacred Cow
Congressional Hopeful Takes on Tax Code
By Vicki Prichard, AP

Tollesboro, Kentucky. The special election in Kentucky's Fourth Congressional District being held to fill the unexpired term of the late Congressman Garrett Jackson is being fought over the most mundane of tax issues. Congressional Candidate Richard Thompson (R-Ky) said he would repeal Section 936 of the Tax Code to bring jobs to rural Kentucky.

"We've got to put the entire United States Tax Code on the table," Thompson, a Republican from Northern Kentucky, told a crowd yesterday at Himes' General Store while campaigning for Kentucky's 4th District Congressional seat.

Against the backdrop of the country store—a longtime staple in the town's humble economy— Thompson told the crowd that he's ready to pick up the "tax ax" and sever irrelevant provisions from the Code in order to offer tax incentives to attract companies to open businesses in economically strapped regions like Lewis County.

"Give me the tax ax and I'll find money by cutting tax provisions which have long since lost their relevance," Thompson said.

As an example, Thompson offered an obscure provision—Section 936—as an archaic and damaging provision that needs to go.

Section 936 allows tax credits to American companies to create jobs in the Caribbean Basin.

"Think of that," Thompson said. "The American government is doing in Puerto Rico what we say we don't have the money to do in Lewis County, Kentucky. It doesn't make sense to me."

Enacted to encourage the economic development of Puerto Rico, Guam and the U.S. Virgin Islands, Section 936 is among several provisions that allow U.S.—based companies under these code sections the ability to repatriate Puerto Rico source income free of U.S. taxes. Ultimately, those companies could bring money earned in Puerto Rico back to operations in the mainland with no tax penalty.

Thompson's opponent in the election, Democratic businessman William Pope, when asked about Section 936 repeal, stated that he was not familiar with the issue, but was running on a campaign to bring good paying jobs to Kentucky. "My years of business experience put me in a better position to accomplish this than my opponent."

Thompson, 47, is a self-described 'Goldwater Republican' from Northern Kentucky, an area of the state that has maintained economic growth and low unemployment figures. He credits his roots in the small river town of Ludlow, Kentucky as helping him relate to the plight of rural communities.

"Because I grew up like these folks, I've probably got a little mean streak of populism in me too," Thompson said.

"Ever been to Kentucky, Bobby?" the man asked his young African-American driver.

"No sir. I had an uncle who was stationed at Fort Campbell about ten years ago, but I never went to visit him. I always wanted to go to the Kentucky Derby, though. Just once, to see what it's like to go to put a double down at a big league track," replied Bobby, knowing the man really didn't care about his response.

"It's overrated. I'd trade my table at the Derby for my table in the club house at Keeneland for the Bluegrass Stakes any day," the man said with no emotion as he hit the speed dial on the car's custom speaker phone.

"Yes, sir." *You smug sonofabitch.* Bobby wished he had the balls to say it out loud, but he was paid well to drive around people like Lawrence Carpenter.

The phone picked up on the first ring. "Good morning, Mr. Carpenter. I assume you're calling about this morning's *Washington Times*?"

Carpenter cut to the chase, "Of course, I'm calling about this morning's article, you nitwit. What are you doing about it? Have you ordered another sweep of the office?"

As Lawson and Alley had assumed would happen, the call went downhill from there. Carpenter leveled detailed instructions, planning the next moves for Lawson and Alley as a field commander positions his soldiers. And, like loyal soldiers, the pair conspired on how to follow Carpenter's orders to the tee. There was far too much at stake at this point of the battle for anyone to not know exactly what was expected of them.

William Pope threw the morning press clips across the room. Before they had even hit the wall, he was laying into his staff.

"What the hell am I paying you people for?" he shouted. "I look like a freakin' idiot in these articles. Why didn't I know about Section 936 of the Tax Code? Why can't I find an issue like that to talk about? Does Michael Griffith have to out-maneuver you guys on everything?"

"Washington is filled with stapler throwers," whispered one of the staffers to a volunteer as Pope stormed out of the room. "There was this one guy from Ohio who used to throw his telephone receiver during staff meetings when he didn't like the answer someone in his crew was giving him. Everyone knew exactly how far the cord reached and sat just outside its radius."

"Maybe," said the volunteer. "But Pope sure has a weird way of showing his appreciation for the work we're doing."

While Lawrence Carpenter continued to give instructions to his minions, a middle-aged woman living north of Kentucky's Fourth Congressional District sat in front of her computer staring blankly at the screen. Since reading the online version of that morning's *Washington Times*, she had logged on and off the web site multiple times, unsure as to whether she actually wanted to proceed any further. After all, the events of the past several months had forever changed her life. Perhaps, her past was best if it simply reamained her past. Still, as she began to slowly type an anonymous entry onto the blog, she knew her own character would not allow something like what happened to her to happen to someone else.

CHAPTER 5

Richard Thompson stood in the shower of his master suite and looked out the glass door at the beautiful woman he called his wife putting on her makeup whom . He closed his eyes as the warm water hit his tired body and he daydreamed about the day Griffith had introduced them at a Republican fundraiser for Ann's boss in D.C.

At the time, Thompson was a law student and Legislative Assistant (a promotion from his job as Legislative Correspondent— he now actually talked to and advised the Congressman on policy). She was the secretary to a freshman Florida Congresswoman.

She was a tall slender blond, with breasts that stole the attention of every man in a 100 foot radius when she walked into a room. He was...well, a policy wonk, true-believer geek who looked like Bill Gates.

So, when Griffith introduced the pair, it was no surprise that Ann was unimpressed. Thompson, however, was smitten. He was a sucker for pretty eyes and Ann had the most beautiful eyes he had ever seen. They were bluish green and seemed to change hues with her mood, but it wasn't their color that captured his stare. They conveyed, along with their color, the look of a woman confident in her appearance and stature in life. Yes, Thompson was smitten. He was so smitten, that in a very un-Thompson like move, he kept dropping by her office to say hello until he worked up the nerve to ask her out.

He caught her in a weak moment one day and she agreed to go out. Thompson had something that Ann wanted desperately he would jokingly tell people in later years. Not stability. Not access to power. Actually, what he had were two backstage passes to the Bruce Springsteen concert at Madison Square Garden in New York.

As they talked on the train ride to New York, Thompson looked into Ann's eyes more than he did at her breasts, something new for one of her dates. As the rails rumbled beneath them that evening, Ann felt what people in Kentucky's Fourth Congressional District would later feel when they met her future-husband for the first time. This was someone who believed he could make a difference. This was someone who could look into their eyes and find their very existence. This is someone they could believe in as well. This was someone Ann could believe in.

If Thompson was smitten before that train ride, he was committed by the time they got to the concert. For her part, Ann gave her heart to Richard Thompson that night. After the concert, rather than taking the late train back to D.C., she looked back into his eyes and suggested they get a room for the evening and catch a morning train home.

That night they discovered another personal attribute which would keep them together over the years. As they entered the room at the Hilton across the street from the Garden, there wasn't the usual uncomfortable first-time feeling of who would do what. When the door closed behind them, nothing had ever seemed more natural and comfortable to both of them.

It was more than a night of desire. True, it was a night when each seemed to spark the other to a sexual climax never experienced before. But it was also a night when both seemed to know instinctively this night was the first in a lifetime of passion.

As Thompson looked out the shower door at Ann, he felt his hunger begin to grow as if it were that first night in New York again. However, his passion was quickly brought back to reality as he began to ponder the day's hectic campaign schedule.

He stepped from the shower and, dripping wet, looked over Ann's shoulder into the mirror as she continued to brush her hair. With a smile, he grabbed her right arm from behind, spun her around playfully and repositioned the brush to his face as if she was a reporter thrusting a microphone in his direction. Looking at his reflection in the mirror as if it were the probing eye of a television camera lens, he responded to the question which he had been responding to in the mirror every morning since announcing his candidacy.

"You know, Dan," he said to the non-existent reporter in the mirror, "we all made mistakes when we were young, and some day I'm going to have to explain them to my children. I certainly don't intend to do so with your cameras rolling."

Thompson cocked his head and continued looking in the mirror to see if he believed his own sincerity, "What we did as kids in college is unimportant. What is important is what we've done in our adult lives. I'm proud of what Ann and I have accomplished and what we've done in this community. I'll stand on that record and not on mistakes I made as a youngster."

"Really, Richard, don't you think if you were going to get the 'pot question' someone would have asked it by now?" asked Ann.

"I know. Griff keeps telling me pot is yesterday's issue. I just want to be ready for it if it comes," he replied. "I certainly can't tell them I spent my time in college shop class making bamboo bongs for Griff and me."

Ann poked him in the belly as she walked out of the bathroom. "You look like you've dropped a couple more pounds."

"I have," replied Thompson, grabbing his stomach and taking a reflective look in the mirror. "The campaign is wearing on me. I swear that someday I'm going to figure out how to turn the rigors of the campaign trail into a weight loss video. If this race were more than a four-week special, I'd have to go and get all of my suits taken in." He paused. "Anything new and fun on the blog this morning?"

"You and that damn blog," sighed Ann. She had been put in charge of reading the daily entries on the Thompson campaign blog site and reporting on them back to her husband. Every morning, she did so dutifully, although silently doubting their value.

"Blogs are the future of politics, babe," he said. "Get used to impersonal voter contact through flat-screen computer monitors. Us geeks are taking over, you know."

"Then in that case, Geek Boy, your precious blog has lots of new, but nothing fun." She paused. "I take that back. There was a new blogger this morning who knew Garrett Jackson in D.C."

"Really? They give any idea of who they are?"

"No. It was kind of weird they didn't fill out the contact form. But they said they might write back later and let you know more about the time they spent together."

"Oh, God, a cyber chit-chatter, that's all I need in the crunch time of a campaign for Congress," said Thompson. "Blogs attract as many nuts as geeks. But, keep an eye out for any more entries from the one who says he knew Garrett. I would like to meet some of the folks who were around him after I left the Hill."

"How'd it go yesterday in Ashland?" asked Ann, changing subjects as her husband stepped off the tile floor of the bathroom and into the carpeted warmth of the couple's master suite.

"Fantastic. Jeff and Suzanne send their love," said Thompson as he ran a towel through his hair.

"They're going to win that county for us single-handedly," said Ann. "How did Josh do on his first big campaign trip with the 'great Michael Griffith'?"

"He did fine. Griff is freaked out he's too young and can't handle it."

"Michael doesn't trust the abilities of anyone but Michael," she said. "He'll warm up to Josh. He just doesn't realize how much the two of them are alike...except Josh dresses nicer...and he has hair."

"Don't worry about Griff. He's uptight about everything these days. And he's royally pissed at me right now."

"Why?" asked Ann.

"Some issue I brought up on the trail," he said, wishing he could start the whole conversation over.

"Please tell me you didn't speak 'wonk' to the folks Jeff and Suzanne got together or at the women's club meeting."

"No...of course not...I wouldn't bring up a wonk issue in front of voters," his voice lowered, "...just the press."

"Richard, you promised. You promised not to go geek on us in public."

"Come on Ann, I don't need it from you, too. Right now, please just be my wife and not another political consultant. I've gotten enough crap from Griff on this one. He bitched at me the entire drive back from Ashland. I barely got to enjoy my cigars or Zevon. Trust me Griff throttled me enough for both of you."

"Good for him," mumbled Ann under her breath.

"Give me a break, I'm exhausted," said Thompson. "The ride

back was grueling. I kept listening to *Accidentally Like a Martyr* and, with all Griff's bitching I truly felt Zevon's pain. Anyway, this is one of the few times I think he's wrong on politics and I'm right. This issue will sell to the voters."

"What's the issue?" asked Ann. She turned to face him when the pause became too long.

"Section 936 of the United States Tax Code," he said with a tone in his voice which sounded far less than confident.

Mindful of his request to be just a wife at this point, Ann turned away from her husband in order to avoid laughing out loud in his face.

Just then the phone rang. It was Michael Griffith. Thompson put him on speaker phone as he continued to dry off from his shower.

"Well, Geek Boy, you dodged a bullet. Josh had drinks with the press corps last night after the women's club meeting and before they filed. The little dweeb spun them like a 20-year vet. He gave me the clips this morning and the tax wonk comments made it into every story in a way that makes you look like a super hero, using your secret geek powers to lighten the burden of the weak and downtrodden everywhere."

"Michael, do you have the clips in front of you?" interjected Ann.

"Front page, bottom fold of the *Washington Times*, 'Create Jobs in Puerto Rico or the Heartland', subtitle 'Kentucky Special Election May Decide.' The stories are stronger in the morning locals. Pope didn't have the first clue what you were talking about. He's quoted as agreeing with you and could only say that he'd be better at getting it done than you would."

"Oh, he's got to be royally pissed this morning," Ann said. "I've heard he's really tough on his staff."

"Tough isn't the word for it," replied Griffith. "We hear he's losing volunteers."

"I swear, Richard, if I ever catch you treating our staff and volunteers that way…"

"What the hell did I do?" said Thompson at his wife's outburst.

There was a long silence on the phone.

"Well, I'm waiting…" said Thompson.

"And the articles are playing well in the District," replied Griffith reluctantly.

"And…?" asked Thompson a second time.

"And, I'm putting it into next week's brushfire, to see if it has any polling traction."

"And...?"

"And, the blogs are eating it up."

"And...?"

"And you were right and I was wrong. There. I said it. Happy?"

"Yes. I'm happy. Will you say it again? I think I'm getting a stiffie," Thompson said, mocking both Griffith and Ann.

"No, but I'm happy for you and your stiffie. I hope the two of you have a long and wonderful life together," said Griffith playing along.

"Thanks. We'll invite you to our next anniversary."

"Thanks for the visual, but I'll pass," said Griffith. "Hey, Annie, when you get a chance, check out Josh's draft of your 'wife's letter' to the female voters. I've hid it on your page on the website. Just go backslash Annie and you'll find it. And, Rick, get your ass in gear. I have your morning money calls waiting for you on your desk."

"I'm the super hero of wonks," shouted Thompson as he clicked Griffith off the speaker phone. Throwing his shower towel around his neck as if it were a cape, he grabbed Ann and ground his naked pelvis against her jeans. "But I shall only use my super powers for good." Ann was laughing now as her husband let her go. Buck naked but for the towel cape, he pretended to fly around the room like Superman and made a noise to simulate the wind was whistling by him as he flew.

He grabbed her waist from behind and humped against her ass. "Ever make it with a bona fide super hero?"

"You want a little money shot before your money calls?" asked Ann, turning around to face Richard and grinding back her answer to the question as she asked it.

"You sure?" he asked as the two made their way to the bed. "I don't have any Springsteen passes to get you out of those jeans."

"I'm sure we can work out something in trade," said Ann as she began to kiss her husband's bare chest. "Michael Griffith's 'Dialing for Dollars' boy is going to be a little late for the game show today."

CHAPTER 6

"I'm going to run down to Chez Nora in Covington to grab lunch with The Fat Man. Does anyone want to join us?" asked Thompson as he made his way for the door of the campaign office. Office was, of course, a funny thing to call the accumulation of second-hand metal tables, plastic chairs, office equipment and cardboard boxes which made up this or any campaign headquarters.

When a candidate is spending his days on the phones raising campaign funds to buy television and radio ads, he doesn't want to spend a whole lot of money on office space and furnishings.

"Overhead doesn't get us any votes," said Griffith anytime someone brought up an idea that would improve the conditions of the office.

But, even for the campaign tight wad Michael Griffith, the Thompson for Congress headquarters was bordering on ridiculous. There was one big room with metal tables shoved into each corner and a bingo style table in the middle which the staff used as a conference table. Each desk had a computer on it. There were two private offices, one for the candidate and one for the campaign manager, but the manager's office doubled as the press room where the staff sent faxes. The walls were covered in textured wall paper peeling apart at the seams. It had a musty kind of smell. The look was certainly a contrast to the mahogany woodwork that outlined Thompson's law office.

"Why are you meeting The Fat Man when you need to be making money calls?" asked Griffith.

"We've got some law firm business to discuss," Thompson replied.

"Can't your secretary handle that stuff?" asked Griffith. "From what I've seen, she seems to run your law practice anyway."

"I do have to show up occasionally," replied Thompson.

"Gee, do you think you can arrange your schedule and 'show up' to be a candidate sometime today?" Griffith mumbled.

"I think I'll just grab some fast food," said Josh ducking his head down and hoping to avoid the fire.

"Come on, Griff," said Thompson. "I've got a responsibility to my partners too. Come with us and I'll let you manhandle the bartender for his vote. You'll like him. He looks like Sideshow Bob from *The Simpsons*."

"Will the two of you be in your normal mode of reciting every line from *The Princess Bride*?" queried Griffith.

"Probably."

"Well, pal, despite my overwhelming desire to sit through a lunch where the two of you laugh your asses off over jokes no one else understands, I think I'll stay behind. Anyway, Josh and I need to go over the poll numbers and the buy."

"How are we doing on the cross-tabs?" asked Thompson following Griffith's lead.

"We're doing good with the 35 plus crowd who watch the news, but we need to get our numbers up with the Thursday night drama watchers," Griffith said.

"Why them in particular?" asked Josh.

"Because, my lad, concentration of upscale television viewers usually consists of a lot of voters who wait until the last minute to make up their minds. Pope is targeting his new negative piece directly at them."

"So do we produce a new ad to take him off message?" Josh asked, hoping this was the right approach.

"No," said Griffith, "I want to see some numbers first. We may simply adjust the buy for the new jobs ad."

"You mean the 936 Puerto Rico jobs ad?" Thompson said proudly. "Ann and I looked at it last night on my secret page on the web. I thought it was great."

"Yeah, but get ready. That may not be enough," said Griffith. "If we take a hit in the numbers over the Pope negative piece, it may be time to respond negative."

"You tell me when," replied Thompson sternly. "I'm ready to swing when you say so. If the sonofabitch throws a pebble at me, he better be ready to duck a boulder back at him." Thompson paused. "But, I'll need a day or so to get Ann ready for everyone who will come up and bitch at her about it at the store. Have we gotten wind of their latest whisper campaign yet?"

"Not yet," replied Griffith. "Their last one about you getting some girl pregnant in high school didn't get any traction. I guess people took a good look at your senior picture and realized that you couldn't have gotten laid in a whore house with a $100 bill in your hand."

"Thanks," Thompson said. "You're on my side, right?"

"Yeah," said Griffith. "And be glad I am. These folks are lowlifes. They'll say anything about you to win."

"I'm really starting to hate this guy Pope," said Josh.

"Don't hate your enemy. It affects your judgment," said Griffith and Thompson at the same time. They were simultaneously quoting one of the few good lines from *Godfather III*, when Michael Corleone tells his nephew Vincent to forget about Joey Zaza, who had made an attempt on his life. The pair looked at each other and chuckled. Their knowledge of when to use the Rules of Battle broke the ice.

"Just go. Enjoy your little geek jamboree. But make sure you're back in time to get those PAC checks at 2:00," Griffith instructed. "The lobbyist from Livius Drugs said he wanted to give them to you personally."

"Right. Honest graft at 2:00. It's on my schedule."

"I'm not shitting you, Rick. This guy is coming in to drop off two checks for the maximum contribution. You know that's huge and I need you to be here acting like you care about his issue."

"And what is his issue?" queried Thompson.

"I don't have the first clue. He's got two max out checks and wants to be your newest best friend. Just be here on time."

Thompson didn't reply. He just put his left index finger across his upper lip and shot his right hand in the air, making fun of the Hitler-like order from his consultant. Josh looked away.

"Just leave. Josh and I have a race to win. For you, by the way," said Griffith in mock exasperation. "Tell The Fat Man I said hello."

"I will," replied Thompson. "And Josh, call Ann to make sure she pulls down the blog entries today so I can go over them tonight."

The Fat Man was Joseph Bradley, Thompson's law partner and, next to Michael Griffith, his closest friend in the world. Bradley was one of those people you meet in life who is a caricature of himself. He stood about 5' 5" and was possibly just as wide around. His scruffy pepper beard made him look like Santa Claus's reprobate brother.

As good as Thompson was in a room, Bradley was that much better in court. He was brilliant at lulling opposing counsel to sleep by his frumpy appearance and then crushing them at just the right moment. He had a picture of a panda bear in his office with a quote from Theodore Reed, the one time Director of the National Zoo in Washington, which read:

"They're so sweet and cuddly and loveable you just want to pick them up and hug them and squeeze them. And they'll beat the hell out of you."

Bradley lived his life by that quote.

Bradley was known for taking on complex cases involving hundreds of boxes of documents, synthesizing them and then putting the case before a jury in such a simple manner that even a fourth grader could understand him. The chief judge in their home county once called Joseph James Bradley the best damned lawyer he'd ever met in 25 years on the bench.

As close as Griffith and Thompson had been in college and D.C., Thompson and Bradley had become just that close after Thompson moved back home to Kentucky.

When Thompson returned home, he and Ann had gotten deeply involved in various community activities. Their zeak for public service went way beyond the desire for public office. They sought out causes which moved them. Charities wanted them on their boards because it was perceived they added passion and vision to the cause.

Thompson carried this passion for always being "on a mission" over into his law practice. Much to the dismay of some of his partners, Thompson frequently took on cases if he thought doing so would protect the little guy. He told his partners he had become a lawyer to stand up for people who didn't have the means to stand up for themselves. If that affected his salary, so be it. But he had not suffered through four years of nights at law school, while working full-time, just to document corporate asset purchases under fluorescent lights. He wanted to fight for those who didn't have a voice. His self-described "mean streak of Populism" gavesome needed meaning and value to his life.

The Fat Man had once told Ann that Thompson's constant quest for a cause to fight for was an incurable "Don Quixote Complex."

But if Richard Thompson was Don Quixote, then Joseph Bradley, "The Fat Man," was the faithful squire Sancho Panza. They became friends, in part, because The Fat Man, too, believed in quests and loved the fight. He added a superior intellect to each and every battle and war. He could zig when others expected a zag. Somewhere in the course of fighting various legal battles side-by-side, this unlikely pair had become fast friends.

And The Fat Man loved movies, especially *The Princess Bride*. He knew every word to every scene and did a great impression of Vizzini, the Sicilian pirate who kidnapped Princess Buttercup.

"How are things at the Fire Swamp?" asked Thompson as he approached The Fat Man sitting at a corner table at Chez Nora, their favorite neighborhood bar.

"Not the same without you around every day. But then again, I guess we'll have to get used to it when we take your name off the letterhead next month. By the way, you look like hell."

"That's only because I feel that way," groaned Thompson.

"Come on, you've been waiting for this moment your entire life," said The Fat Man.

"Joey, I've been around candidates all my life, but I never knew how hard it was to have your name on the ballot."

"Really? How about when you ran for council in Ludlow?"

"That doesn't count, man. That race was retail politics. Ann and I knocked on doors and literally met every voter personally. Hell, most of them we met twice. Now, I'm meeting people in 30 second television spots and slick direct mail pieces. I'm trying to make eye contact with as many people as I can, but the district is so damned big. I don't know how these guys who run for three or four years before they get elected do it. I'm half way through a short special election and I'm dog tired."

"That's because you've fallen victim to one of the classic blunders. The most famous is 'Never get involved in a land war in Asia. But only slightly less well known is this: Never go in against a Sicilian when death is on the line,'" said The Fat Man doing his best Vizzini impersonation.

"You realize that has no relevance to anything," said Thompson laughing out loud.

"I know, but it always makes you laugh and you look like you need a laugh right now."

"Laughs I can use."

"You know it's weird to turn on the television and see an ad selling you."

"Wait until you see the next one. It's on the 936 Puerto Rico jobs issue."

"Your geek boy ad?"

"I got your geek boy right here," said Thompson as he grabbed his crotch in a gesture of defiance against his 'geek boy' title. "It polls off the charts and the focus groups love it. Check it out on the web. I'll have Griff download it on a secret page for you."

"How much are you buying?"

"We've bought so many gross rating points that if this ad were selling Coke, no one in the district would ever buy Pepsi again. This one could put the race out of reach."

"Don't get too cocky now."

"Griff tells me I need to go fishing in the Keys for the next couple of weeks so I don't have the opportunity to fuck it up." Thompson turned and faced the man behind the bar. "Jimmy, send over the regular."

Jimmy Gilliece and his wife Pati were the owners of Chez Nora and he didn't even have to take their order. It was always the same. Both men judged a restaurant by the quality of its pork chops, and Chez Nora served up the best pork chop in town, a thick cut presented on a bed of mashed potatoes and covered in a warm mango salsa. "You better watch out, Jimmy," Thompson told the owner as he took his first bite a few minutes later, "you're going to start giving bar food a good name."

The food and the caffeine laden sodas came in mass quantities as the two men spent a couple of hours going over a laundry list of pending cases and other issues facing the office. Most of the time, Thompson would have thought of this work as dreadfully boring. But today, dealing with the issues involved in managing a law firm was a welcome relief from the day-to-day activities of the campaign. The pair was deep into the budget and staffing portion of their law firm's executive committee minutes when Thompson's cell phone went off.

"Forget about your 2:00?" asked an irritated Griffith.

"Shit. I'll be there in ten minutes. Keep this guy on ice and I'll zip up the Cut in the Hill," said Thompson referring to the short stretch of interstate between Chez Nora and the campaign office.

"What's up?" asked The Fat Man.

"Griff's pissed," Thompson replied.

"Isn't Griff always pissed?"

"Yeah, but this time I deserve it. I've got a lobbyist coming in to give me two max PAC checks and I let the time slip away," said Thompson as he hurriedly picked up his papers.

"Don't tell me that. I'm voting for you. I really don't need to know you're selling out."

"I'm not selling out to anyone."

"You're meeting with lobbyists and taking PAC checks, aren't you?"

"Yes, but there's not a bogey man behind every PAC contribution."

"Maybe," said Bradley, unconvinced.

"Did you ever think people are giving me the maximum contribution because they share my vision for good government and a stronger democracy?" snapped Thompson.

There was a short pause before both men burst out laughing.

"Have a fun time storming the castle," shouted Bradley as Thompson moved quickly to the door.

The Fat Man was back at the office when the phone rang at about 3:45. It was Thompson.

"Hey, what's up?" asked The Fat Man, picking up the phone only because he saw on the caller ID screen it was Thompson. "Griff still pissed that you were late?"

"No, in fact, now I think he's pissed that I actually showed up," said Thompson, only half jokingly.

"What's he pissed about now?" asked The Fat Man.

"Well, that's a funny story," replied Thompson.

"Ha ha funny or weird funny?" asked The Fat Man.

"Weird funny," replied Thompson. "Remember what I said today about people giving campaign contributions and only wanting better government?"

"Yeah?"

"Today's meeting didn't go well," said Thompson.

"How so?"

"This joker comes in and, almost immediately, wants me to back off 936 reform. It was really uncomfortable. He came with two big checks to back him up and clearly wanted me to drop 936."

"How'd you handle it?"

"I politely asked him to leave and take his PAC checks with him."

"Good for you."

"I guess so," replied Thompson, "but I just chased a guy with big bucks out my door."

"So, why are you calling me…moral reinforcement?"

"No, I need a favor."

"Name it," was the obvious response of Thompson's Sancho Panza.

"Skip the fundraiser tomorrow night, get online and find out all you can about a lobbyist named Virgil Lawson."

Lawrence Carpenter's phone line was ringing about the same time Thompson hung up with The Fat Man.

"Well, how'd it go?" asked Carpenter.

"Bad," replied Lawson with a sound of tentative fear in his voice. "He turned down our money."

"Then he knows," said Carpenter sternly.

"I don't see how he'd know about…"

Carpenter interrupted. "I do not pay you to not see. He knows and you better figure out how to silence him before the election."

"I understand," said Lawson.

"You god damned well better understand, Virgil," said Carpenter in a firm, even metered mono-tone which let Lawson know the importance of the issue had just been raised to its highest color level.

"I do," replied Lawson in an answering voice meant to convey respect. "I'm flying back tonight, but Frank is staying around to go to Thompson's fundraiser tomorrow evening. He's got checks with him."

"You stay, too," said the cool voiced Carpenter. "We need to move to 'Plan B', and Frank may need your help. I'll work the deal. Silencing Richard Thompson is still your number one priority. We'll need to make sure tomorrow night goes like clock work. You got the check from the girl, too, right?"

"Yes, sir. They'll be in the basket tomorrow night," was Lawson's reply. The call ended. Nothing more explicit needed to be said.

CHAPTER 7

Money is the tit milk that feeds the growth of politics in America.

Candidates for public office usually enter races with the best of pure intentions. Under the skin of almost every first time candidate there is a foundation of idealism which almost dares them into public life. People talk about politicians' egotism and unquenchable thirst for power. But those are often acquired personality traits which reveal themselves later in political careers. It takes the taste of a little power to thirst for more. For most first time candidates, like Richard Thompson, there is no power. They truly believe.

First timers are faced with their initial moral crisis with the realization they must raise campaign cash to convert their wild idealism into 30 second TV spots. Winning candidates attack their fundraising activities with the internal justification that all those high brow motives don't mean a damn if you can't get in front of the voters. Losing candidates never get it and take their idealism to their political graves.

Michael Griffith had a candidate one time who was so darned proud of his yard signs and bumper stickers that when he visited Washington on one of his campaign trips, he had samples in his brief case. In his usual gruff tone, Griffith told the candidate if he didn't raise the money, he should just pack up those signs and bumper stickers and store them in his basement for his grandkids' amusement someday. Because without cash, all those stickers and signs were not worth shit. The candidate fired Griffith on the spot, eventually lost the race and today probably has a box of stickers and signs stored somewhere in his basement.

To win, candidates need money from the moment they announce their intention to run for public office. On day one, there is the need for office space (even dirty, smelly office space with peeling wall paper costs money), desks, telephones, faxes, copiers, computers, and, of course, staff. The younger ones will work for nearly nothing with high hopes of making their way to D.C. following the election. Baby-faced Josh Barkman was handling Richard Thompson's press on such a dream.

It's the consultants who cost the big bucks. Today's candidates need at least a media consultant, a general consultant and a pollster. If the campaign can find a firm like Peller Marks, which handles multiple tasks, there can be some savings. Still, for each consultant who signs onto the campaign there are monthly retainers of $20,000 or so, plus 15% of all the ads and mail they place for the campaign. If they can turn the race into a victory, the campaign owes them a victory bonus pushing $25,000 or more. That's right: the campaign pays consultants a bonus for doing what they were hired to do—win.

All the money starts flowing out of the campaign checking account before the first campaign ad is run or the first piece of mail is sent. And when the ads go up on television and radio, money starts pouring out like a flood of green goo.

When you add up the costs for cameramen, key grips, sound men, makeup artists and editing room time, one single ad may take $20,000 to produce.

Placing the ad on the air depends on the number of gross rating points, or "GRPs" the campaign wants to buy. A GRP is an estimate of the exposure a particular campaign ad gets in a specific media market. The general rule of thumb is that 1000 gross rating points means an average television viewer sees the ad 10 times. Heavy viewers may see the ad 15 to 20 times, while light viewers may only see it 5 or 6 times. One thousand points per week is a pretty big buy for a campaign. In a short special election, where there isn't the opportunity to gear up to a big buy, 1200 to 1750 points per week for a month is more the norm.

The cost of placing a particular ad during a particular show depends on the number of GRPs the underlying show generates and the media market's cost per point. In the Northern portion of the Fourth District, voters tune into the Cincinnati, Ohio, market at a GRP cost of about $300 per point. The same ad on the same show costs $200 to air in a smaller media market like Huntington, West Virginia, which covers the Eastern end of the district.

When planning the media budget, it becomes easy to understand why money plays such an important role. Consider 1,000 points per market in four markets at an average cost of $300 per point for four weeks prior to election day and it isn't hard to understand why campaigns cost millions of dollars to run.

And it's not just the television ads that cost big money. Radio costs money. Direct mail costs money. Even those annoying automated phone messages that clog up answering machines across the country just before election day cost 35 cents per call.

The cost of running in the Fourth Congressional District of Kentucky is complicated by the nightmare of its geography and demographics.

Geographically, the Fourth runs along the Ohio River about two to three counties deep from the outskirts of Louisville to Ashland, Kentucky, which is just across the river from Huntington, West Virginia. In between is an area as diverse as America herself. If you drove from one end to the other, it would take upwards of five hours. On I-71, from Oldham County outside Louisville, it takes over an hour and a half to get to Northern Kentucky. Then you weave through the interstate interchanges just across the Ohio River from Cincinnati on to the Double A Highway for a three hour drive to Ashland. Griffith didn't know if it was true, but he complained to all of his consultant buddies back in D.C. it was the longest district in the country.

Targeting messages is complicated by the demographic diversity of the voters in the District. To the west, Oldham County is home to the highest per capita income families in Kentucky. On the east side, Lewis County has one of the highest percentage of families living on government assistance. While Ashland is a dying steel town trying to replace foundry jobs that have been steadily shrinking on an annual basis, Northern Kentucky, which is home to the Greater Cincinnati Northern Kentucky International Airport, has a thriving economy.

Thompson loved the diversity of the District and Griffith hated it. That's because all the variation Thompson loved about his stomping grounds was a logistical nightmare for Griffith.

Griffith had to coordinate four different television markets to get Thompson's message out and none of them were fully in the Fourth District. Louisville stations made it into the western end, but also leaked into three other Kentucky Congressional Districts and one in Indiana. The stations in two markets, Cincinnati, Ohio, and Huntington, West Virginia, weren't even based in Kentucky, but had to be bought to cover Northern Kentucky and the Ashland area. About 70% of each of those buys was going to be wasted on Ohio and West Virginia voters.

And then, of course, Griffith had to buy the station in Lexington that covered University of Kentucky basketball. It not only had some direct penetration into the Fourth District, but every cable network in Kentucky streamed that station so their customer base could follow their beloved U.K. Wildcats on a year around basis. Even in the summer time viewers watched Lexington news broadcasts for tidbits about the up coming Southeastern Conference college basketball season. This campaign was not going to be cheap.

The good thing happening on the money end was that Pope was making mistakes. The polls were showing he had started his negative attack far too early. Negative attack ads affect the numbers of the person throwing the jabs as much as they do the person getting hit. Apparently, no one had told Pope he should have some strong positive name identification before he started attacking Thompson. As Pope went negative, his numbers went down and Thompson stayed even.

Griffith was elated. Mistakes cost money and the other guy had made the first one.

For his part, Thompson was spending a large part of his time as a candidate should, by raising money. Each morning started out with money calls to major donors. Griffith wanted him to do these early in order to catch people before their first business meeting of the day. About 10:30, the PAC calls would start. Late in the day, Thompson would call veteran members of Congress to try and pry money out of their campaign accounts.

No road trip was made without stops by the offices of prospects, and donor reply envelopes were constantly within quick reach in Thompson's inside coat pocket.

Then, there were the fundraisers. Thompson was holding them in the district, across the state, in the District of Columbia and anywhere else a group of like-thinking folks would gather together with open check books.

It's not always comfortable to ask for campaign contributions. In most instances, people contribute because they want someone who is like minded to them being elected. But there are times, surprisingly rare times, when people expect something in return. Most of the time people want access to the Congressman in order to express a position on an issue. Occasionally, it's something more. Occasionally, someone wants a straight up quid pro quo.

The Holy Grail of campaign contributions is an individual or political action committee which "maxes out." Under Federal election finance law, an individual can give $2,000.00 for each election cycle and a political action committee can give $5,000.00. Primary and general elections count as separate cycles. Thus, to make a maximum contribution an individual would contribute $4,000.00 and a political action committee would contribute $10,000.00. A special election, such as the one featuring Thompson versus Pope, is two cycles. Candidates need as many maximum contributions in their campaign war chests from individuals and PACs as they can muster.

Thompson didn't like the fundraising part. No one particularly does. It's demeaning at times to call friends (and outright strangers) to pan handle cash for the sole purpose of shameless self-promotion. It's not like you're raising money for cancer research. You're asking major donors for maximum contributions so you can put a picture of yourself on television. As uncomfortable as it was, Thompson did it every day anyway, justified in knowing he had to do so in order to win. He had felt the press of people who expected access. And after meeting Virgil Lawson, he had met a person expecting a quid pro quo.

When Lawson and Griffith stood to greet the late arriving candidate, Thompson had felt uneasiness in Lawson's hand shake.

"Mr. Thompson. Virgil Lawson. I'm pleased to finally meet you and to be a part of a winning campaign."

"Thank you," replied Thompson. "Don't believe what you read in the papers. We're running like we're 20 points behind."

"I like your attitude, but I also like your poll numbers," said Lawson.

"The only poll numbers I really care about are the ones on election night." Thompson's canned response sounded even less genuine than usual. Griffith kept a straight face.

"Agreed. I've been talking with Michael here about the campaign and your upcoming new television ad on jobs," said Lawson. "It's an interesting approach. I don't think I've ever seen anyone use that issue before. Where did you come up with that one?"

"It's just an issue I've been following since my days on The Hill. I thought now was the time to do something about it." Thompson was quickly becoming bored with the meeting.

"Are you sure that Section 936 of the Code isn't too mundane to move voters?" countered Lawson.

"Not when it's couched in terms of jobs leaving Kentucky and going to the Caribbean Basin," was Thompson's quick reply showing he was suddenly reengaged in the conversation.

"Well, that's actually why I'm here today, Mr. Thompson," said Lawson in a tone meant to cut to the chase.

"I thought you were here to be part of a winning team."

"I am. But I'd also like to talk to you about Section 936. I represent several business interests and unions in The Basin and…"

Thompson cut him off. "It's my position, Mr. Lawson, and I'm not changing it."

Griffith began to shift nervously in his chair as Thompson and Lawson leaned forward in theirs.

"I'm not asking you to change your position, Mr. Thompson," said Lawson. "We'd just like for you to hold off on the hard rhetoric until we have a chance to take you to some of the American owned plants in The Basin which benefit from…"

Thompson cut Lawson off again. "I'm not running for Congress to get free trips. I'm running to change things in Washington. And one of the things I intend to change is Section 936 of the Tax Code."

"I understand, Mr. Thompson, but we really believe…"

"Quite honestly," said a now angry Thompson, "I don't give a damn what you or your interests believe. In fact, I hope before election day I let everyone in this country know Section 936 is taking jobs out of this country. Mr. Lawson, I think you should take your checks and leave."

Lawson waited a moment, then stood up. Griffith handed him back the two checks. Once Lawson had closed the office doors, Griffith looked at Thompson in disbelief. "You just gave back two maxed out checks."

"Feels good doesn't it?" asked Thompson.

"It feels like we're two max checks poorer," said Griffith.

"It's kind of liberating," was Thompson's retort.

"It's kind of stupid," Griffith mumbled under his breath.

"Come on, Griff, it was abundantly clear Lawson was giving me maximum contribution checks to get me to back off Section 936 reform. He can give me all the bullshit reasons he wants about representing interests in the Caribbean Basin and how much 936 has helped the impoverished people who lived there. But I know the issue better than Virgil fuckin' Lawson. For every comment he can make in support, I've got a reply."

"It's your campaign pal," said Griffith. "Your ass better be in here extra early tomorrow making calls, to make up for what just walked out the door."

As Thompson sat in front of the computer on his desk, he knew it wasn't Lawson's opinion that bothered him. He could disagree with facts and opinions. But Lawson's delivery had seemed forced… insincere. He usually had a pretty good instinct about when to turn and walk away. Virgil Lawson had set off that internal radar inside his head.

"Max out or not, something just didn't feel right," Thompson said to himself, while simultaneously assuring himself they'd make it up at the fundraiser the next evening.

When it comes to money, the candidate always has the final call. He is the one who has to live with the consequences of each and every decision made in a campaign. And Griffith knew that, once made, there was no need to try and change the decision or complain about it outside the room. As Michael Corleone warned his brother Fredo when he sided against him on a financial issue and instead took the side of Moe Greene, "Don't ever take sides against the Family again. Ever."

CHAPTER 8

"You thrive on nights like tonight," Thompson said to Griffith as the pair stood around the general aviation hanger on the outskirts of Greater Cincinnati Airport, waiting for the private jet carrying former Vice-President Douglas Byrd.

"Chaos, baby. Pure chaos," Griffith replied.

"You've created an entire resume around managing chaos, haven't you?"

"Better than anyone in the business," said Griffith.

"You're weird," replied Thompson.

"And you helped make me this way," Griffith shot back at his old frat house roomie.

While Griffith and Thompson stood exchanging small talk, Ann was on the other side of town giving last minute instructions to the campaign staffers and volunteers who were invading the home of Brian and Vicky Columbus. In just a few hours, people would be entering the Columbus' front door and making their way through the maze of campaign volunteers directing them to the food and open bars. Those who had made a maximum contribution would go to a special holding area and await the arrival of Thompson and the former Vice President.

Contributors who give maximum contributions to campaigns like to get their photos taken with big name politicians to commemorate the writing of a four-figured check. You can tell how financially active a person is in politics by viewing the number of "grip 'n grab" photos on the brag wall in their den.

"Okay, folks," Ann said to the young volunteers assembled to assist in the fundraiser, "'Grip and Grab' is a very precise description of what you will be doing tonight. We will be forming a line in the hallway which will lead to the Columbus' family room. When we're ready to start taking photos with Richard and the Vice-President, one of you will literally 'grip' the contributor out of line and place them in position for a 'click'. When the 'click' is over, someone else needs to 'grab' them from the line and quickly move them to the bar. Don't let the contributor say much more than 'cheese' to the Veep. We're allowed a maximum number of fifty-five clicks, so let's make them all count."

Since leaving politics as a candidate, Doug Byrd had remained active in political fundraising for Republican candidates. Thompson had met the Vice President with Congressman Jackson a year earlier at a celebrity golf tournament in Washington. Jackson and Byrd had been very close, and the Vice President, along with Thompson, had spoken at Jackson's funeral.

At their first meeting Congressman Jackson had introduced Thompson to the Vice President as his potential successor one day. At the funeral, Byrd remembered the comment Jackson had made and told Thompson if he decided to run for Jackson's seat, to give him a call. "If you were good enough to have the blessing of Garrett, you're good enough for me," said Byrd. After he got the nomination, Thompson called the Vice President. Byrd's only response was to ask "when" and "where."

The sky above the airport was a bright blue as Thompson and Griffith stood on the tarmac looking for the incoming Lear 35 carrying Vice President Byrd.

"Pretty heady stuff, boy," said Griffith as he looked upward at an approaching airplane. "VPOTUS is coming in for your election."

"It's surreal, Griff," said Thompson.

"How so?" he replied.

"Think of it. Doug Byrd was one of our idols back in college. We walked door-to-door for him in Iowa and New Hampshire. Now he's coming in for us."

"Now you're the one that controls the strings," said Griffith doing his dead-on Vito Corleone impersonation. "If he actually gets in," said Griffith pulling out another smoke. "Where the hell is that plane?"

"Calm down, Griff," replied Thompson. "He'll be here soon."

"All I know is Ann is tap dancing with a room full of people back at the Columbus' house who maxed out to get their picture taken with the two of you and the wheels are not down yet."

"Oh, my God, do you think Josh told the pilot that Cincinnati's airport is actually across the river in Kentucky?" asked Thompson, his voice mocking a gasp.

"Okay, he's doing better than I thought he would," said Griffith. "Josh..."

"They've just radioed in and are about five minutes out," said Josh as he walked up on the pair.

"What's the run down again for when he arrives?" asked Griffith.

"I'm going to get the cameras set up to shoot the Boss meeting the Vice President on the tarmac. The two of you will mug for the cameras and act like you're the oldest of friends. I've got a podium set up inside the hangar for a couple of questions from the press and then we'll be on the way to the fundraiser."

"Great," mumbled Griffith.

"Boss, you'll have an AP reporter in the car with you on the drive to the Columbus' house. He wants to get an exclusive with the VP."

"And, Josh, what do we get out of that exclusive?" queried Griffith.

"Good will?" said Josh.

"Great. Hey, Josh, please tell me—how many votes will your little good will tour get us in the Gupser's Mill precinct?"

"Lighten up, Griff," said Thompson. "Byrd's advance gal wanted it and I'm fine with it. Josh, tell the press corps it's five minutes until show time."

When the plane landed and taxied to the door of the private hangar, a small cadre of photographers and television news crews had gathered behind Thompson. Griffith, knowing a consultant's role is to walk on wet cement and not leave foot prints, had made his way behind the press corps and camera lenses. Right on cue, when the Vice President stepped from the plane, Thompson was there to greet him and the two shook hands and had some private words before turning to greet the press.

The Vice President's wave to Griffith over the top of the press corps would be the front page photo in the locals the next day.

The press conference was soft ball questions and answers. "We met through our late dear friend, Garrett Jackson." "I'm here because Richard Thompson will be a great Congressman for the Fourth Congressional District of Kentucky." "I don't know how much we'll make tonight, but we can always use more."

The press interview on the way to the fundraiser was more specific and, at times, more intense. The reporter had come well prepared with questions on a wide range of issues. Thompson wasn't paying much attention until the reporter reminded Byrd that when he was in the Senate, he had voted for the legislation establishing Section 936 of the United States Tax Code.

Byrd handled the question beautifully, talking about the policy considerations facing the nation at the time. "I don't know if the Caribbean Basin Initiative is still relevant or not," said Byrd. "Maybe it's run its course. Maybe it hasn't. I don't know. I'm backing Richard Thompson because he's the type of leader who will take a good look at that program and make an honest assessment about its effectiveness in today's economic and political world."

Thompson breathed a sigh of relief. He certainly didn't want to get into a debate with the Vice President in front of a reporter over this issue.

The fundraiser itself was a whirlwind of activity. When the caravan carrying Thompson and the Vice President arrived, the house was already packed. As the crowd roared, they quickly ducked into the photo room and, after some small talk and photos with the host family, the flow of people through the photo line "grip" and "grab" began.

(GRIP-SHOVE) "Aref and May, meet Vice-President Byrd," a staffer would say after removing the guests name tag. (TURN-CLICK-FLASH-GRAB-PULL)

(GRIP-SHOVE) "Mr. Alley, meet Vice-President Byrd" (TURN-CLICK-FLASH-GRAB-PULL)

(GRIP-SHOVE) "Wade and Robin, meet Vice-President Byrd." (TURN-CLICK-FLASH-GRAB-PULL)

The line depleted quickly.

By the time Thompson went to the podium to introduce Vice President Byrd to his supporters, they were ready for a good speech. Byrd did not disappoint. He spoke passionately about his old friend Garrett Jackson and the values he carried with him to Washington. He told the crowd in detail how Richard and Ann Thompson were the kind of team Kentucky needed to replace Jackson in Congress. He ridiculed Pope for the negative manner in which he was attacking such a good and solid citizen, and he complimented Thompson for not stooping to Pope's level. And he spoke about Section 936 of the Tax Code, repeating the statements he had made earlier to the AP reporter. When he did, Thompson looked at Griffith and winked.

Byrd closed his remarks by standing between Ann and Richard Thompson, holding both of their hands and thrusting their arms into the air in a political victory salute. He exited the stage, shook some hands and headed back to the airport. In all, he spent just under two hours on the ground.

During those same two hours, the nightly phone calls started.

There were two sets of caller ID blocked calls going out that night. The first set was the final night of calls of the real poll. Campaigns are constantly polling and tonight's calls were testing any movement in the head-to-head numbers and the effectiveness of Pope's negative ad. These calls were quick hits, called a "brushfire" poll: "Have you seen, read or heard anything about Richard Thompson?" "Based upon what you've seen, read or heard, are you more likely or less likely to vote for Richard Thompson?" "If the election were held today, who would you vote for?"

With six hundred quick calls over two or three nights, the campaign would be able to tell if its campaign ads and mail are moving the numbers and effecting voters.

The other calls going out were for the phony poll. Not far from the fundraiser, volunteers were sitting in a small warehouse set up with 25 phone lines calling voters with a short list of questions. The questions were phrased so the voters would think they were part of a poll. In fact, the questions were being used to identify what would move that particular household of voters. The responses voters give on these calls would get spooled into a computer in a manner which would determine what campaign literature would make its way to that household.

The veterans' mailer may not go to the same household that gets the pro-life mailer. A mailer with warm and fuzzy pictures of the wife and kids goes to some households, while the same piece with photos meant to elicit strong emotions of patriotism goes to others. A supportive voter gets put in a queue to receive GOTV (get out the vote) and someone for the opponent gets cut out of all lists. The theory here is simply to let sleeping dogs lie in the hope that apathy may keep them from getting off their collective asses to vote against you on election day.

While the bourbon was flowing, the pictures were being snapped, and the calls were being made, the reporters were at their desks pounding out their stories to beat the deadline for the morning editions.

Through it all, The Fat Man sat in front of his office computer pouring over web sites and databases. He missed the chance to get his picture taken with Vice President Byrd, but he knew what he was doing was more important. Several of the searches were easy. Printing all of his hits as he went along, Bradley had found Virgil Lawson's lobbying clients at the web site for the Clerk of the House and the Secretary of the Senate. He had found out to whom Lawson had given money by dialing up the Federal Election Commission web site and www.opensecrets.com. Bradley had even found Lawson's name on some web site thanking Lawson and a hundred or so other people for sponsoring a charity dinner at $1,000.00 per person.

But something was missing. Somewhere in the realm of cyberspace there had to be a wealth of information about a lobbyist named Virgil Lawson, not just a few snippets.

The Fat Man popped open another Mountain Dew, and added another hundred sheets or so to the printer.

The next morning, everyone was exhausted. Elated, but exhausted.

"Well, we won the day yesterday," smiled Josh, uttering a frequent campaign line that follows a good day of campaigning.

"Not a bad day. I don't know if we won it or not," said Griffith in his normal emotionless delivery.

"Not a bad day?" asked a shocked Josh. "Last night we raised over $280,000, our top line numbers are up, the Vice President's visit got national coverage and you call it 'not a bad day?' Bullshit, we won that one."

"Did I stutter?" Griff gave Josh a cold look. Then, slowly and over-articulating, he replied, "I don't know if we won it or not."

"Who pissed in your beer last night?" Josh mumbled as he turned and left Griffith's office.

But deep down inside, even the crusty Michael Griffith was happy about the way this campaign was going. Money was coming in. The ads were working. The numbers continued to go in the right direction. Even the kid seemed to be working out. As he read the political tidbits column of one of the Washington dailies, he wondered what the boys at the Capitol Hill Club would think when they read that Wonk Boy had gotten Byrd to support him on 936.

There was one post script to the fund raiser. It was so well attended, with so many people coming through the door, no one even noticed the several envelopes dropped in the contribution basket by one attendee who got his photo, quickly went to the bar and gulped down a double bourbon on the rocks. If anyone had noticed, they'd have known the guy with simply "Frank Alley" on his name tag was an out-of-towner. Twenty minutes after Byrd's speech, he had asked for a Jack Daniels in a state where the locals are quick to point out that JD is Tennessee sippin' whiskey, **not** Kentucky bourbon. Whatever the drink, after the very unpleasant phone call he had just had with Lawrence Carpenter about the Vice President's comments on Section 936 reform, he needed another.

CHAPTER 9

It seemed odd to many, but during the campaign, Thompson didn't like trips to Washington. While D.C. was home to many fond memories for Richard and Ann, campaign trips were strictly business. A three day trip was a whirlwind of breakfast meet-and-greets with industry lobbyists, appointments with trade associations stretching from one side of K Street to the other and money calls from a barren cubicle at the National Republican Congressional Committee. It was fast paced, not fun and took Thompson away from Kentucky voters three days at a time.

Traveling around in a private black Lincoln Town Car all to himself did have its novelty appeal. If nothing else, it made these unbearable trips a little more comfortable. But calls home were constant.

Thompson had just finished a lunch meeting with insurance industry lobbyists at a swank French restaurant on Pennsylvania Avenue just down the street from the Library of Congress. When he jumped into the back of the Town Car with his jacket pockets filled with PAC checks, he did that one thing which seemed to calm him while on the road. He called Ann.

"Hey, babe, how are the kids?" whispered Richard Thompson into his cell phone so the driver of the Town Car could not overhear the conversation.

"We're good," she said recognizing the depressed tone in his voice, "But, from the sound of your voice, we're doing better than you. What's wrong, honey? Normal D.C. blues?"

"Remember when I told you that if we did this, we were going to have fun?"

"Yeah?"

"Well, am I having fun yet?" asked Thompson, the thrill of last week's fundraiser having obviously worn off.

In a big time political race, the spouse has several different roles to play. In fact, at the start of any race, Griffith would give a couple a list of what it takes to be the candidate's spouse. Ann Thompson, loving spouse of candidate Richard Thompson, was no exception. Ann had a personal written job description which set out her many campaign functions, ranging from balancing duties with the family to participating in various campaign activities. She would wear many hats and have to switch them often, sometimes in the same conversation.

From the tone in her husband's voice, Ann knew her cue. Now was the time she needed to switch from being a wife to a motivational speaker. "You, of all people, knew that being away from me and the kids was part of the gig when you put your name on the ballot. Remember what Hyman Roth said in *Godfather II*? This is the business you have chosen for yourself," Ann said with an inner laugh, realizing Griffith's Godfather Rules had worn off on her too.

"Anyhow," she continued, "put this all in perspective. This is your last trip as a candidate. Our next trip to Washington, you'll be Congressman-elect Richard Thompson." After a silence she added, "We love you and we are proud of you."

"Thanks, babe. I love you, too," said Thompson as he looked out the window of the Lincoln at the line of sweaty tourists waiting to get into the Washington Monument. "So, what else is up? Was there anything new on the blog yesterday?"

"No, but remember the blog entry we got last week?" asked Ann, "the one from the lady who said she knew Garrett?"

"Yeah." Thompson paused. "How do you know it's from a woman?"

"It's easy to tell by the way she writes," said Ann. "Women writing on blogs aren't nearly as crass as men. We aren't suddenly emboldened by anonymity like men."

"All right, I get the message, Gloria Steinem. What about the blog?"

"Well, she logged on again and said she'd read the articles on 936 and might call you someday soon to talk about it."

"And what's so strange about that?" asked Thompson. "Some people—other than you and Griff—actually find the issue intellectually stimulating."

"It was something else she said about Garrett at the end of the blog. She said we should 'beware of the color red in politics'. It just sounded funny."

"Hang on to it. Maybe I'll try to call her when I get a chance."

"That's just it. She wants to talk to you but still doesn't sign her name, fill out a contact form or give her phone number."

"She...or he...is probably just a crank," said Thompson. "I wouldn't worry about it until after the election."

"You're probably right. Now, finish your business up there and get home. I'm horny." When words of motivation didn't work with her husband, sex talk always did.

"Me, too. All right. Thanks. Kiss the kids for me and I'll see you tomorrow."

Griffith had decided to stay behind on this trip to tweak the ad placements over the final week or so of the campaign. When Ann called the campaign office to update him on her husband's sour mood, Griffith got on the phones to organize a group of their old drinking buddies to greet Thompson's Town Car at the curb of the Capitol Hill Club. These guys were senior lobbyists in D.C. They were the grey-haired power players and had been so for decades. Years ago they had taken a liking to Thompson and Griffith. When Griffith called, they jumped to help out.

"Hey everybody, Wonk Boy is back!" shouted an overweight man with long hair.

"Shut up, Charlie. Next month it's going to be Congressman Wonk Boy to you," laughed another in a southern Tennessee drawl as he opened the door of Thompson's car with a royal bow. "When you're a big swinging dick in Congress, please remember it was 'the Sport' who was properly kissing up."

"Come on downstairs, boy. Griff cancelled out your afternoon calls from the NRCC and said we're to buy you precisely two Maker's Mark Manhattans."

"Why only two?"

"He said if you had more than two, you'd drop your pants, put on one of the waitresses' aprons and attempt to fly around the Club."

"Thanks, Ann," Thompson mumbled to himself.

"And according to Griff, you've got to be somewhat sober for your dinner tonight with Elmer Fudd."

The buildings at both party headquarters have clubs in them, but even the Democrat lobbyists in town will privately admit they spend more time at the Republicans' Capitol Hill Club. The green awning which covers the brick sidewalk leads into the marble floors of the Club. There is a grand stairway from the lobby which leads to a sit-down restaurant on the second floor and more private fundraiser rooms than any other building in town. Walk into the Club on any given evening and you'll discover 5 or 6 events for Republican Members of Congress.

But the bar in the brightly lit basement is where the real action takes place. It has a non-smoking section, but the room is filled with enough second-hand smoke to shut down the lungs of a triathlon athlete. It's the place to go to find a stiff Manhattan, bold political punditry and a good gin rummy game. Most nights there is a former Member of Congress sitting at the piano playing sing along music. He's not employed there—he just loves to play the piano and sing.

Thompson sat down with the boys and savored the smell and taste of the first sip from his Maker's Mark and sweet vermouth.

"So how's it going, junior?" asked Sarge, an old Viet Nam era Marine helicopter pilot who represented a defense contractor, as he started to deal the first hand of gin rummy.

"The numbers are great. But I'm going to keep running…"

"Cut the crap, son," interrupted the man with the southern drawl whom everyone in town knew simply as "Sport." "Don't give us the bullshit canned response. We were writing that kind of crap for administrations while you were chasing cheerleaders. We're your friends. Shoot straight with us. How are you and Ann holding up?"

"Hell, Sport, I don't know. I guess we're holding up all right."

"Who are you kidding? Ann's holding you up."

"Ain't that the truth," replied Thompson as he looked at his cards.

"On da high side, no one has killed Griffith yet. Ya got dat goin' for ya," said one of the men, an Italian lobbyist from New Jersey, as he pondered his first bid.

"Yet. Yet is the operative word," said Thompson to the laughs of the rest of the men.

"So, something is bothering you," Sport probed. "What is it?"

"I don't know, I guess it's just the uncertainty of the whole thing," said Thompson as he folded his cards and tossed them on the table. "I don't know what I am right now. I'm not practicing law. I'm not a Congressman yet. We've put our lives on hold. These days if someone asked me what I did for a living, I'm not sure I could answer the question."

"You want to know what you are, Richard?" asked the old Marine.

"Yeah, please tell me, Sarge."

"Son, you're a candidate. That's what you are."

"Great. I'm a candidate," said Thompson reluctantly.

"God damned right, you're a candidate. This town, our jobs, hell, this bar wouldn't exist without candidates. People, like you, willing to put their asses on the line is what makes this whole place work. God damned right you're a candidate, and we've seen more than our share. Forget if you win or lose. It doesn't matter. We've seen lesser men than you win and better men than you lose.

"What is important right now is you're a candidate and **you believe**. In fact, you believe enough you've put your name on the ballot. You believe enough to suffer the slings and arrows of assholes who hate your guts because they disagree with you or because they're jealous and want to be you. You're a candidate, son. You're doing something all of us down here wished we would have tried when we were your age, but we never really had the balls.

"Trust me son, win or lose, you'll never look in the mirror some day and ask 'what if.' You're candidate Richard Thompson. Stick out your shoulders and be proud of it. I know that win or lose, we're all proud of you for giving it a shot."

Thompson took another sip from his Manhattan and, for the briefest of moments, as Thompson sat amongst his old drinking buddies and smiled, it felt like he had never left D.C. in the first place.

When it came time to leave, Thompson thought briefly about canceling his dinner. But he knew Griffith and Ann would kill him if he cancelled out on the chance for one-on-one time with the man who could make or break a first year Member, Congressman Marcus Lackner.

CHAPTER 10

Institutions attract people who will prostitute themselves for their own personal gain. It's not always intentional. But the power of certain institutions can corrupt a pure soul like cheap gin. Absolute power corrupts absolutely. The United States House of Representatives is no exception.

Barry Goldwater said those who seek absolute power, "even though they seek it to do what they regard as good, are simply demanding the right to enforce their own version of heaven on earth." He concluded those are the ones "who always create the most hellish tyrannies. Absolute power does corrupt, and those who seek it must be suspect and must be opposed." Of course, Goldwater also said if everyone in D.C. who was guilty of chasing women and drinking had to leave town, "there'd be no government left."

In any event, the halls of the House are filled with 435 men and women who were each elected to be the voice of their District in the governance of the United States of America. They have come from a variety of backgrounds, but for the most part, they've never been put in the spotlight like this before in their lives. It's a position of power and prestige like none other in this country. Suddenly, their picture is on the front page of their local papers. People are asking them for autographed photos as if they were sports stars or celebrities. Staff is waiting on them hand and foot. All the lobbyists at the Capitol Hill Club are buying them drinks and **everyone** is laughing at their jokes.

When Marcus Lackner was first elected to Congress in the late 70's, he was a young dashing progressive Republican from South Florida. It didn't take him long to realize that often being at odds with his own party on core issues would not help him make his way up the ladder of Republican leadership. So, in the 80's, he started moving to the right on key issues. Reagan was President and all he needed for reelection in his overwhelmingly Hispanic district was to be anti-Castro. He could get away with philosophical shifts from time to time.

Those very strategic shifts started to get him recognition as a young man who would go places in the party. In the years when the Republican Party was in the minority in the House of Representatives, Lackner became one of the party's primary bomb throwers. As Ranking Member on the Rules Committee, the panel which decides what bills make it to the Floor of the House for a vote, he learned how to manipulate the Jefferson Manual of Procedural Rules to get legislation through the Congress. When the Republicans took over the House in 1994, he had become chairman of the Rules Committee and one of the key players in making sure the Republican agenda was accomplished.

On the other hand, in 2006, when the winds of change swept the Democrats back into the majority, Lackner wasn't totally displeased to be in the minority again. With so many years in the House, he was disturbingly content with the new prospect of still holding some power without the pressure of having to deliver.

In the early years, Lackner's innate ability to get legislation through Congress attracted more than just favorable "op ed" pieces from the *Miami Herald*. It also attracted Washington, D.C.'s power crowd, along with invitations to the elite events the town offers on a nightly basis. Reserved seats at the Thomas Moore Society dinner, tee times in power foursomes at the male-only Burning Tree Country Club, and front row seats at the Kennedy Center can change a man over the years.

And it changed Representative Marcus Lackner.

He became eaten up with the power and prestige of being a United States Congressman. The change was gradual, but relentless. As Lackner moved little by little to the right, his waist line grew incrementally larger and his ethics became increasingly "practical."

The transformation happened so slowly Lackner himself hardly noticed it, and, even when he did, he convinced himself he was becoming wiser and more realistic with age.

The crowd he ran with back home in Florida began to change as well. He began to have regular meetings with the financially well off Cubans of South Florida, many of whom supported the Anti-Castro movement on the island nation just to the south of Key West. He looked the other way at the otherwise unsavory actions taken by some of those "new friends" in the belief such noble ends justified the use of some relatively distasteful means.

Thompson greeted Lackner as he stepped from his black Lincoln Town Car and made his way to the entrance of The Palm. "Keep it close, Bobby," said Lackner to the driver as he stuck out his hand to Thompson. "We should be about an hour or so."

One of the better eating establishments in town, The Palm is known for its green checked tablecloths and walls adorned with caricatures of its more famous regular customers. Thompson contrasted his memory of the once dapper young Congressman with the devastatingly accurate caricature of Lackner on the wall—an overweight figure with a receding hairline and drooping jowls. *It's no damned wonder that, behind his back, everyone calls him Elmer Fudd,* Thompson thought to himself.

Watching Lackner order from the restaurant's most expensive "premium" wine list, you'd never know The Palm was known for its far more other sensible list "40 wines under $40." When Lackner ordered a bottle of wine pressing four figures, Thompson wondered if anyone in Ludlow, Kentucky would believe that a single bottle of wine actually cost more than a month's rent.

"Well, young man, how goes the campaign?" asked Lackner. "The NRCC tells me you're polling like a four-term incumbent."

"They're being too kind, Congressman." Thompson waited for the 'Call me Marc' response, which never came, and then continued. "The polls do look favorable. But, quite honestly, I'm not going to take anything for granted. I'm running like I'm 20 points down and will do so until the polls close on election day."

"They showed me the ads you've been running. The 936 issue ad was quite a departure for Michael Griffith."

"Thank you, sir. We're proud of that one."

"You may be the only candidate in the country to ever get traction off such a strange and boring policy issue. I understand it's tracking well for you. How in the world did you decide to use that one on the campaign trail?"

"Well, sir, Michael Griffith, my staff and even my wife are probably asking the same question. Years ago, when I started working for Congressman Jackson, one of the first letters I had to respond to was one from some woman in Catlettsburg, Kentucky who had read in *Readers Digest* the government gave tax breaks to companies in the Caribbean Basin. The mills in the Ashland area were laying off workers and she was upset the government was spending money on jobs in Puerto Rico and not in Eastern Kentucky. That was back in the days before internet research. And I spent several hours over at the Library of Congress before drafting a response for the Congressman to review. Maybe it was because I was young and green, but the issue always stuck in the back of my mind. Every time I went over to the Library of Congress, I did a little more work. It just seemed more and more to me that we should repeal 936."

"You know, son, there's a damned good policy reason for that section of the Code. The Basin is important to us from both an economic and defense basis. We can't really afford to send direct Federal funding to the area, so we support them by allowing tax credits to American companies which locate there. Garrett understood and supported us on that point."

"Yes, sir. But Congressman Jackson also understood his constituents came first." Thompson didn't particularly like some stranger lecturing him on how his old mentor would have felt about his position.

"Well, I've got constituents, too," replied Lackner. "And some of my constituents are depending on 936 for their futures."

"I understand , Congressman, but I think its time has run. I don't agree it's valid anymore, and I think the people of Kentucky's Fourth Congressional District don't agree either."

"A lot of Members support 936. You're going to look a little silly when you come up here and can't get any changes accomplished."

"Sir, as I told you, I've done some serious research on the issue. I've looked at the tax benefits versus the jobs created. Somebody's making money off this deal, but it's not the working class poor of Puerto Rico. I have a list of 23 companies using this credit who haven't actually created a new job in years. I have a list of drug companies who use the credit as a means of moving money between the US mainland and Puerto Rico to skirt taxes. It may have been valid at some point in time, but it's being abused today."

"Reagan was the one who initiated this provision. He thought it was important," Lackner responded.

"Yes, sir," said Thompson. "And Barry Goldwater said the Tax Code created more criminals than any other single act of government."

"You're committed to the issue. I like that. But I've got several supporters in my District who would really like for you to back off this issue," said Lackner as he sipped from his stemmed goblet of over-priced wine.

"I appreciate your interest, Congressman, but I've dug in my heels on this one," Thompson said softly, not quite sure where the conversation was going next.

"Look, son, this is a place where your success can be accelerated by who your friends are. A favor here or there for influential friends leads to return favors. Switch the commercials. Go with some standard right-wing stuff to get voters to the polls and I could be of great help in your campaign—and even more once you get here."

"Sir, I'm not sure where this is heading, but I feel quite uncomfortable. Is this about my race, or are you trying to get me to drop an ad? I'm set on 936, Congressman. Pardon my blunt nature here, but end of story."

"Very well then," said Lackner pausing for a moment, "let's order up some food. The prime rib is excellent and you'll love the creamed spinach."

That was about the last comfortable exchange the pair had for the remainder of the evening. They discussed everything from family to politics to sports, but following the men's exchange over 936, Lackner seemed disengaged. Thompson didn't like disagreeing with a

Member before even winning a seat in the House, especially when that Member was as big and powerful as Congressman Marcus Lackner. Nevertheless, Thompson felt compelled to stick by his guns on this one. Once elected, he could look for common ground with Lackner. For now, Thompson had the bully pulpit and the issue was getting traction with the voters. Besides, Thompson believed he was right.

What Thompson didn't realize was it wasn't his position on tax credits that had diverted Marcus Lackner's attention. It was the phone call he was going to be forced to make following dinner.

"Well, how was dinner?" asked Lawrence Carpenter in a sharp voice over the cell phone.

"Hold on a minute. I'm just getting into the car." As soon as he was settled in and had given the driver instructions to take him home, Lackner returned to his call. "I like the kid. He reminds me a lot of myself when I was first elected. He's young and full of his own ideals."

"Cut the crap, Marc," said Carpenter clearly ignoring Lackner's title and name. Lawrence Carpenter did not suffer fools gladly and he had long ago come to think of Congressman Marcus Lackner as more amusing than formidable. "Can I go on home or does your lobbyist pal, Mr. Lawson, have more work to do tonight?"

"This kid knows the issue better than most Members and he believes in his position. He didn't take the bait. I don't think he knows about the deal, but it means too much to my friends." Lackner paused before he spoke again. "Do what you have to do."

"Pity. He would have been a good Member for you."

CHAPTER 11

A candidate for public office spends so much time on the road, staying at hotels and friends' houses, the first waking moments of any morning can seem a little blurry. Where am I? What time is it? The room spins slightly. You look around and it takes a second or two to get your bearings.

These are just a few of the waking thoughts that can run through your mind when snapping out of a deep REM sleep. Waking up snuggled next to a warm, soft, naked body with the lovely scent of a woman filling the room can reassure you that you're safe in your bed at home.

Except, Thompson was in D.C., not at home, and Ann **did not** have red hair.

He froze for a moment and, staring at the ceiling, tried to recall the night before.

I left Lackner at the Palm, returned to the Grand Hyatt for a night cap and went straight to bed. Didn't I? Oh fuck, I can't remember. Come on, you didn't have that much to drink. I spoke briefly to a young redhead who had sat down next to me at the bar, but I went from there straight to my room.. I think?

His breath began to shorten as he tried to remember what happened the night before.

Jesus, I can't remember anything after the bar.

"Good morning, stud," said the redhead, exposing her breasts to Thompson as she rolled over to face him. She kissed at his chest with the familiarity of someone who had been there before. "How about a back rub and a quickie before you head out this morning?"

"Ma'am, I'm not sure who you are or how you got here," said Thompson, his voice quickening, "but, God, somebody's made a huge mistake."

The redhead ran her hands softly along Thompson's inner thigh, up to his crotch and gently tugged at his manhood. "You didn't say it was a mistake last night," she whispered while sucking on his ear lobe. "And, it wouldn't be a mistake this morning."

There isn't a man alive who hasn't pictured himself in this position on a business trip to somewhere... waking up in bed with a beautiful woman whose only thought is to have sex and leave. Nobody will ever know about it. Code of the Road. What happens in D.C. stays in D.C.

"Come on baby. Fuck me," her hand working quicker on his penis.

Her deep kiss seemed to send Thompson's last remaining shred of fuzziness out the window. He was kissing her back when his morning haze was shattered with a mental picture of his wife Ann. Suddenly, the thoughts of her smell, her hair, her kiss...her tears if she could see this moment, literally threw him from the bed. He shot up and struck an uncomfortable position trying to cover his quickly receding rigidness.

"I'm not sure what happened last night, but whatever I did, I'm very, very sorry. I'm married and very much in love with my wife. This is so wrong. I am so sorry, but you'll need to leave."

The woman grinned a disappointed smile at Thompson and slowly slid the sheets back to expose her body. When she stood up, her 5' 11" frame was both lovely and athletic and she was in no hurry to find her clothes. He never really liked tattoos on women, but the one on the small of this girl's back sure looked erotic. She slowly walked around the room putting on articles of her clothing that were strung around the room. Her movements were like a reverse striptease. Her beauty, nudity and the way she moved were definitely working. Even though he was asking her to leave, he couldn't help but watch her every motion and record in his mind her every gesture. He was asking a beautiful young naked woman to get dressed and leave his room.

On the way out, the woman backed Thompson against the wall, pressed her body against his, looked him in the eye and asked one last time, "Are you sure you want me to leave?"

"No, I'm really not, which is why you have to go," was his nervous reply.

The woman leaned over and softly kissed Thompson on the cheek. "You're a sweet guy and your wife is a lucky woman. Don't be so hard on yourself about last night."

When the door closed, Thompson fell back stunned.

He sat naked on the edge of the bed and for one of the few times in his life, he didn't know what to do next. He was short of breath and visibly shaking. He felt sick to his stomach and was fighting back the urge to throw up. The morning shower was as much to calm his stomach and clear his head as it was to cleanse his body.

As Thompson emerged from the shower, he looked closely at himself in the hotel bathroom mirror. Unsure of his own actions the night before, he threw the towel at his own reflection.

He had to tell someone, but he couldn't figure out what to say or who to say it to. He couldn't even remember what had happened. Griffith would kill him if he found out. He had to tell Ann, but feared she'd take the kids and leave him. His only reaction was to wonder out loud again and again what had happened.

The meetings, phone calls and meals which consumed the remainder of the day were a blur. When the plane landed at the airport, the sudden jolt of the wheels hitting the tarmac woke Thompson from a sound sleep. For just a moment, in the confusion between sleep and being awake, he hoped that waking up next to a naked redhead in D.C. had been part of a dream within a dream. But the runway lights and the roar of the engines as they reversed to slow the plane down brought him back to reality. The cob webs of a tiring business trip couldn't mask the guilt and shame he felt low down deep in his stomach.

CHAPTER 12

The Fat Man wondered out loud to himself if Thompson really cared about the information he had given to his law partner.

Joe Bradley was known in the legal community for the anal retentive preparation that went into his presentations, and his accumulation of information regarding Virgil Lawson was no exception. Hours of late nights at the office were neatly gathered together in one three-ring binder. He knew people at the office always teased him because of his conspiracy theories, and the information in the binder was still a little thin, but what The Fat Man had already compiled in that one little binder had raised enough red flags that Thompson should have given it more attention.

But Thompson was distant that day. Even one-liners from *The Princess Bride*, didn't get their normal scripted response.

Maybe the faithful squire Sancho Panza needed to stay up even later last night to gather a little more information, The Fat Man thought to himself. *Thompson constantly kept saying this was the big leagues. Maybe conspiracy theories were no longer enough. Or, maybe D.C. was already so full of conspiracies they didn't even merit attention when Thompson was in his D.C. mode. More facts, more proof and less (or at least more supportable) theories.*

Virgil Lawson had turned out to be a private solo lobbyist with an expensive address in downtown Washington. He didn't show too many clients and only one with an interest in the Caribbean Basin, Livius Drugs. In fact, his office was in the same building as Livius' corporate office. Livius' PAC had been a big supporter in the past of Congressman Marcus Lackner of Florida. *Keep looking, I guess. There's some connection here. I just know it.*

At the campaign office, the 936 issue had seemed to garner interest from across the country. Reporters were calling. Special interest groups were requesting private meetings with Thompson to talk some sense to him. The voters were responding with calls and letters of support.

When Thompson got back from his 8:00 a.m. meeting with The Fat Man, Griffith was laughing that the issue had even drawn the attention of a true-blue D.C. "badge fucker" (one of the D.C. political groupies who get a head rush out of having sex with powerful men—so named because of their glances towards special lapel badges identifying Members of Congress). As Thompson hung up his suit jacket, Griff approached him with an ornery smile. "Hey, geek boy, check this out. Some crazy broad Fed Xed you an autographed naked picture. 'To my stud, Love, Miss 936'."

Thompson froze when he saw the photo of the young redhead he woke up in bed with just yesterday morning. He didn't know how to respond to Griffith and the crew of laughing staffers gathered around the desk displaying the photo. Thompson felt his heart rate increase immediately as he began to sweat under his fresh white button-down shirt. He tried to hide his shortening breath by simply turning and walking into his office.

Thompson's abrupt departure caused the staffers to quit laughing and look uncomfortably to their mentor, Michael Griffith. The look of fear that they had gone too far with the Boss was evident on their faces. "Don't worry, gang," Griffith told the assembled young staff. "It's just crunch-time jitters."

Griffith followed Thompson into his office.

"You know, Rick, we're down to the final ten days of crunch time," said Griffith in a brother-to-brother fashion. "I don't need my old roomie wigging out on me now."

"Not today, Griff," said Thompson.

"Today, Richard!" snapped Griffith. "It's full-tilt gonzo from now until election day. I've got you maxed out for the next ten days. The bus tour starts Wednesday. I'm getting pulled in 14 different directions every hour of the day. I've got to spend my time winning this race. Ann tells me you're as distant as a third cousin. You didn't even want to talk to her about the blog when you got home last night. I can't be holding your hand 24-7. If you're flipping out, that's natural. But, come on, it's max out time for you now."

The silence from Thompson was deafening. Maybe Griffith should have yelled at Thompson like he would at any other candidate he advised.

"Come on, pal. Talk to me."

"I'm fine," said Thompson. "What's on the schedule for today?"

Griffith wasn't reassured by Thompson's cold response, but he decided not to press any further. Candidates were known to feel the pressure as elections grew closer. After all, it's the candidate's name on the ballot facing acceptance or rejection. Griffith would always go back home to Virginia the day after an election. A candidate has to live in his community with election results for the rest of his life.

Griffith had worked once for a candidate who was so wigged out he refused to leave his house the weekend before the election. The entire campaign crew pictured the guy wandering around his house in nothing but fuzzy pink slippers and a robe, mumbling to himself about who hadn't supported him like they should have. And now the guy's in House Leadership. If Griffith could win with a candidate in pink fuzzies, he could win with Thompson getting a little moosey on him in the final days.

So, Griffith just forged ahead and went over the day's schedule. A mailer was dropping that day which would hit its well-defined targets in the next day or two. Griffith was switching the message on the ads. 936 was going to be pulled the next day in favor of the warm and fuzzy "vote for my values ad" with Ann and the kids. 936 had run its course and now was the time to move from issue ads to ones which would reassure the voters Thompson was the right choice. Griffith was upping the GRPs in the Huntington market. 936 had gotten traction in that market and an increase in warm and fuzzy GRP's just might push the head-to-head polls a couple of points in the Kentucky counties who watched the Huntington, West Virginia, television stations.

"And you, my friend, you're going with Josh back to Lewis County for door-to-door in Vanceburg followed by a late afternoon rally at the Republican headquarters in Flemingsburg. Josh has some Lexington stations lined up to be there. Then, you've got the night off for dinner with Ann. Her sister is watching the kids and I've got you a suite at the Marriott for the night."

Ann had spoken to Griff that morning about Thompson's weird mood. Maybe a relatively "easy" day of campaigning for him and a night alone for the two of them would do the trick.

"And don't worry; Josh is actually starting to like Meat Loaf, John Prine and Warren Zevon. Take a few minutes to return a couple of calls and hit the road."

As Griffith turned and closed the door to the candidate's private office behind him, Thompson pondered the emotions he felt which, at the moment, were running in fifteen different directions. He had apparently slept with a red headed woman from Washington who was now sending him naked photos of herself.

Good Lord! What have I done to myself and my family? It may end my marriage, but I've got to tell Ann.

Everyone knew Ann Thompson mattered more to Richard Thompson than anything else in the world. She was his soul mate, best friend and mother of his children. So it wasn't a surprise Thompson felt he must tell his wife of his betrayal. Maybe his shame and true, sincere regret would be enough for her to stay.

The only question is when do I tell her?

If he told her before the election, he knew she wouldn't leave before election day. Ann Thompson had worked on Capitol Hill for several years before she met her husband. She was no dummy. She was smart enough to know this election had implications far beyond choosing who would represent the Fourth Congressional District in the United States House of Representatives. No, Ann would see the election through and make her own personal decision after the polls closed.

He briefly contemplated waiting until after the election to tell her, but quickly rejected it. Waiting would just compound the betrayal.

Tonight. We've got the night off. I'll tell her tonight at dinner.

Thompson didn't have long to ponder how he would tell Ann about his D.C. affair, as Josh was already pushing him out the door and into the campaign car. With tonight's dinner on his mind, door-to-door in Vanceburg was probably the best place for Thompson to be today. Another coat of paint couldn't hurt, and he would be seeing a lot of friendly faces. Lewis County has been a Republican stronghold since it was formed from parts of three other counties following Reconstruction. When it was formed, Republicans were placed in office and have been there ever since. Lewis County may be the only county in Kentucky that has a monument to Union soldiers on the front lawn of its county courthouse.

So, as planned, Thompson and the Lewis County Judge-Executive (the chief elected official of a county in Kentucky) walked for hours knocking on doors and asking the good folks of his county to "vote for a good Republican who is going to remember us when he gets to 'Warshington.'"

And the reception at the G.O.P headquarters in Flemingsburg around 4:30 was just as strong. Josh had done a great job of advance by getting about a hundred folks to the rally. The main road off the Double A Highway which leads to Flemingsburg was covered with Thompson campaign yard signs and larger 4' x 8's' billboard signs. Josh had indeed gotten television news from Lexington to the out-of-the-way rally, reminding them of the huge amount of cash the campaign was dumping into their stations in the days to follow. Daily newspapers from Ashland, Lexington and Maysville were there as well. This day was definitely getting Thompson's mind off his own personal shame and, if only for a moment, back into the excitement of crunch time campaigning.

By the time Thompson was a minute or two into his speech in the old store front, he was back on track. This is where he was at his best and the thrill of a crowd was pumping him up. Pacing back and forth on an old hard-wood floor with his shirt sleeves rolled up and his tie loosened got his blood pumping stronger with each passing phrase.

Josh was in the back of the crowd on his cell phone to Griffith, giving him the skinny on the day and proudly announcing their candidate was back. Griffith reminded the young man he had dinner plans set up for the candidate and his wife, "So try to keep him on schedule." But sticking to a schedule was difficult when Richard Thompson was on a roll. He finished his speech and answered press questions as he worked his way through the crowd, shaking everyone's hand once, if not twice.

We definitely won another day, thought Josh to himself.

As they were saying their goodbyes to the throng of loyal supporters, a man approached the car. His dress, demeanor and lack of accent showed he was definitely not a local. "Mr. Thompson, may I have a private minute of your time."

"We're on a tight schedule," snapped the ever loyal staffer. "Give me a card and I'll set up a press call for tomorrow."

"I'm not with the press. My name is Frank Alley. We met at your fundraiser with the Vice President. I'm a friend of a lady friend of Mr. Thompson's in Washington." Thompson and the man stared at each other for a moment. "Privately, Mr. Thompson?"

"Look, Mr. Thompson has to be back…" said Josh.

"It's all right Josh," said Thompson interrupting the young man. "I'll handle this. Let's use the storage room in the back for a minute."

Once in the dimly lit storage room, Thompson swung around to face Alley. "I assume you're going to tell me what this all about?"

"It's about you, Mr. Thompson, and a certain redheaded female friend of yours in D.C."

"I don't know any redheaded females in D.C.," said Thompson.

"Oh, now, Mr. Thompson," Alley said mockingly. "Please don't try to be coy with me. You know who I'm talking about. Doesn't 'Miss 936' ring a bell?"

"I don't have any idea what you're talking about," replied Thompson in a lame effort to deny what was causing him to shake noticeably.

"Why are you making this hard on both of us, Mr. Thompson?" asked Alley. "Okay, let me see if this helps your recollection any… remember your bedroom at the Hyatt…beautiful girl…only hair on her body is the red on top…nice firm tits…a little tattoo on the small of her back…" He stopped, pulled a pack of cigarettes from his coat pocket and lit one, all the while looking at Thompson with a knowing stare that challenged the sincerity of his denial. After he exhaled his first puff, he laughingly asked Thompson, "Should I continue? Or, is this image suddenly ringing a bell?"

"Who the hell are you and what do you want?" asked Thompson in exasperation.

"I told you, I'm Frank Alley and I want what everybody in politics wants, Mr. Thompson. Just a little access—a little piece of your time to talk to you about your personal vendetta against Section 936 of the Tax Code. I represent some people who would like you to back off your stance on that issue…at least until after the campaign."

"This doesn't make any sense to me," said Thompson. "Why should the people you represent care so much about this issue?"

"Don't worry about why, Mr. Thompson," replied Alley. "Just rest assured my clients are serious about their request and willing to back up their request."

"Back up their request? With what?"

"Friendship," said Alley matter-of-factly. "The kind of friendship that can help advance the career of Washington's newest rising star. You'll need the tools of the trade in D.C…money…access…power…and my clients can help you with all of those."

"Doesn't exactly sound like the kind of new friends I want to make at this point in my life," said Thompson. "What if I refuse to back off?"

"Oh that would be very bad for your career," said Alley. "If you refuse, we'll have to tell the press about your relationship with the redhead."

"I don't have a relationship with her," said Thompson. Then, he thought *Hell; I don't even remember what happened.*

"That's not what the pictures indicate," said Alley, as he showed Thompson photos of what appeared to be him and the redhead in the throws of wild sex. Alley cocked his head sideways and held the photo kind of crooked in the other direction. "I think this one is my favorite," he chuckled. "It would make a nice Christmas card, don't you think?"

Thompson picked up the photos and slowly looked at each one of them. *Shit. Someone was in the room taking photos. That's it. That's why I can't remember. I was set up. I must have been drugged. This fucker set me up.*

"You cock sucker," mumbled Thompson at Alley. "They're fakes and you know it. I ought to kick your ass right here in this storage room."

"Oh, let's be calm now, Mr. Thompson," said Alley, showing Thompson the Glock under his coat. "You really don't want to take a swing at me. There's a very civil solution here."

"Fuck you and the civility you rode in on. I'll take my chances."

"Good for you," said Alley gleefully. "While you're driving home today you can tell your young press secretary to prepare a release on how these photos don't show a candidate for United States Congress on his back getting laid by a beautiful redhead. How do you start a release like that? ...For Immediate Release...I didn't fuck her?" He paused. "Cat got your tongue, Mr. Thompson?"

Thompson exhaled slowly as he looked at the bare light bulb on the ceiling shedding dim light on the walls of the dirty storage room. "So what do you and your clients want, Mr. Alley?" asked Thompson point blank.

"We want what everyone wants, Mr. Thompson. Good government. And for us, good government means that you back off on 936. Pull your ads. Change your speeches. I have your poll numbers and cross-tabs. You can win without it. Do my clients this small favor and they'll remember it throughout your long career in D.C. Don't do it and, well, you'll have no career in D.C."

"I don't want any favors from your client, Mr. Alley."

"It's a little too late for that now, Mr. Thompson. They've already done favors. They're maximum contributors to Citizens for Thompson, your official campaign committee."

"Who?"

"Don't worry about who. Be assured, Mr. Thompson, my clients are businessmen. They want you to win and to have a long and successful career in the United States Congress. We'd just like to persuade you to grant us our little favor. The photos and the contributions are just a little insurance policy so that, if you try to run to the authorities, we know it will affect you as much as us. Politics makes strange bed fellows. Right?"

Alley threw the photos of Thompson and the redhead on a stack of boxes containing election day sample ballots in the storage room. "Do we have a deal?"

"What about when I get there?" asked Thompson.

"What about it?" snarled Alley.

"How am I going to just drop the issue when I get there? I've made certain promises to the voters that I'm going to pursue this thing."

"You weren't listening, Mr. Thompson," said Alley. "I didn't ask you not to pursue it once you become Congressman Thompson. Just drop it right now, on the campaign trail. Once you get to Congress, you can drop a bill in the hopper to repeal it. Hold hearings on the issue. Hell, pass a bill with a fucking White House Rose Garden signing ceremony. My clients really don't care. Just shut up about it right now."

"I ask again," Alley smiled. "Do we have a deal?"

"We have a deal. The ads will be down tomorrow," said Thompson in a low voice knowing full well Griffith had already pulled the 936 ads to switch to the new warm and fuzzy, family values spot.

Alley put out his hand to Thompson.

"Stick it up your ass," Thompson said to Alley, as he used his hand to open the door to the storage room rather than shake.

Alley didn't particularly care about Thompson's disgust for him right now. He was finally going to have a phone call to Carpenter that was going to be a pleasant one.

As Thompson got in the car, he felt remarkably calm. He quietly slid the envelope containing the photographs into his briefcase on the back seat. The meeting in the storage room had lifted a huge burden off his shoulders. *I didn't do it. I didn't cheat on Ann. I'm not a sonofabitch. I didn't do it.*

Suddenly his thoughts shifted. *Who is Frank Alley? More importantly, who are his clients? Why do they want me to back off 936 until after the election? Should I care? Or, should I just go on with my life like nothing happened? Bullshit, why don't I just quit. I'll just drop out. I don't need this shit in my life. No one needs to know any of this stuff. No one needs to know, except Ann. I've still got to tell her. She'll freak, but she'll know what to do.*

Thompson popped Warren Zevon's *Learning to Flinch* into the CD player as Josh sped back up the Double A toward home. "Send lawyers, guns and money," he mumbled to himself, "the shit has hit the fan."

CHAPTER 13

Ann had left the kids with her sister and checked into the Marriott earlier in the day. She needed an hour or two by the pool with a good book before walking the three blocks or so from the hotel to her and Richard's favorite haunt. When Josh dropped Thompson off at the end of the campaign trip, Ann was already at the bar.

"Good evening, Congressman," said Jimmy as Thompson came through the front door of Chez Nora. "Pork chops are on the stove. Do you want your regular table?"

"Jimmy, in a week or so I promise you can call me Congressman," replied Thompson. "Until then, don't jinx it. And tonight, can we have the Judge's Chamber upstairs? We need a little privacy."

Jimmy smiled at the couple. "Yes, sir. Ann told me she wanted to get back to the room pretty quickly tonight."

After heading up the stairs and sitting down at the table in the private room, Richard Thompson looked into his wife's eyes a long time before saying anything to her.

"What?" asked Ann.

Campaigns and naked redheads were out of his mind. He was looking into her eyes just like he did on their first date, trying to figure out why someone like her ever ended up with someone like him.

"What?" she repeated.

Her question snapped him back into the reality of the situation. Thompson looked at his wife and posed the same question he was always asking her, "Why are we doing this?"

Ann was used to her husband constantly questioning his own integrity. It was one of the things she loved about him. Richard Thompson knew that he was good in a room. He knew he could get even the most cynical skeptic to follow him into hell if he wanted. So, occasionally, he wondered out loud to Ann if he was running for Congress because he believed or just because he believed he could win.

"Honey, do we really have to have that discussion again tonight? We've got no kids...a room. Jimmy's going to get us out of here quickly..."

"This isn't rhetorical tonight, babe." He paused and took a deep breath before beginning. "I've got something I've got to tell you... Remember when I was up in D.C. the other day? Something else happened. I was set up."

"What do you mean set up?" she asked laughing.

"I mean set up, set up. The morning after my dinner with Lackner...please don't flip out about this, but I woke up in bed with a redhead."

Ann started to laugh, thinking her husband's weird sense of humor was in overdrive. Her stomach turned over and she nearly threw up when Richard gently placed the pictures on the table.

She began to look through the photos. "Jesus Christ, Richard," her eyes filling up with tears as she gasped out the words. She stood up and started to walk out of the room.

"Please honey, don't leave. I need you more right now than I ever have in my life. This is real. I'm being set up. Please don't walk away."

Ann stopped and, without turning, said coldly, "You have exactly one minute."

"Today, some guy at the Fleming County stop approached me and said if I didn't drop the 936 ads, he'd release these to the press. I don't know who this girl is or how I got into bed with her. The last thing I remember about the whole evening was dinner with Lackner. I woke up the next morning and I'm in bed with this broad. I swear."

"My head is spinning right now Richard," said Ann still with her back still to her husband.

"You've got to believe me," he pleaded.

"Why should I?" she asked.

"Because of the pictures," he said in quick sentences. "Look closely at them. I'm asleep."

"And when were you going to tell me?" she said, her back starting to show some signs of relief.

"Tonight. I swear I was going to tell you tonight, Ann. Then, this guy brings me the pictures and threatens me. Please don't leave, Ann. I don't know what to do."

She turned and looked into Thompson's eyes. "Look me in the eyes and tell me you didn't screw this girl."

He paused and looked squarely into her eyes. "I'd never and I didn't."

Ann believed her husband couldn't look her in the eyes and lie about something like this.

"Who else knows about this?" asked Ann as she sat down, cutting to the point and purposely avoiding any more glimpses at the photos.

"No one knows right now. And apparently, as long as I do what some puke tells me to do in the next couple of days, no one except me, you and her ever will," he said pointing to the redhead in the photo.

"So, what do they want from you?" she asked.

"It's odd, Annie. All they want is for me to shut up about 936. Pull the ads. Take it out of my speeches. And we've already done that. I didn't tell the asshole who gave me these pictures today, but new ads go up tomorrow."

"When I told you talking like a political wonk would get you in trouble, I never envisioned this," she said as she gathered up the nerve to look at the photos. She held up one of them in the same manner Frank Alley had done earlier in the day, turning it askew to get a better angle. "I don't think that's possible," she said describing what she saw on the photo.

He picked up one of the other photos. "Look, if you look close enough on this one you can see I'm not even in her. I'm asleep, in more ways than one."

"Do you have any idea who she is?" asked Ann as she tried to get a better look at the face of the girl in the photo.

"That last picture, the autographed one, was sent to the office today," said Thompson. "Josh noticed the style is like the promotional photos for strippers. The envelope was marked from D.C."

Ann sat back trying to take it all in. "What's our options?" she asked.

"Right now, I'm considering dropping out." Thompson surprised his wife by his first preference.

"You can't be serious," was her response.

"Think of it, Ann. I've worked my ass off to accomplish what we've got in this world. Now, because of politics, I've put my family in a position where something like this can erase it all. I don't need this shit in my life. I really don't."

"I thought you believed? Isn't that why we're doing this?" asked Ann.

"I don't know any more, babe. I just don't know," he replied. "I used to think I believed. But, I'm so good in a room that I'm starting to doubt myself. I know when I walk into a room I can own it. Now, I'm not sure if I believe or if I just believe I can convince people in the room to think I believe."

"You've always told me life is more about asking the right questions than it is finding the right answers. If you're asking the right questions about why you should be a candidate, then you probably should be one. You're a candidate and you know it."

"You're right. Deep down I know you're right," he said. "But, I've got to wonder if all of this is worth it. Do you think I should quit?"

"And watch you walk around the house for the rest of our lives singing *Objects in the Rear View Mirror May Appear Closer Than They Are*. I don't think so."

"But it's true. Financially it's a bad deal. We're taking a cut in pay to be treated like this. I'll make a helluva lot more money practicing law than I will being a United States Congressman."

"Yes, you will, and you'll be unhappy the rest of your life. You've been around the business your whole adult life. You know not everyone gets a shot like this and chances are you won't get a second one. This is your time. No one ever said this was going to be easy. We'll get through this. It's time to drop any thoughts of quitting. It's time to get back on the fucking horse." Ann didn't drop the "F-bomb" often, so it got Thompson's attention.

There was a pause as Ann stared at her husband almost challenging him to oppose her conclusion. "So, what do they want from us? What's option number two?" she asked.

"Well, like I said, we've already pulled the ads," said Thompson. "To these assholes it will look like we're playing along. On one hand, we could forget about it and act like nothing happened. We win, go off to Washington and live happily ever after."

"And on the other hand?" asked Ann.

"On the other hand, we can try to find out who is doing this to us and why," said Thompson.

"Your call," said Ann.

"No way," Thompson replied. "This isn't about the race babe, it's about us."

"I don't know that I can push my brain that far tonight, Richard."

"You have to. Whatever we decide, it's going to have a huge impact on our lives. This decision is forever. I can't—no, I won't— make it without you being 110% on board."

Ann paused while she pondered the options. She looked at her husband. "Moderation in the pursuit of justice is no virtue."

Richard Thompson smiled. "You've been reading my Goldwater books, haven't you?"

"No. I've just been listening to you for so many years I've started to believe, too," she replied. She forced a smile in spite of the situation.

"So, what's the answer?" asked Thompson.

"I can't live the rest of my life with someone holding this over our heads," Ann said, holding up the photos and dropping them back down on the table. "Bastards like this will never let us go."

She paused, as if to clear her head of the images on the table in front of her.

"Don't you have a client with a private jet over at Lunken?" Ann asked, referring to a small general aviation airport on the outskirts of Cincinnati.

"Yeah. It's a real nice, six-seat Areostar," replied Thompson.

"Well, call him and tell him the campaign has to make an emergency trip to Washington."

"When?" asked Thompson.

"Now. This evening," she said. "If we're going to find out who's behind all of this, it starts with finding the bitch in these photos. And the sooner we find her, the sooner we can get to the bottom of this whole mess."

"He's what?" said Lawson.

"I told you," said Alley from his cell phone. At Carpenter's insistence, Alley had been following Thompson since their meeting earlier in the day to make sure he didn't go to the police. "He's at some little airport just outside Cincinnati getting on a private jet."

"Where the hell is he going?" came the obvious next question from Lawson.

"I'm not sure, but you better be on the ground at Dulles in an hour to make sure he's not coming to D.C."

"Shit. Carpenter had me fly back so I could stay at the office tonight and plan the logistics of the wire transfers for the closing."

"Well, if he's coming to D.C., you'll need to worry about more than the wires at the closing."

CHAPTER 14

In a town where sex and politics seem to run hand-in-hand, D.C. strip clubs are remarkably mild by comparison to those in other major U.S. cities. They are all located in a very small area of the downtown, away from The Mall and tourists, but easily found by convention-goers in the business district.

The girls, while totally nude on stage, don't interact much with the audience. Tips are either given at the stage by patrons or left on the tables for the girls as they walk through the audience following their dance. No $20 lap dances. No high-priced, B-girl drinks. Some clubs have private areas which allow more interaction between the girls and the customers, but for the most part, D.C. clubs are basic tits and ass on stage and nothing more. The guys standing in single file at the stage, each waiting to give $1 tips to his favorite girl, makes the scene look like an adult amusement park, with grown men behaving like hyperactive little boys in the line for the roller coaster ride.

For an hour or more, Thompson had been wandering from club to club, showing the photo of "Miss 936" to the dancers, bartenders and bouncers and, in return for a $5 or $10 tip, they would tell him if they knew who the mystery girl was and if they knew where she worked. As there were only 6 clubs in town, he was about $175 into tips when a when a cute, curly haired, bleached blond named Jade said she recognized the redhead. For an extra $40, Jade identified her as a stripper named "Amber Burn" who was working down the street at the Sultry Club, just around the corner from The Palm.

The Sultry Club was a huge upgrade from the clubs which Thompson had been in earlier in the evening. The Sultry Club contained two different stages on separate floors. On the lower floor was a brightly lit stage, with neon lights and mirrors, where anyone entering the club could go to enjoy the women who danced there. However, there was also a "Platinum Room" on the second floor—a "more private room," as the guy at the door described it—where a patron could go and enjoy his evening from the confines of a private bar and a dimly lit booth.

At the Sultry Club, Thompson paid the guy at the door the extra entry fee to be seated at a private booth in the Platinum Room, away from the crowds on the first level. He ordered up a Guinness and watched the girls come to the neon-framed stage one at a time, each for their three dance set. Just as the Sultry Club was clearly nicer than the ones he had visited earlier, Thompson couldn't help but notice the women were more pleasing to the eye as well. They did not have the hard look of girls from the other clubs and their bodies and movements oozed with eroticism.

It was clear the Sultry Club was the top gentlemen's club in D.C. in both the quality of the facility and the attractiveness of the women who danced there.

Once in the "Platinum" section of the club, Thompson also noticed the patrons, like him, who had paid extra got a smaller crowd and a better view without strobe lights. It was also apparently the room where the bigger tippers went for more action. In this private section, the girls were allowed to "visit" with customers at their tables following their dance. Platinum customers could approach the stage, give their favorite girl a tip and, at the end of the set, the girl would come over to his table.

That's why, when a certain redheaded stripper named "Amber Burn" spun around the pole and strutted to the front of the stage to face Richard Thompson, she did so as if she was greeting any other Sultry regular who wanted a little private time. It was only after she recognized his face that she froze.

Thompson gave her a $100 bill and said, "After your dance, why don't you sit down and have a drink with me. We've got a lot of catching up to do."

When "Amber" sat down at Richard Thompson's table, she was wearing a sheer top that allowed him to see the nipples of her breasts and a short skirt that scarcely covered her bare crotch. She pulled a cigarette out of her purse and held it out for Thompson to light. "I assume you're not here to take me up on my offer from the last time we were together?" she asked with a nervous laugh.

"No more than you really give a shit about Section 936 of the United States Tax Code."

"Is that what that 936 thing stood for?" she asked. "Are you some sort of tax guy or something?"

"No, actually I'm a lawyer who is...hold on...Don't you think it's my turn to ask the questions?" She shrugged. "First, what's your real name? I really feel funny calling you by your stripper name."

"Fair enough. You paid for the time," she said, constantly puffing through her cigarette. "I'm Tammy. Tammy Stewart. Next?"

"What the hell happened at the Hyatt last week?"

"Oh, my God, you were wonderful," she said as she snuggled up next to him in the booth. She rubbed the inside of his thigh. "I've never been fucked like that before in my life. You did things to my pussy I've never felt before. Look, why don't we just leave and we can have a repeat." She leaned over and whispered in his ear. "It'll be the best $100 you've ever spent."

"Cut the shit, Tammy," said Thompson as he pulled out the photos and tossed them on the table. Tammy grabbed the photos and looked them over in detail. She moved away from her place of intimacy next to Thompson and looked aimlessly towards the stage.

"Do you still want to go and earn another $100?" asked Thompson snidely.

"No, but if you want to know more about those pictures, it's gonna cost you more than what you paid up at the runway," Tammy replied.

He pulled out another $100 bill and placed it on the table. She caught a glimpse of the wad of cash in his wallet and smiled inwardly. *This could turn out to be a profitable evening,* she thought to herself as she grabbed the bill and tucked it into her small purse.

"I met you at the bar and tried to put the make on you," she said. "When it was clear you wouldn't take the bait, the guy sitting on the other side of you slipped something into your drink. We led you to your room, stripped you down, took some pictures and I went to sleep. Probably the first thing you can remember is when we woke up together the next morning."

"So who was the guy? Who are you working for?"

"I don't know. He comes in every now and then, and gives me cash to go to hotels and take pictures with naked, passed out, wrinkled old men. Then, he comes in a couple of days later and asks me to send a note to the lucky guy with a picture of me showing my tits."

"Why?"

"I don't know why. Find the guy who pays me and ask him."

"No. I mean why do you do it?"

"I make good money when I do it. At least it's easier than having some guy slobber all over your thigh while you swing on a brass pole."

"Jesus, you've done this with lots of other people, haven't you?"

"About a dozen, I think. Eleven men and one woman."

"Nice career."

"Don't look down your nose at me," snapped Tammy. "I saw how hard your dick was when you got out of bed that morning."

"So?"

"So," said Tammy. "You wanted a piece of my ass and you know it. You're no better than me, you were just afraid of being caught." She was as confident in the statement as she was in her moves on the stage.

"Maybe," said Thompson. "But I didn't go upstairs willingly, did I?"

"No, you didn't and, normally, they always go upstairs on their own. I usually don't have to slip 'em anything until we get to their room. You were the first guy we ever had to drug just to get upstairs. He slipped you the mickey and then we just acted like you were drunk and we had to get you back to your room. I was kind of hurt that you didn't want me."

"And how about the morning? Is that on film? Do you fuck each of them in the morning just before you leave?"

"No. I don't," she said with more than a little anger in her voice. "You think· I want to fuck those old codgers? I'm just supposed to make sure they know what I look like and get out."

"Look, they wanted a quick piece of ass and they got what they deserved. You were different from the rest of 'em. You were nice in the bar. You didn't even seem to realize I was coming on to you. I felt bad we had to drug you to get you upstairs. So, I wanted to make it up to you the next morning. No cameras. No one watching. Just you and me."

"Great," replied Thompson. "Even my blackmailer wants to throw me a pity fuck."

"Call it what you want. If you wanted to leave here right now, I'd go anywhere you wanted and fuck you like you've never been fucked before." She slid back over next to Thompson and put her hand on his inner thigh and spread her own legs just enough to let him see her intent. "You'll even go home with a little money left in your wallet."

"Anywhere I want to go?" he said looking into her eyes.

"Anywhere you say," she replied, rubbing closer to his crotch and sensing she had finally gotten through to him. She squeezed his penis through his pants. "And I do mean anywhere."

"Okay," Thompson responded. "Then how about you go with me to the F.B.I. to tell them what happened."

"No way, honey," she said. Tammy quickly pulled back her hand and sat straight up in the booth. "I'm not sure who these boys are who had me hit on you, but I know this. With the money they're paying, they're playin' in a game that's outta my league and probably even outta yours, too."

"I don't care," said Thompson.

"Well, I sure as hell do. I'll fuck you, but I ain't fuckin' with these boys. Come on, let's go to the back room. I'll blow you in the hallway for another $200."

"Fuck you. I'm out of here," said Thompson. "I've got a plane to catch."

Thompson stood up, walked away from the table and headed for the door. Once he was out on K Street he paused, took a deep breath and started trying to hail a cab.

As soon as a cab stopped, he told the cabbie through the rolled-down window he needed to get to the private aviation terminal at Dulles International. The driver nodded in agreement.

Just as Thompson opened the door to get in, Tammy suddenly ran out the front door of the club, coming directly at him. Actually, it would be more accurate to say she was *trying* to run, but doing a damned poor job of it in her new, Ebay purchased, red stripper stiletto heels. Without a word she brushed past him and jumped into the back seat of the waiting taxi.

Tammy tried to pull the door closed behind her, but Thompson had his right hand on the top of the door frame. He was able to hold the door open long enough to get into the seat next to her.

"Jesus Christ," Thompson shouted. "First you try to fuck up my life and now you're trying to steal my cab. Get out. I flagged this guy down. Go get your own god damned cab."

"Fuck that, get me out of here," said Tammy. "Driver, take us around the block a couple of times." As the cab slowly pulled away from the curb, the driver, not knowing quite what to do or who his fare was repeatedly glanced back in the mirror. Tammy fumbled in her purse for her cigarettes.

"You're shaking. What's wrong?"

"I think you were followed here," she said, as she lit up a smoke and took a first calming draw.

"Followed? By whom?"

"I don't know his name. But a couple of times, when the guy who paid me to set you up would come to the club, he'd bring along another guy with him…real sleazy type…always trying to feel my ass and shit. Right after you left, I saw him. He's in the club tonight, by himself, at a booth in the corner."

"Good. Let's stop the cab, go back inside and you can just point him out to me. I'll take it from there."

"No fucking way. I don't know who you are or why they want you set up, but they must know you're here. And I don't want to get in any deeper with them than I already am."

Tammy and Thompson were both silent for a few seconds, as the cab continued to crawl around the block through the D.C. traffic. Both of them were trying to get a handle on whatever in the hell was happening to them and what to do next.

"Look," Tammy resumed. "I just got scared when I saw him and I freaked out a little bit. I don't know if he saw me with you, or not. I know for damn sure I don't want to talk to him tonight."

"You don't have to," Thompson replied. "Like I said, just point him out to me and I'll do all the talking."

Tammy took another long and soothing draw on the cigarette, and as she exhaled she seemed to have made up her mind. "No, just drop me off at the back door of the club. I'm gonna go back in and try to act like nothing's happening. I'm supposed to be back on stage in about 15 minutes. Anyway, I'm pretty sure I don't want that scum bag to even know I was gone."

"Then I'm going in the back door with you."

"No way. Not a chance."

Thompson was beyond exasperated. "Listen, somebody is fucking with my life here and you're already up to your tits in it. I've got enough to go to the feds with you and you alone right now. Do you really want to go to jail for these pukes? I don't want to turn you in, but I will. I swear to God I will turn your little cheap ass over in a heartbeat."

Tammy began to cry. "Please don't go to the cops or anybody. I'm not the one who's after you. I just needed the money. I don't need any trouble like this."

"You've already got trouble," Thompson responded. "And you've got a choice to make. Show me who the real bad guys are, so I can fuck with them and leave you out of it. Or, don't show me who they are, and I'll go get the F.B.I. to come and talk with you about trying to blackmail me, and you can fuck with the F.B.I. Your choice."

In response, Tammy sobbed deeply and fixed a look on Thompson that was half accusatory and half pleading.

Thompson couldn't play the bad cop role for long with a woman who was crying, even if she was a stripper who had helped to set him up. He changed his approach and his voice became much more conciliatory. "Look, Tammy, I've got three kids. I don't want them knowing about any of this crap. I don't know why these guys want me set up either. I may never find out unless I get a good look at this guy." There was a pause. "Come on, Tammy. Look, if you wanted to fuck me to sorta pay me back for what you did, do this one thing for me and we'll call it even."

She thought about it for a few seconds, biting the red lip stick covering her lower lip. "Even?"

"Even," he replied.

Tammy's crying quickly subsided—perhaps a little too quickly.

"All right," she said in a small voice. "Cabbie, make a right at the alley and stop by the red door." After a short silent drive, she jumped from the cab. "Wait here while I clear it with the guys inside."

The door flew open a minute or so later, and Tammy waved for Thompson to come on in. Thompson handed the cabbie an extra $50 and asked him to stay in the alley and keep the engine running. "We may need to make a quick exit," Thompson told the driver.

Griffith and Thompson had spent a lot of time at strip clubs back in their college days, but they never went backstage to the girls' dressing room. He instinctively froze for a moment as he stood in a room with 8 or 10 beautiful women in various stages of undress.

A stunningly attractive young brunette woman in orange heels that matched her lip stick, and who went by the stage name of Suzi Q, was the first to notice Thompson was in the dressing room. "Oh look girls," she said as she slapped Tammy on the ass. "Amber's got a date for the night. If you bring him home tonight don't make those loud squeaky noises when you come. I've got an English exam in the morning and I need my sleep."

Thompson's feet felt as if they were set in concrete. A goofy smile broke out over his face as he peered across more bare skin than he had ever seen since peeking into the shower at a girl's dorm in college. His eyes shot from side to side until he felt a tug on his arm. "I thought you were married," Tammy said sarcastically as she pulled him through the gaggle of exposed breasts. "Cool your jets, Romeo—half of them are lesbians."

They entered a dark hallway, maneuvered past a woman giving a man a blow job against the wall and proceeded up a set of stairs to the room where the deejay played the music for the girls on stage in the Platinum Room. The small room smelled like three-day-old bong water. It had windows with one way mirrors so the deejay could see the girls on the stage, but no one in the crowd could see the deejay inside.

"Look behind that couple over there. That's him. Over at the table in the corner."

"Sonofabitch," said Thompson.

"What? Do you know him?"

"Yeah. His name's Virgil Lawson."

"Who is he? How do you know him?"

"He's a big-time K Street lobbyist. I pissed him off a few days ago when I wouldn't take a couple of checks from him." He leaned back against the wall of the sound booth to contemplate the situation.

"So what are you going to do now?" asked Tammy.

"Now? Now, I'm going home," replied Thompson.

There was an awkward silence as the two looked at each other. "I'm sorry," she said, not sure how to say what she was sorry for. "I really am sorry."

"I know you are," replied Thompson as they headed out the door of the sound booth and headed back down the stairs. "Do yourself a big favor and find another line of work."

"What do you mean by that?" she asked, sounding more than mildly offended.

"No, no, no—don't take it wrong. Look you're pretty. You're smart. Somewhere in there you have a heart. You don't expect to do this your whole life, do you? Show your tits to men for money?"

They stopped at the bottom of the stairs. The guy in the hallway getting the blow job was moaning in climactic pleasure. Without needing to reach an agreement over their next movement, the pair decided to wait a minute or two before attempting to maneuver past him again.

"I've never really thought about it. I started doing it young and I've never really thought much about doing anything else," she replied.

"Well, at some point you're gonna have to think about your future," Thompson said in a voice low enough to avoid distracting the couple blocking their exit. "Eventually, there'll come a point in time where gravity will take over and likely kill your career."

"My future. Right," she said in an equally low voice. "I'm too busy trying to make ends meet to sit around and think about my future."

"Doesn't all this make you feel …well…cheap?" Thompson asked.

"In the beginning, yeah, it did. Standing naked in front of a bunch of drunks for money is sort of humiliating. But, I got the body to make money with my ass. When I first started dancing, I cried myself to sleep just about every night. But, then, I guess I just got used to it."

"You got used to it?" asked Thompson sincerely. "How do you get used to doing this for a living?"

"I don't know. It just happened," she replied. "One day, I just decided to quit crying. I guess after a while, when I walked into a club to dance, I'd check a part of me at the door. Then, one day I forgot to pick that part of me back up on the way out."

"It doesn't have to be that way," Thompson said.

The guy in the hallway finished his transaction with the young lady on her knees in a series of unmistakable groans and expletives. After a few moments of awkwardness, Thompson and Tammy made their way down the now empty hallway.

"You're a sweet guy. But you're from another world. People like me don't get second chances. Go back to your wife and kids. And remember, we're even." Tammy looked at him in a sad sort of way and kissed him gently on the cheek before she opened the door to the brightly lit dressing room. She pointed the way out of the club to the alley and the waiting cab. But, as he walked through the dressing room, she didn't follow.

The flight back to Cincinnati was a mixed bag of emotions for Richard Thompson. He was relieved to confirm nothing sexual had actually happened between him and Amber ...Tammy... whatever her name was.

The lawyer part of his brain also took comfort in knowing he had done nothing more culpable than make small talk with a woman at a hotel bar. Everything past that point had been beyond his control.

Tammy Stewart had not turned out to be quite what Richard Thompson had expected. He had flown to D.C. not even knowing her name and fully prepared to hate her for what she had done to him and his family. Yet, she had turned out to be a sad little pawn in a game she herself neither understood nor even cared about.

But the face he could not get out of his mind was that of Virgil Lawson. *Lawson is the one who was doing this to me*, Thompson mused. *Or, more likely, he's one of the front men for whoever is willing to ruin my life.*

Lawson was clearly participating in this personally and taking huge risks to do so. And, so was his employer, whoever that might turn out to be.

Marcus Lackner? Maybe. But why would Lackner care so much about Section 936 of the United States Tax Code simply being debated on the campaign trail?

Lackner and Lawson were both clearly unhappy with me talking about 936, but I can not see any reason they would otherwise necessarily have anything to do with each other. With Lackner it was probably just a Republican political thing—don't rock the boat with the G.O.P. by calling attention to corporate welfare disguised as "tax incentives." Party unity's important, and D.C. is a tough town, but it isn't likely that somebody in the Republican leadership would be arranging a set up for one of the party's own candidates, complete with strippers and photos.

On the other hand, Lawson, as a lobbyist, played both sides of the aisle, so he would have no constraint against setting up someone who was a Republican candidate in a special election.

Maybe he was working in conjunction with the Pope campaign. According to people in the community, Pope is a loose cannon. Could he stoop so low as to set me up with a stripper? He's already been spreading rumors about me. Maybe, he wanted pictures to back it up. But, if it was Pope, he'd want more than to have me back off an ad. He'd want me out. Or worse yet, he'd have already dumped the photos in unmarked envelopes to the press.

If Lawson was hanging out with the guy who helped Tammy get me up to my room at the hotel, and Frank Alley ended up with the pictures the next day, then clearly Lawson and Alley were working together.

But for whom? And why?

Was it politics? Or, was it business?

Alley said they don't care if it's actually repealed. They just want me to shut up about it for a few more days. It just doesn't make any sense.

Thompson pulled out The Fat Man's three-ring binder and began to pour over the information his law partner had gotten on Lawson, until the plane landed softly at Lunken. Mentally, emotionally and physically exhausted, Thompson barely kept his eyes open long enough to see the friendly confines of his own bedroom.

Chapter 15

"Nine days left folks! What were the overnight top lines?" asked Thompson as he bounced into the campaign office.

Ann had lectured him before he left the house that it was time to put his game face on with the campaign staff. "You've got to put this whole Tammy thing aside and start acting like it's the final sprint to the finish line. You can make a crowd of voters believe; now it's time to make your staff believe, too. They need you on your A-game now."

As tough as it was going to be, Thompson knew his wife was right. So as he drove to the campaign office that morning, he turned up Meat Loaf as high as his ear drums would allow. He pulled into the parking lot with a new outlook and determination which masked his concerns over the events of which had taken place the night before. "Come on, boys, give me your best shot!"

"You're in a good mood this morning," laughed Griffith. "It looks like your poll numbers weren't the only thing up over the last 24 hours. Did you wear the cape last night?"

"Bite me. Nine days. What's the number?"

"Good news, pal," said Griffith as he passed the freshly printed pages to his candidate, "you've gone up over 50%. We've got a seven point margin and rising. You've got to be caught with a live boy or a dead woman to lose this one. Check out the *Cincinnati ADI* cross-tab. These numbers will dry up Billy Boy's money in the final days."

"Anybody endorse this morning?"

"None this morning, but we expect the *Post* and *Daily Independent* to be out later today. After that meeting with the editorial board in Ashland, I don't expect we'll get the *Independent*, but our best bet is they don't beat you up too bad. And," said Griffith, "the closer is in the can."

Thompson shot over to Griffith's computer screen to get his first look at the 30 second ad produced to close out the campaign on television. Thompson played it over and over again as Griff and Josh looked over his shoulder. They waited for his response with anticipation. Thompson turned to the pair with a scowl on his face and looked them squarely in the eyes for a couple of seconds, which to Griff and Josh felt like an eternity. Then, a smile broke out on his face.

"Damn boy, you've saved your best for this one," said Thompson as he high fived Griffith. "When does it go up?"

"Thursday," said Griffith proudly. "And with this we waltz to victory next Tuesday night."

"Beauty. What's on the schedule for today?" asked Thompson.

"Easy day. Money calls in the morning. The list is on your desk. You've got lunch at the senior center in Campbell County. Door to door in Grant County and then attend dinner at the Grant County GOP monthly meeting. We drop the social security mailer to the 50+ list today. And the final letters to the editor and press releases get mailed out to the weeklies today."

"Put the mail schedule on my secret page. I want to look at it when I get home tonight." Thompson paused. "And let's pull the letters to the editor on 936. I think that issue has run its course. Replace them with some standard family values crap."

Campaigns write their own letters to the editor and then find supporters to send them. It doesn't take much to change them before they are sent in to the papers.

"Wonk Boy is backing off his super issue? What's wrong? Cape fall off last night?"

"No, I'd just like the letters to close with the same message as the closer ad."

"You're the candidate," said Griffith. "I just want your name in the paper. I don't give a damn about the issue. We can bang new ones out in an hour or so."

"Change them?" Josh asked Griffith in a tone he hoped would reverse the decision back to the status quo.

"Josh, I'm surprised at you," replied Griffith. "All of our people are businessmen. Our loyalty is based on that. Now, one thing you should learn is to try and think as people around you think. Now on that basis, anything is possible."

"Michael Corleone to Tom Hagin, *Godfather II*, right?" asked Josh.

"Right," replied Griffith. "You're catching on. Oh, Rick, I almost forgot. Call The Fat Man at the office. He's called here four times already this morning looking for you. He's all fired up over something."

"We've got 'em on the run," was The Fat Man's opening line.

"What the hell are you talking about," replied Thompson.

"I figured it out," said The Fat Man.

"Figured what out?" replied Thompson. "Please slow down and let me know what's going on with you."

"Well, I know you were disappointed with my research so I kept looking," said The Fat Man. "Then it hit me. When that Lawson guy was in your office he asked you to back off 936 until election day. Why that day, I asked myself."

"Did you answer yourself, too?" Thompson asked.

"I did after I did some more online research. Lawson does lobbying work for Livius Drugs, right? You probably saw that in the binder."

"Right." Thompson hadn't noticed but was playing along.

"So," said The Fat Man "I went online and looked at Livius' recent Securities and Exchange Commission filings. Lo and behold, I find a filing that they're buying a drug manufacturing plant in Puerto Rico. And here's the rub. Guess when the closing is set for?"

"I don't know, but I assume you're going to tell me," replied Thompson.

"The day before the election."

"And what does that have to do with anything?"

"I'm not sure, but I know I'm onto something."

"And how do you know that?" asked Thompson.

"Well, I called them," he replied. Apparently, The Fat Man had decided Thompson wasn't acting quickly enough on the information he had provided. So, just as he usually did in their law practice, he took matters into his own hands, did his research and had placed a call to Carl Bontiff, the President of Livius Drugs Company in New York, to ask about their acquisition of Caribbean Drugs.

According to The Fat Man, the call was great. But, as he related the blow-by-blow of the conversation, Thompson felt the knot in his stomach continue to grow.

The Fat Man had had Bontiff on the run from the start of the call. Bontiff acted like he knew nothing, but The Fat Man perceived the guy on the other end of the phone was hiding something. He had kept pushing. He had kept prodding. But Bontiff wouldn't give a straight answer to any of the probing questions about Livius Drug's pending deal to acquire Caribbean Drugs. Not even when The Fat Man accused Livius' top brass of using political contributions as bribes to Thompson.

The Fat Man was elated his call had touched a nerve somewhere, because Livius Drug's law firm had faxed a letter that morning demanding Bradley and the firm cease and desist from all calls to Bontiff and other agents of Livius. With great glee, he read to Thompson the parts of the letter claiming Bradley had defamed the company, possibly tortuously interfered with a pending business transaction and had violated the Lanham Act.

"We've got the lyin' rat bastards on the run!" he exclaimed to Thompson.

"Jesus Christ, Joe," burst Thompson into the call. "What the hell prompted you to do this? I didn't tell you to do this. Send a letter apologizing and comply with the cease and desist. What the fffffuu…'" Thompson paused in an effort to avoid totally losing his cool with his friend and law partner, "…heck were you thinking?"

"What are you talking about, Rick? Last week you wanted me to find out everything about these guys. Now you get a couple of campaign contributions and you want me to back off."

"Just do it, Joe," whispered Thompson over the phone. "Look, I can't tell you why, but these bastards have got my balls in a vice. It's not the contributions. This is bigger than the campaign. You need to back off, at least for the time being."

"Yes, you can."

"Can what?"

"Can tell me. Among other things, I'm counsel to you and the campaign. Remember? Our conversations are lawyer-client privileged."

Thompson paused. "This is more than what you bargained for as a volunteer. I don't want to get you into this."

"Griff says you're going to Grant County tonight. How about I drive? You tell me what's going on and I'll decide if I want to get involved."

Later that evening, after he had dropped Thompson off at home, The Fat Man went back to his office and sat blank faced in front of his computer. The story Thompson had told him was more outrageous than he could have ever imagined. His best friend was being set up. Strippers and political graft were not going to look good if those allegations saw the light of day.

The Fat Man couldn't decide if he was more shocked by the story Thompson had told him or by the fact he was online buying a plane ticket for himself to Puerto Rico.

CHAPTER 16

The life of a business deal is nothing like the producer of a television reality show would have you believe. For the most part, there are no power hungry men or wicked women in Gucci shoes sitting around in chi-chi restaurants over three martini lunches conjuring up evil ways to conquer the world's market share of widgets. While merger and acquisition deals may sometimes seem threatening and even vaguely mystical to the outside world when they are ultimately announced or leaked, they are the result of countless hours, days and weeks of discussions between the men and women who put them together.

Gordon Gecko was a great character in *Wall Street*, but you'd really be hard pressed to find his type in the angel finance firms which deal in mergers and acquisitions.

Business people do meet over lunch, but it's usually by coincidence at one of the members-only business clubs where they go to entertain customers, at a Chamber of Commerce function, or at some other industry-specific national convention. The competitors generally know each other, either personally or at least by reputation. Because they are usually in the same line of business or related lines of business, they are very likely to have worked for the same company, had the same boss, or shared the same customers at some point in their careers.

If and when they sit down together to talk aloud about a combination, they start talking about the "what ifs" of a union of their two businesses. The prospects of two firms with similar ambitions working together for the economic well being of both gets the free market blood flowing.

They fight over the tab and agree they should keep talking.

Those early dreaming sessions lead to more formal meetings. The top management from both companies conduct a joint "visioning" session to see where a union could take them. In reality, these sessions are more often referred to as "asshole" sessions, because both sides are looking at the other to see if they have any real assholes in top management they'd have to deal with after a merger.

If the "visioning" session works out, teams from the two companies start getting down to the brass tacks of drafting an initial term sheet: Are we really merging or are you buying us? How much will it cost? Who stays? Who goes? Who gets the golden parachute?

The devil is in the details, and lawyers are the devils who put the details on paper. Days and weeks are spent negotiating the language in the sale documents. Lawyers argue for hours, sometimes clarifying the substance of the details, but more often than not simply changing "beautifuls" to "lovelies." In an asset deal, you have to spell out in great detail the assets being purchased and excluded. In a merger, great effort is put into identifying both the known and contingent liabilities the surviving company might be accepting by "merging in" the other. In either format, hours upon hours are spent deciding who is going to survive with a job and who is going to get a big buyout to leave. Both sides often have a "no material adverse change" clause that would allow the company to back out if something goes badly awry in the time gap between the hand shake and the actual closing.

While all of this is going on, executives in each company are directing what is generally referred to in the merger and acquisition community as "due diligence." Due diligence is exactly what the words indicate. Someone at the acquiring company has to check out all of the key details about the company being acquired to make sure the transaction is a good deal. The process is a lot like a buyer's home inspection, but with hundreds of boxes of business documents to examine rather than water pipes and floor trusses. It's like checking to see if the deal has termites or not.

Teams are assembled to audit the acquired company's financials, assemble and review on-going contractual obligations and assess employee relations. The executive who heads up the due diligence team is usually someone high up on the company food chain whom everyone in the company that's doing the "buying" respects and depends on to make sure the company being acquired doesn't have any significant hidden defects.

Thus, when Livius Drugs made an offer to purchase Caribbean Drugs, it was not outside of the norm that Livius' Chief Financial Officer, Lawrence Carpenter, volunteered to take on the massive task of supervising the due diligence for the acquisition. Carl Bontiff was the President and CEO of Livius Drugs selected by the Board and its shareholders. True, he was the dashing young CEO featured on the cover of *Success Magazine* as one of the top rising young execs in America. But everyone on the inside looked to Lawrence Carpenter as the man who had taken Livius to its current spot as a Fortune 500 company. Heading the due diligence team on a major acquisition was the type of thing that Carpenter was known for in the business world.

Since Bontiff and Carpenter were not even remotely close, Bontiff was glad to have Carpenter engaged in anything. Carpenter had brought the deal to the attention of Bontiff and maybe Carpenter's involvement in the implementation of the acquisition would help form a bond previously missing between the two.

Lawrence Carpenter had come to Livius Drugs more than twenty five years before, after spending his first six years out of college at the accounting firm which had done the company's books since its formation. He knew the company from the financials up. His financial advice, especially his advice on where the company should make its growth moves, had earned him respect in the business world as the man who took Livius Drugs from its mid-spot in the market as a specialty drug company producing over the counter cold remedies to one of the largest prescription drug manufacturers in the country.

Carpenter's tax background allowed him to analyze the tax benefits of Livius' acquisitions and product ventures like no one else in the industry. When President Ronald Reagan got the Congress to pass his Caribbean Basin Initiative, Carpenter had spearheaded Livius' moves to establish a Caribbean based drug manufacturing facility in Puerto

Rico. The move had made him an instant player in some of Washington's mid-level power circles. He was often called on to testify before Congress regarding the benefits of using tax incentives to create jobs in U.S. territories. Carpenter's rise to prominence had been impressive, and he had the Mercedes convertible to prove it. But he wanted more.

Unfortunately, when boards of directors of publicly-traded companies go out looking for new leadership, they feel they owe it to their shareholders to do "a national search." Boards want a new fresh perspective. They look for a person who can fit into the company's corporate culture and develop new paradigms (whatever the hell those are). In doing so, Boards often fail to see the leadership that has developed within the successful corporate culture they created.

And that's exactly what Livius' board had done two years ago when its CEO retired. They decided the company needed a fresh perspective. Oh, they had made sure Lawrence Carpenter was one of the three finalists for the job. But, with all due respect to Carpenter, they never really had any intention of hiring from within. When the dust settled, the board went outside the company to hire one of Wall Street's new wiz kids, Carl Bontiff, to give Livius the fresh look they so badly desired.

To all outward appearances, Carpenter took the news well. Inside his mind, however, he began to believe he was not chosen because of some intra-company scheme to keep him out of the top spot. He looked at board members with the jaundiced eye of someone who believed they were always talking behind his back, going silent just as he walked into the Board Room. He trusted no one, especially Bontiff and the other new faces whom Bontiff had brought with him into management at Livius. Carpenter's desire to be the ongoing architect of Livius' future waned as his inner-demons searched for a conspiratorial cause of his corporate misfortune.

As Carpenter's anger grew, he began to look for a way to get what was rightfully his. He deserved the package that would have landed him a retirement home in Belize, not Carl Bontiff. He didn't care about the next quarterly report of Livius. He had a lot of time and effort invested in the company. Hell, in Carpenter's mind he **was** the company. And the shallow, uninformed idiots on the board had taken it away from him. Worse yet, he had to suffer the daily humiliation of watching everyone fawn all over the next young hotshot CEO with a blow dry and shallow "can do" attitude who didn't know one tenth as much about the industry as Carpenter did.

Carpenter wanted to leave, to move on to a life of umbrella drinks and easily impressed young women looking for a rich father figure to have sex with on the beach in front of a mansion in a Caribbean paradise. But he did not have quite enough in stock and options to fund the kind of truly luxurious life he wanted—at least not **yet**.

It was only when Carpenter met Gilberto Guidos last year that Carpenter realized there was still a viable strategy for getting a personal "golden parachute" for himself from the boys at Livius that would allow him to enjoy everything he ever wanted for the rest of his life.

Shortly after Bontiff's hiring, Carpenter had met Guidos, an aspiring young union leader, at a lunch meeting in Puerto Rico. Their worlds were light years apart, with two simple exceptions. Both had secret agendas and both needed money to get them accomplished.

Guidos had been one of the more popular rank-and-file union members at the Caribbean Drugs plant near San Juan, Puerto Rico. He was dynamic and one of the union members whom other rank-and-file members just-naturally looked to for leadership. Nevertheless, despite his apparent popularity, his attempts to move into formal union leadership had been thwarted on numerous occasions.

Many within the union blamed Guidos' inability to get elected to a leadership position on his statements in support of anti-Castro rebels in Cuba. "The workers don't give a damn about Cuba," they'd tell him. But Guidos himself suspected his losses in prior union elections were more likely the result of corrupt union leadership and their ability to direct the money from union dues rather than the result of any of his anti-Castro political leanings.

Guidos was certain he had won his last campaign, and he was convinced the existing union leadership had cooked the outcome to have him lose by a couple of dozen votes. Even after getting roughed up by goons on election night, Guidos had declared his candidacy for a spot in the next union election. He could clear up much of the corruption, get better results for the workers and make sure some of those dues were currently going into the pockets of corrupt union leaders went to the rebels in Cuba.

One man's corruption is another man's cause.

But Guidos needed seed money to get elected. He needed support from the mainland. He needed men like Lawrence Carpenter and Marcus Lackner.

And Lawrence Carpenter soon realized that, somewhat to Carpenter's surprise, he needed—or at least could use—a man like Gilberto Guidos. The dues structure of the union was such that, with some help from Carpenter and some creative accounting, Carpenter and Guidos could both have access to an almost unlimited flow of funds, out of which they could each fund the righteous cause which he championed. For Guidos that meant helping to fund potential freedom fighters who would rise up when Castro finally—and, thank God, inevitably died. For Carpenter, it meant getting enough ongoing kick backs from union dues to buy the house in Belize and to live off the vig of Guidos' secret bank accounts for the remainder of his days.

The plan, as devised by Carpenter, started off with a move that was relatively straight forward. Livius Drugs would acquire Caribbean Drugs. Caribbean Drugs had grown dramatically, it had a strong cash flow and the deal made business sense. On paper and in the Board room, it was pretty easy to justify.

What was not written down was Carpenter's plan to use his political connections from South Florida to fund a secret bank account to buy out the existing union leadership at the Caribbean Drugs facilities and put Guidos in place to succeed them. The anti-Castro friends of Congressman Marcus Lackner, who badly wanted Fidel, Raul, Fidelite and everybody else named Castro out of power, would be more than glad to put cash into that account to get the existing union leaders out of the way.

Guidos would take over as head of the union. Once in place, using a series of complex account transfers designed by Carpenter, Guidos would increase the benefits to the union workers, direct excess cash to the anti-Castro forces in Cuba—and direct a healthy ongoing stipend to Carpenter, as architect of the scheme.

The key to making the set up work without detection were typical of many embezzlement schemes.

First, it was helpful that—courtesy of the intentional confusion generated by the outgoing union leadership as a cover for their own sins—very few people really understood the flow of funds that came out of the workers' pay checks as union dues. A couple of extra vaguely named accounts and a few extra wire transfers would be sufficient to confuse all but the most persistent and curious of potential auditors. The fact that the total of the various amounts coming out of the workers' checks did not quite add up to the total of the amounts going into the union's various accounts would go unnoticed.

Secondly, it was comforting to know that Carpenter himself—in his capacity as Chief Financial Officer at Livius Drugs—would be in a position to get an early warning if anybody ever did detect the inconsistencies.

Finally, and from Carpenter's standpoint this was just icing on the cake, the diversion of funds by the prior union leadership had been so large and persistent that the union members themselves had come to have very low expectations. So long as the total amount diverted to the anti-Castro forces and Carpenter himself was less than the old union leaders had been taking out, the union members would perceive a **net increase** going into the various union programs.

Guidos, the new union leader, would be perceived as a young and dynamic hero who had helped the workers.

Lackner wanted to be seen as anti-Castro. His role in this arrangement, though blatantly illegal, would indirectly win him the support of the South Florida Cuban community. To the extent the appreciative and discreet anti-Castro element in Cuba went out of their way to make it clear they were proud to have a friend in the United States like Congressman Marcus Lackner, he would be seen as a brother in the battle against Castro.

And Carpenter would get even with the bastards who screwed him out of the CEO spot by living out his days at home on a beach in Belize, fully and perpetually funded by a flow of cash, right from under their noses.

The funny thing about the trio of Lackner, Guidos, and Carpenter was they all three believed that everything—the kickbacks, the illegal actions—was completely justified. Guidos believed, quite correctly, that through this arrangement he could simultaneously improve the lives of the underpaid workers at Caribbean Drugs and benefit the cause of the anti-Castro forces in Cuba. Lackner believed that by helping Guidos win the presidency he could do his part to help his anti-Castro constituency in South Florida defeat Communism in Cuba. And Carpenter, well, Carpenter believed it was time to take what was rightfully his from Livius Drugs.

The deal was set to close on July 16, the Monday before the Tuesday special election in Kentucky's Fourth Congressional District. All contingencies in the purchase contract had been met, except one.

Bontiff had insisted on one contingency in the purchase contract which, at the time, had not given Carpenter any reason for pause. It was the relatively standard clause which would allow Livius Drugs to terminate the deal, without penalty, at any time based upon any material adverse change prior to closing that might affect the profitability of Caribbean Drugs. It really didn't seem like any big deal at the time of the negotiation.

But then some Congressional candidate in a special election in Kentucky had started talking loudly and vigorously about repealing Section 936 of the United States Code. The national media had picked up on it. Next thing Carpenter knew, Bontiff and the Board had started looking at what the profitability of the Caribbean Drugs acquisition would be if there were no tax credits available in the future and the possibility of calling off the deal.

Carpenter had already seen his ascent to the role of Chief Executive Officer at Livius Drugs thwarted. That failure, at the hands of the Board had fueled his innate paranoia.

Carpenter was convinced Richard Thompson knew about the deal and was conspiring to end it. Perhaps members of Livius' Board of Directors who were secretly opposed to the deal were funding Thompson's campaign, and encouraging him to speak out against Section 936. After all, how unlikely was it that a Congressional candidate from a small town in Kentucky, and Garrett Jackson's hand-picked successor, would, without strong encouragement from someone, make Caribbean Basin tax credits a central issue in his campaign? And talk to the national media about it. And just happen to do so in the two weeks leading up to the closing on the deal that would give Carpenter his one-way ticket to paradise.

Carpenter decided he had to act, and act quickly, if the deal were still to become a reality. If those stories about the headstrong candidate from Kentucky stopped, he could check-mate Bontiff and the Board and force the issue on the Caribbean Drugs deal. If the stories continued, the lawyers kept calling and the deal died before July 16, someone would pay. Others had already done so and he had no problem with adding one more to the list

Carpenter was not afraid to go to any lengths to insure the deal's success. Richard Thompson was not going to stop him. After all, one Congressman was already dead and another had been forced to resign her seat. Carpenter considered the death of some unknown candidate for Congress just the third in his Congressional trifecta.

CHAPTER 17

"...And so that's why I wanted to start out our bus tour this morning in Ludlow, Kentucky, the town my family has called home for four generations and in front of this building where my dad once sat as president of such a fine organization." Thompson paused and looked into the faces of the many friends and family who had come out early in the morning to help kick off the campaign bus tour from the parking lot of the Ludlow Vets. He couldn't help but smile a sincere grin of appreciation for their loyal support.

Thompson reveled in being from the small Kentucky river town. It seemed a day didn't go by without Thompson telling some one the hit movie *Lost in Yonkers* was filmed just across from his boyhood home. "Ludlow today looks more like Yonkers in the 40's than Yonkers does," he would laugh. When he wasn't talking about how the movie had been filmed there, Thompson was telling people how Christopher Walken's first big role as an actor was as a 12 year old, starring in the NBC summer replacement show *The Wonderful John Acton* about an Irish shopkeeper in Ludlow, Kentucky. So it was appropriate that Thompson kick off the final event of his campaign for Congress in his hometown.

"Next time we're together, we're going to be celebrating that a kid from Ludlow, Kentucky, can make his way to the halls of the

United States House of Representatives. Thank you for coming out so early. God bless all y'all, God bless Ludlow, Kentucky, and God bless the United States of America."

Even though technology has taken over nearly every aspect of modern day campaign activities, the old-fashioned bus tour remains one of the staples of electioneering in the South. The candidate and his wife jump on a bus along with staff and volunteers for three or four grueling days of non-stop campaigning. Each county has at least one stop where everyone unloads and holds an old-fashioned political rally organized by the local party faithful. In some counties there is more than one stop. Lunches and dinners are planned with great care to insure the bus stops at establishments frequented by locals and operated by supporters.

There is an advance team which travels from stop to stop, making sure the podium is set up and the microphone and speakers are working. As soon as the bus arrives, the advance team is off to the next stop. Then, there is a trailer car which breaks down the sound system, packs up the podium and picks up any staffers or volunteers left behind when the campaign bus pulled out. The advance team and trailer car are constantly trading equipment back and forth from stop to stop to the point they have to take inventory at the end of the day to see who has what.

While the bus is on the road, the candidate is on the phone talking to reporters and radio talk shows. And while he's talking to one reporter, someone else is setting up the next call. Loyal supporters jump on the bus for a leg at a time to impress their local folks they're traveling with the candidate. Occasionally, a local reporter who has been friendly during the campaign gets to jump on for a leg, too.

Every morning on the Thompson for Congress tour there was a staff meeting at 6:00 a.m., in which the first order of business for the staff was Griffith's review of any movement in the polling numbers from the previous evening. Next, Josh would go over the morning press clippings for Thompson and Pope that he had been able to pull off the internet. Finally, the group would discuss the schedule for the day and any changes in assignments. This morning meeting was also where the message for the day would be tweaked, revised and tweaked again.

At the end of the day, after dinner, one room at the new hotel was used as a "war room" to debrief every one of the day's activities. What went right? What went wrong? Maker's Mark could always be found in the smoke-filled "war room" and, at the end of the day on the bus trip, bourbon and cigarettes were a necessity for getting unwound and ready for sleep.

Griffith did his best to keep Thompson out of these morning and evening campaign staff meetings. The candidate needs his rest to look as fresh as possible on the trail. The less he worries about details, the better. After the morning staff meeting, Griffith would meet privately with the candidate and his wife to let them know the good or bad of the day's poll numbers and press. Before the evening meeting, Griffith would always ask the pair for their input on the day.

Ann's job, secretly given to her by Griffith, was to keep her husband occupied when these meetings were going on. "My advice to you," he told Ann on the day before they left, "is to get ready for lots and lots of campaign sex."

"Leave that to me," assured Ann. "By the time I'm done with Ricky each night, you'll have to call him 'candlelight.'"

"Candlelight?" asked Griffith.

"Yup, one long blow and he'll be out like a light."

"Never underestimate the power of the pillow, babe," replied Griffith, slapping her on the ass as if she were the quarterback and he was the coach.

Of course, what Griffith didn't know at this point was that Ann and Richard Thompson actually planned to spend their mornings and evenings on long distance phone calls to The Fat Man in Puerto Rico.

Griffith had hated the thought of the bus tour because it was going to be nearly impossible to plan and would keep him away from noodling numbers at his desk. Josh had hated the thought of the bus tour because of the exhausting schedule he had to execute. Only Thompson had been looking forward to the tour because it was the best way to make maximum use of voter touch time just prior to the get out the vote final push.

And, though everyone pretends to hate them while they're happening, the truth of the matter is, campaign bus trips are fun. In some respects, the bus tour is what political hacks live for. It's the excitement of the hunt, just before the actual kill. Not to say that tempers don't flare on the bus. When you take fifteen or so people and force them to bunk up at hotels for four days after spending all day each day traveling on a bus, the blood pressure seems to mount with each passing mile.

It's the old-fashioned nature of the bus tour that makes it fun. Despite the laptops, air cards and cell phones that may make their way on to the bus, no technology is actually necessary to the core activity. It's just old-time, meet the voter with a sincere smile and a firm hand shake. When you hear politicos colorfully weaving their war stories from the campaign trail about stapling their hand to a sign or getting chased down a sidewalk by a big dog, chances are they are telling tales from the bus tour.

This particular bus tour was being complicated by all the national media attention the race was getting. Griffith had been right in his early analysis. This was a mid-term special election which was as much a reflection on the President as it was on either Pope or Thompson. Bus tours' schedules have time built in for media availability at each stop, and normally that means local media…the local weekly newspaper and the local A.M. radio station.

This time, the national media wanted to follow along, but they were writing stories which voters in the Fourth District would never read.

Josh convinced Griffith to let him rent a separate, smaller bus for the national media trailing the bus tour. "A bus for the enemy?" groused Griffith. "Never. They can't help us. They can only hurt us."

"I thought you taught me to keep my friends close and my enemies closer?" was young Josh's convincing reply.

More *Godfather*—the kid was learning.

Griffith okayed the media bus.

As they prepared to leave the first stop, Thompson worked the hometown crowd as he made his way to the bus, sincerely thanking each and every person who was there. Finally, Thompson made his way to the place where Ann was loading the kids into his mom's car. Bus trips may be fun for politicos, but they are no place for the kids. They would be much better off staying with their grandmother for the next few nights. Thompson and Ann never took them to any campaign stop simply to use as a prop for newspaper photographers.

Richard Thompson, the Dad, kissed the kids goodbye as Ann fastened their seat belts. "Now you guys be good for Grandma. We'll call you each night and we'll see you in a couple of days," said Ann.

"Daddy loves you guys," said Thompson. "Make sure you get them to the next to last stop on Friday, Mom," he added. "I promised them they could ride along for one leg of the trip. Anyhow, I'd like them to be with us when we step off this cruiser for the last time."

"Guys, I know it's the kids, but we've got a schedule to keep," said Griffith in a low, calm voice. He knew not to push either one too hard when it came to the kids. One of the reasons Thompson was a good candidate was because he was a good dad.

At one point or another in a campaign, every candidate tells someone he's running for his children's sake. For the most part, reporters and voters see through the fake-sincerity of the delivery. Most candidates who say that are repeating a line learned in some campaign school. Some, like Richard Thompson, came to actually believe their service as an elected public official can make a difference in their children's lives. It was part of why people believed the empathy he exhibited on the trail.

Thompson and Ann went to the steps of the bus, and turned and waved to the supporters standing around the parking lot of the Ludlow Vets. The morning fog was just starting to lift off the Ohio River, which runs directly behind the building, as the trailer car college kids started breaking down the equipment for the drive to their next stop.

"Hey Griff," shouted Thompson as he bounded up the steps to the aisle way of the bus. "How far is it from Ludlow to Washington, pal?"

"According to my calculation, it's about a four day drive on a bus. But if you don't sit down and let us get started, it could be longer."

"Did I ever tell you guys that *Lost in Yonkers* was shot just across the street from my boyhood home," said Thompson loudly.

Griffith hit him in the back of the head with a paper wad as the bus pulled out of the parking lot. "Yeah. Yeah. And you used to listen to Pure Prairie League play in a garage in Latonia. We know. We know."

"God, I love a bus tour!" shouted Thompson to those assembled on the bus.

As wheels went up in Ludlow, Kentucky, wheels went down in San Juan, Puerto Rico.

While The Fat Man gathered his belongings, he looked outside the window of the commuter jet that had taken him south. The plane had stopped on the tarmac in front of the entrance to the terminal, and The Fat Man noticed a group of men in suits and a couple of local police standing alongside the building.

"Mr. Bradley?" asked the approaching stewardess.

"That's me."

"How was your flight?" she asked.

"Big man, a long flight, and a small jet are not a good combination," he said to the stewardess as he continued to look at the men outside. He stood, stretched and headed towards the plane's steps which took him to the tropical heat and humidity waiting outside. As he exited the plane, the men approached him.

"Joseph Bradley?" asked one of the men.

"Yeah?"

"Scott Petrina, Federal Bureau of Investigation," said the man as he showed Bradley his identification. "I'll need you to come with us."

CHAPTER 18

Thompson sat at the tiny desk in the small hotel room, his laptop computer plugged into the dial up connection in the hotel, working intently on his daily campaign blog.

If campaign bus tours, yard signs and door-to-door are old school, then campaign web sites, the Internet and blogs are definitely new school.

No one is exactly sure who started the blog craze. It probably started several years ago when, for a small fee, some computer geek bought a catchy domain name and set up an interactive website where everyday people could publicly pontificate on topics of the day. It may not have seemed like much at the time. It was just a way for some guy to talk online with others who were also interested in politics.

But everyday people took the bait and bit hard. As they logged on, the number of websites available for blogging exploded, allowing those everyday folks to become anonymous political columnists.

Today, blogs are everywhere. People go home at night and scan their favorite sites to join the threads of comments on the latest news story or comment of the day. And the blog sites vary like politics itself. There are sites featuring comments to the left. Others, lean to the right. Newspapers have them so readers can comment on their news articles and editorials.

Bloggers take their roles in online public debate very seriously. They assume anonymous identities such as ANTI-RINO (Republican In Name Only), PROPREZ and ChazFosterKane.

When Richard Thompson put up his campaign website, he insisted there be a blog page for people to visit and offer online comment and debate. Thompson believed blogs were the 21st century's answer to the Federalist Papers. He truly felt anonymous public debate could influence public opinion in much the same way three of our country's founding fathers, Alexander Hamilton, James Madison and John Jay, had done under the name of Pablius when they disseminated the essays that became known as the Federalist Papers through the media to garner support for the new Constitution. "Maybe, Pablius was the first blogger," Thompson had once said to a reporter.

Thompson spent endless hours reading the blogs. He even posted his own comments from time to time under the identity of AuH2O GOP (Au=gold, H2O=water; GOP=Republican; Goldwater Republican).

Thompson typed away:

> Today's topic–how big does government have to become, before it gets too big? Barry Goldwater said that a government big enough to give you everything you want, is also big enough to take away everything you have. How far are we from a government which has gotten too big? Go to it and I'll log back on at the end of tomorrow 's bus tour to see how you're doing. If you're looking to say hello in person, don't forget to check out our schedule on the press page.

That ought to get them talking online tonight, he thought to himself.

"Hey, Ann, your lady friend was back on the blog today," Thompson shouted to his wife in the hotel room shower.

"Someday, we need to try and figure out who she is," replied Ann, as she let the warm water run over her tired body.

Thompson shut down his laptop and stretched out on the bed. The phone rang and the candidate, sprawled across the bed, stretched to answer it.

"Richard Thompson," he said.

There was a pause as he listened.

"What the hell do you mean you're on your way back?" said Thompson as be rolled to a comfortable position, trying to let the stress of the first day of the bus tour drain from his body. "You just got there."

"I know I just got here, but it's time for me to come home," The Fat Man said from a pay phone at the San Juan Airport.

"What's wrong? Are you all right?" queried Thompson.

"Oh, I'm all right, but I need to get out of here. I can't tell you what's going on over the telephone. I've got a flight into Huntington, West Virginia, with a layover in Atlanta tonight. I'll get a car and meet you at the Ashland Plaza tomorrow night."

"Are you sure you're all right?" Thompson asked, not knowing if he believed his law partner's previous answer.

"Yeah. Yeah. I'm fine."

"Good," said Thompson. "I'm not sure I believe you, but good."

"Man, there's much more here than meets the eye," he informed Thompson. "But I can't tell you about it over the phone. In fact, the sooner I'm out of here the better."

"I'll have someone call the Plaza and get you a room up on the top floor. The top floor is one of those security access floors you can't get to without a room key. It's even got a little private lobby with free booze and cookies."

"Cookies?" said The Fat Man in anticipation.

"Raisin oatmeal, usually. They're blocking out the entire top floor with rooms for Griff, Ann and me. Everyone else is on lower floors. I'll make sure you're up there with us so we can talk privately."

"Speaking of Griff, does he know about all of this yet?"

"Naw. It's crunch time," said Thompson. "I've had to wrap his head in duct tape to keep it from exploding all day. I'm afraid if I told him about this now his head would literally shoot off his body."

"Good point."

"Besides, I need him focused on the race. He'd want to help us out and he can't." He paused. "Bud, I think we're going to win this damned thing."

"Don't jinx your Mojo," warned The Fat Man. "See you tomorrow night."

"Yeah. Just please be careful. Night."

Thompson hung up the phone; flipped on the television and looked for ESPN. The tail end of William Pope's negative ad came on the television.

"Do you really want some Washington insider and his special interest pals representing you in Washington? Vote for William Pope for real change. I'm William Pope and I approve this message."

"What was that all about?" asked Ann as she emerged from the bathroom with nothing on but an untied robe covering her wet naked body. "Oh, God, not that ad. Please, honey, I don't want to hear that lying sonofabitch calling you a Washington insider tonight. You grew up in Ludlow for God's sake. Turn it off, please." Ann's reaction to Pope's negative ad proved Griffith's old adage that campaigns are often harder on the spouses than on the candidates themselves.

"The Fat Man's on his way back from San Juan," said Thompson. "He's flying into Huntington and he's going to meet us tomorrow at the Plaza."

He didn't know what was more distracting, the phone call from The Fat Man or the anticipation of what was under Ann's robe. He wasn't sure, but he suspected Griffith had given Ann his standard campaign advice and told her she needed to be loose and easy with the campaign sex over the next couple of days to keep him relaxed.

"Flying back tonight? He just got there," she said.

"I know."

"Is he all right?

"He says he is."

"Do you believe him?"

"I guess so. I know one thing for sure. He's doing better than I am right now," said Thompson as he got up off the bed and walked towards his wife.

"What do you mean?" she giggled as he slowly pulled back her robe to reveal her glistening bare body. She was very concerned about what was happening to The Fat Man, but she also knew one of her duties on this trip was to keep her husband relaxed. And the "sex kitten wife" role was one which she enjoyed very much.

"I mean, he's not being tormented by the sight of your glorious wet body," he said as he started to gently lick a single droplet of shower water from her neck. "You know I'm still a little hepped up from today's tour."

She put thoughts of Puerto Rico out of her mind and pushed back with her pelvis in that familiar move which was an indication of things to come. "You do look a little tense from the bus trip today. How about I take care of 'that' for you," she said unzipping his fly and reaching aggressively inside his pants.

The next few minutes confirmed why candidates were happy to pay Griff so much for his advice.

CHAPTER 19

Suzi entered her brownstone just off DuPont Circle by conducting the same ritual she did every morning after dancing at the Sultry Club. In the foyer, she quickly took off all her clothes and walked naked to her bedroom.

Like an emergence from a cocoon, this final strip of the day would transform her from Suzi Q the stripper to Suzi Plummer the political science student. She wasn't sure if it was the smell of cigarette smoke embedded in the clothes that made her disrobe so quickly each morning, or the disgust that the clothes seemed to represent for the acts she had performed in them only hours earlier.

Either way, in her first week as a stripper, she had begun this private home strip upon entering her domain. Naked, she would proceed to the shower to wash away the smoke as well as the lingering feeling of grubby hands on her near perfect body. She'd wait until morning to pick up her clothes from the entry, as if they had been left by some stranger the night before; then go to classes at George Washington University.

Suzi Q was a young brunette so named by her fellow strippers, but named Susan Michelle Plummer by her parents. She had come from California to the District of Columbia with high hopes of getting her political science degree and proceeding to a job on Capitol Hill.

Early in her freshman year, an upper classmate she had befriended introduced her to the night job of stripping. True, she had come to town for an education and a career, but a little extra money on the side didn't hurt her lifestyle. Little money, hell—she was making a bundle and enjoying college life on an executive's budget.

About eight months earlier, she had met Tammy at the Sultry Club and the pair quickly became friends. With the money they were making, Suzi had been able to leave her dormitory and the two had agreed to share the fashionable apartment they now inhabited in the brownstone section of D.C. near DuPont Circle. Tammy always had extra money from another job she apparently was working on the side. Suzi didn't ask what it was and Tammy didn't offer.

While neither considered themselves lesbians, they had enjoyed each other's sexual company on more than one occasion. After a long day of classes and a longer night of stripping, the last thing Suzi needed (or wanted for that matter) was a boyfriend. Tammy seemed to fill a sexual void which Suzi needed in the little personal time she had.

That sexual energy had been building up over the last couple of days, since Tammy had left town quickly to go find some guy she had met at the club who lived in Kentucky. Tammy came home one evening, with a fresh red mark under her eye, saying she couldn't go back to the club until she talked to this guy. Tammy had had a long string of failed and often abusive relationships, and Suzi assumed this trip to Kentucky probably involved yet another one. Tammy had been in such a hurry to leave that she and Suzi had switched cars, Tammy having left hers in a parking lot by the club and come home by cab the night before she left. Suzi thought to herself how pleasant it would be if Tammy were with her now to help unwind the tensions of the day.

But she wasn't. So, like every other night, Suzi dropped her clothes by the door and walked into her bedroom towards the small bath, casually swinging the door closed behind her.

Suddenly, after taking just two or three steps into the room, she had that strange tingly feeling one gets on the back of the neck when you know someone is behind you.

She turned to meet the shadowy stare of a man standing just beyond the bleak light coming into the room from the street lamp outside and now partially back lit by the sharp light coming between the door and its frame.

"Who's there?" she asked in a voice barely able to speak as fear engulfed her.

"Where's your room mate?" asked the male voice from the shadows.

"I don't know. Who are you?" she asked, looking for something to cover herself with.

"Don't," came the stern order. "I'm enjoying the view far too much. Rest assured, I'm not here to hurt you. Just tell me where Amber is and I'll be gone."

"Why? Is she a friend of yours?"

"I said I wouldn't hurt you, but I'm not a man of much patience," he said calmly, but in a cold voice sent yet another shiver down Suzi's body. "I'll ask the questions. You will provide the answers. Agreed?"

"Yes," she said in a trembling voice.

"Now, let's try again. Where is Amber?"

"I don't know," said Suzi.

"Turn around," the voice demanded. After a half second of hesitation, she complied.

He walked up behind her and placed a leather gloved hand on her smooth, firm ass. "Now, understand that if I want to hurt you, I can," he said in her ear. As she stood frozen in place, she tried to remember where she had heard the familiar voice. "I told you I don't want to, but I am losing my patience. You will not like what happens to you if I lose my patience." He ran his other gloved hand along her waist line, reaching up under her breast and cupping it in leather.

"I'll give you one last chance," he said grabbing her breast so firmly it hurt. "Now, where is she?"

"I haven't seen her since a couple of nights ago. I swear." Suzi began to cry quietly.

"Good, now was that so hard?" he said as he continued to run his hands around her body from behind. "So, where did you see her that night?"

Suzi took a deep breath before she answered, trying desperately to maintain her composure. "Well, she left work early that night. She skipped her last set and then didn't come home until way after I got home. She came in and she asked me if she could borrow my car for a couple of days. That's the last I've seen of her. Please don't hurt me."

"Good girl," he said in a voice showing he was beginning to become aroused. "Where was she going?"

"She said something about Kentucky."

The man slipped his glove off his hand, unzipped his fly and pulled his penis from his underwear. He quickly ran his gloved hand across Suzie's flat belly and pressed his penis against her back side. With a push he attempted to bend her over at the waist and enter her from behind.

She jumped at the feel of his rigid prick against her back and spun around to face her attacker. "Oh, my god," she said in a voice of obvious recognition. "It's you. Why are you looking for Tammy?" She had recognized Virgil Lawson from the club. He was a regular there and one of the guys who would frequently shell out big bucks for blow jobs from the girls in the back hallway.

"Tammy. Yep, that's her real name."

"I didn't say that."

"It's okay, I've already gone through the things in her room. I know everything." He reached his gloved hand into his coat.

Suzi started to scream, but in one movement Lawson placed his ungloved hand over her mouth and backed her up against her bedroom wall. The act of removing the knife from his pocket and depositing it into Suzy's stomach seemed to happen in one fluid motion. The look of terror on her face was suddenly replaced by pain, shock and then nothing as he lifted the blade abruptly up her rib cage towards her sternum.

"Sorry you figured out who I was, dear. You would have been a sweet fuck," Lawson said. As Suzi's body slumped to the floor, the knife remained implanted in her rib cage.

Lawson moved carefully to make sure he did not leave any foot prints in the blood. When he opened the door back out into the hallway, the light that flooded in revealed Suzi's lifeless body but no foot prints.

Lawson's eyes darted around the apartment for a few seconds as he considered his options. Then, decisively, he went to Tammy's bedroom, got a pair of her sneakers and painfully shoved the balls of his feet into them, his heels hanging over the edge. While carrying his own shoes, he went back into the dead girl's bedroom, stepped in the blood, turned and abruptly walked out into the hallway, leaving small bloody footprints along the solid wood floors.

Lawson walked to the door and slowly stepped over Suzi's stripper clothes before he silently exited the apartment and entered the morning air of Dupont Circle. When he got to his car, he tossed the shoes in the back seat, and replaced them with his own black wing tips before driving home.

CHAPTER 20

Day two of the bus tour was starting out in Maysville, Kentucky.

The breakfast rally put on by the Maysville Republican Women's Club was great, except for the fact two Pope supporters were in the crowd taking notes and, hoping to catch a slip-up on tape for YouTube, shooting digital video. Josh recognized them from a Pope event he had infiltrated several weeks earlier. Political rallies usually occurred in public places, so sending volunteer spies to each other's events to keep track of any changes in the opponen'ts stump speech or other campaign tactics is routine. Catching a candidate in an on-stage gaffe is icing on the cake.

Josh told Griffith who they were. Rather than confronting them and causing a scene, Griffith told the local Republican State Senator who they were and had the pair introduced from the podium. To the cheers and jeers of the crowd, they made a hasty exit. Josh was pumped.

The next stop was a radio interview at WFTM-AM. The station itself was located in the front of an old tobacco warehouse, and the call letters stood for **W**orld **F**amous **T**obacco **M**arket. The owner of the station was also the news director, ad salesman and general manager. When the station played music, it was a country format piped in from some outside streaming source. But the old man who ran the place still had a red-felt covered turntable in his booth to spin occasional Johnny

Cash, Ferlin Huskie or Loretta Lynn records out of his private collection of 45's. To be the proprietor of a small radio station in eastern Kentucky and not spin tunes by the favorite citizen of Butcher Holler, "Miss Loretta," is the moral equivalent of a Federal crime.

As Thompson sat in the crowded booth doing a live interview, the national media corps wandered around the station.

"I didn't know little stations like this still existed," said one reporter to Griffith while quietly playing with the red felt turn table.

"I'm claiming dibs on a story about this place after the campaign," said another.

The interview went well and the troops loaded up again for the 20 minute trip to Rick and Ann's favorite campaign stop, Himes' General Store. There was no rally planned there today. The bus was simply going to run down the main drag (there are only two streets in Tollesboro to begin with), pull off at the store and give Thompson about 45 minutes to spend walking door–to–door. What the campaign didn't expect was a parade…literally.

Jeff Himes was there to meet the bus as it pulled up to the city limits of Tollesboro. Sometimes it seems every man in eastern Kentucky has a car that he works on in his spare time, and the one Jeff Himes was proudest of was an old Woodies Jeep. The Woody and two county police cars were sitting on the side of the road when the bus pulled up.

"What's going on, Jeffrey?" asked Thompson as he stepped from the bus.

"Well, we figured we're all voting for you in Tollesboro. So rather than spending your time walkin' door-to-door and talkin' to people who are already on your side, we're going to send you off to Washington with a parade."

Just then the advance car pulled up to the bus, and Josh was inside. "Boss, they called me while you were at WFTM and said they wanted to do this. I figured the press will eat it up. They've got the street lined with flags and yard signs and everybody in town is out on their front porch waiting for you and Ann to drive through."

Jeff put Thompson and Ann up on the front hood of his old Woodies and, with the sirens from two county police cars blaring in front of them, led the bus down through Tollesboro, Kentucky. They waved to people, many had come to know Richard and Ann Thompson as if they were one of their own.

One of the local reporters would later describe the scene in his column, noting how natural it all seemed as Thompson was shouting out first name greetings to those who lined the street and they were replying back with a familiarity that normally only comes with years of personal interaction. One of the east coast reporters described the same scene by snidely suggesting to his readers he thought he might have seen Andy, Opie and Aunt Bea somewhere in the crowd.

The volunteers in the bus were whooping and hollering as they waved to the people lining the street.

When the impromptu parade went past the general store, Suzanne was standing out front on the steps waving a Thompson for Congress yard sign. "You know, he's never let me sit on the front hood of his baby," she shouted joking about the Thompsons' perch on the hood of the Woodies.

"Don't think we don't appreciate it," replied Ann as she blew her a kiss.

By the time they got to the other end of town, Thompson surmised they had seen every registered voter in Tollesboro in five quick minutes. The pair jumped from the hood to thank Jeff before they got back on to the bus.

"No need for a longer stay here, Rick," said the beaming Himes. "These folks are all for you. You can get up the road a little ahead of schedule. You can get on up to the truck stop and take a few minutes there."

"Will do," said Thompson as he shook Himes' hand. "We'll see you guys Tuesday night, right?

"Final game of a Cincinnati Reds' World Series couldn't keep us away," Himes laughingly replied.

"Now you're just lying to us," Thompson said. "You know damned well if the Reds were in the final game of a World Series that night, we'd *both* be at the ball park. Priorities are priorities!"

As Thompson got back on the bus, Josh was giving instructions to the driver. "There's a truck stop up the road, just before you turn into Vanceburg, about 10 miles or so. We're 20 minutes ahead of schedule, so pull in there and let's take a breather."

The extra time would give Thompson an opportunity to sneak around the back of the building to call The Fat Man who should have just landed in Huntington.

When the bus pulled into the truck stop just outside of Vanceburg, it got some stares from the locals eating at the diner inside. But the crowd got back to normal pretty quickly as the Thompsons went around the diner introducing themselves to everyone and asking for their votes on Tuesday.

"Oh, you're the lady who sent me the letter today asking me to vote fer her husband," said one patron who had evidently gotten a copy of the campaign "wife's letter."

The same woman gently patted Thompson himself on his arm, saying, "That was a really nice letter and the picture of your kids was precious. You've got my vote, honey!"

Once he had gotten around to meeting everyone in the diner and, at Griffith's insistence, in the kitchen, Thompson got a cup of coffee to go and ducked around the back of the building to call The Fat Man.

A few minutes later, the bus was ready to depart and everyone was on board but Thompson himself. "Where the hell is our candidate?" shouted Griffith.

"I saw him walk around the back of the building," said one of the volunteers.

"I'll get him," said Ann, knowing her husband was probably on the phone discussing something other than the day's activities in Kentucky's Fourth Congressional District.

"Josh, go get him," barked Griffith.

Josh nearly knocked Ann down as he jumped at Griffith's order, leapt down the steps of the bus and ran towards the back of the building. There he found Thompson huddled against the wall with his back to the bus, talking on his cell phone in hushed tones. Josh could have sworn he heard him utter the words "Federal Bureau of Investigation."

"Am I interrupting something?" said Josh. But it was Thompson's reply, or rather lack thereof, that gave Josh pause.

Thompson turned quickly and stared at Josh as if he were a kid who had been caught with his hand in the cookie jar. "I've got to go," he said softly into the phone as he walked quickly toward the bus. Josh followed closely in his wake.

"How long was he standing there?" whispered Thompson to Ann as he sat down in his seat.

"Not long," she replied. "What did he hear?"

"I don't know."

"Now that we have a candidate on the bus, can we please proceed to the next stop?" shouted Griffith to the bus driver. Griffith shot an accusatory look at Thompson, which either Thompson didn't see or chose to ignore.

Thompson spent a large portion of the remaining time on the bus that day drafting a new blog topic he would add to his campaign web site that night in Ashland. He hunched over his laptop, rather than bantering with the other folks on the bus.

Fifteen minutes or so passed before Griffith plopped down in the seat across the aisle from Thompson and Ann. "What's going on, junior?" he asked.

"I'm just trying to figure out what to put up on the blog site tonight," Thompson replied.

"God, you make me nervous with that blog thing," said Griffith. "I liked campaigns a hell of a lot better when people couldn't correspond with the candidate so easily. So, what's the issue tonight? Whether the computer geeks will shed their shackles of key board bondage, unite and take over the world?"

"Cute," said Thompson. "Actually, I'm following up on my Goldwater theme. The one last night about big government got a lot of good comments. Do you know what Goldwater said about politics?"

"I'm afraid to ask," Griffith replied.

"He said politics is the art of achieving the maximum amount of freedom for individuals consistent with the maintenance of social order."

"I don't follow you," said Griffith.

"All of this, the campaign, the television ads, the bus tour, are all about preserving individual freedom."

"And," led Griffith.

"And, I want to see how my regular bloggers respond to that thought."

"Just be careful," said Griffith. "Let's not start something controversial on the web just a few days before the election."

"I could have used Josh's favorite Goldwater quote," replied Thompson.

"What's that?" Griffith asked.

"Goldwater said sex and politics are a lot alike. You don't have to be good at them to enjoy them."

"Great," said Griffith. "Let's stick with the first one."

The bus took a sharp right up a hill past a sign which read "Flatwoods Kentucky–Home of Country and Western Star Billy Ray Cyrus." They were approaching the final stop of the day, a rally at a diner owned by a Thompson supporter.

The exit from the bus at a campaign stop is an event in and of itself. First, all of the staff get off and quickly disburse into the crowd to execute their appointed job duties. As this is happening, the television cameramen and still photographers are all scrambling around for the best angle to get a shot of the candidate exiting the bus. Finally, the candidate and his spouse exit the bus to the rowdy cheers of supporters waving hand-made signs, who are urged on by some of the volunteers who just got off the bus and strategically dispersed among them.

At the diner in Flatwoods, as the Thompsons stepped from the bus for their final stop of the day, everyone cheered, right on cue. It was a pretty good turnout, and in all the excitement, Thompson didn't notice the pretty young woman standing off to the side of the crowd in a tee-shirt and jeans. A ball cap and sunglasses pulled down to cover her bleached blond hair allowed her to be just one more person in the crowd, albeit a person in the crowd, who, if one looked closely, had a remarkably good body. But, as it was, no one actually did seem to notice her—no one, that is, except for Ann Thompson.

When Ann Thompson first spotted the woman, she immediately thought of the photos. The image of the redheaded woman who had, figuratively and literally, tried to screw her husband was etched in her memory. Ann looked probingly at the face behind the sunglasses for what seemed to Ann an eternity, but which in reality may have only been a second or two. The blond in the ball cap and sunglasses, perhaps in reaction to Ann's gaze, turned away and looked sheepishly down to the ground.

Despite the blond hair and sunglasses, Ann was certain it was "her." There was something about the shape of her face, her height and the look of her body which were too consistent with the woman in the pictures for it not to be her.

Ann clasped her husband's hand tightly and pulled him through the crowd of supporters so quickly that he nearly tripped.

"Honey, what's wrong?" whispered Thompson as he held the door open for his wife.

"She's here," said Ann, hissing through a fake smile as if nothing were wrong.

"Who's here?"

"Your stripper. Amber."

"You mean Tammy."

"Oh, you're on a non-stripper, first name basis now? Whatever her name is, she's here. She's right behind us."

Thompson turned to look. "Where?"

"Right thhhh…" she stuttered as she wheeled around, to no such blond standing in the crowd. "I could have sworn I just saw her."

"You're imagining things, hon," said Thompson. "Let's get this rally done and head to the Ashland Plaza for the night. We could both use a drink to unwind and then get a good night's sleep."

CHAPTER 21

The Ashland Plaza is not standard fare for campaign bus stops. Unlike some of the budget hotels you're forced to stay in because of the location, the Plaza is actually very pleasant and relaxing. There's a full service restaurant, indoor swimming pool with a hot tub and a sports bar.

Griffith gave the campaign kids the night off as soon as they finished their staff meeting. After a brief meeting with the Thompsons, Griffith headed to the bar.

As soon as he was confident Griffith was going to be gone for a while, The Fat Man emerged from his room to spend time with the candidate and his wife. They met in the private lounge on the secured top floor of the hotel, just opposite the elevators.

"So let me get this straight," said Ann. "You didn't even make it out of the airport at San Juan?"

"Nope," said The Fat Man, already into his second oatmeal raisin cookie. "As soon as I walked off the plane, I was taken to a secured interrogation room by an F.B.I. agent and a Puerto Rican police officer. That's when they told me about the investigation…"

"Operation Caribbean Guns," interjected Ann.

"Yeah…involving some union goon who's trying to run guns to anti-Castro rebels in Cuba and the right-honorable Marcus Lackner. Damn, these cookies are good."

"Focus Joe. Stay with me," Ann instructed her husband's cookie munching law partner.

"So, do you remember that Securities and Exchange Commission filing I found which indicated Livius Drugs was purchasing Caribbean Drugs?"

"Yeah, so what?" said Thompson

"That's the deal the F.B.I. is investigating. They're spending all this time and effort hot on the trail of money-laundering businessmen and corrupt politicians who are planning to run guns to anti-Castro rebels. Then, some geek...no offense..."

"None taken," said Thompson.

"...in a race for United States Congress starts talking about Caribbean Basin tax initiatives in his election. The brass at Livius starts thinking about backing out of the deal. Originally, the F.B.I. can't figure out if you're a good guy or a bad guy. So, they start an investigation of you."

"Me?"

"Phone taps, surveillance, you know, the whole nine yards."

"You don't think they heard us having sex, do you?" asked Ann. "We get pretty loud at times."

"I don't know, and I really could have gone the entire evening without having that visual planted in my brain," said The Fat Man with a grimace on his face. "If they know about the photos with the stripper, they didn't tell me."

"Thank God. I don't need that one in my file."

"No, they think Richard Thompson is pretty much a blundering idiot who has fallen into this whole thing by mistake."

"Hey! I'm standing right here. I do have feelings, you know."

"Go with it. You're not a target of the investigation."

"I'm fine with that. I can be an idiot."

"What do we do now?" asked Ann.

"We play their game. They need help finishing the sting and they want you to be part of the bait. They want you to get to Lackner."

"I'm supposed to sting the Ranking Member of the House Rules Committee? From my own party? And when I'm not even elected yet?" Thompson looked at his law partner with disbelief. "Joe, why don't you have another cookie and explain this to me, in small words even

I will understand, why I wouldn't be fucking crazy to play along with something like that?"

"Well you really aren't going to have any choice," said The Fat Man.

"Yes I will," replied Thompson. "The F.B.I. isn't going to run my life for me."

"Well, they will in this instance," said The Fat Man. "Their investigation of you links you to the whole scheme."

"No way," said Ann.

"Way," he replied. "At least circumstantially, way. Rick, do you remember the fundraiser you had the other week?"

"Yeah, so what?"

"Well, do you remember getting any out of state checks that day?" The Fat Man broke a cookie in two and munched on one half. "Maybe, a couple from Florida?"

Thompson thought for a moment. "Every donor who writes a check gets a hand written note card thanking them for their contribution. I do remember writing a couple to some people from Miami with Hispanic names. And Alley mentioned he had dropped a couple of checks in the basket at my fundraiser."

"Three to be exact," said The Fat Man, reciting what the F.B.I. had told him. "Those checks are from some Cubans in Florida, who are the bag men in this whole scheme. You should not take checks from people you don't know."

Ann rushed to her husband's defense. "Come on, Joe. Most of the checks we take are from people we don't know."

"Well, apparently in this case those people you don't know are the subjects of an on-going F.B.I. investigation, which, coupled with Rick's recent quiet dinner with Marcus Lackner makes him look like he's on the payroll, as well," said The Fat Man.

"Hey, wait a minute,," Ann insisted. "I thought the F.B.I. considered Richard as someone who had simply stumbled into all of this?"

"They do, but they're the F.B.I. They've got enough on Rick to go to the United States Attorney for a conspiracy R.I.C.O. indictment. Sure, he'd probably beat it, but they know the publicity it would generate would be devastating to him. As a practical matter, they can make him do whatever they want. And, right now, they want him to be the bait to sting Marcus Lackner."

At that moment, all heads turned towards the ding of the elevator, announcing its arrival on the top floor.

"Oh, shit, that must be Griff," said Thompson. "I haven't told him you're here."

"Too late now," said Ann, putting on her best political fake smile as the elevator door opened. "Hey, Griff, what are you doing coming back to your room so early?"

Her question was soon answered when the blond Ann had spotted at the campaign stop in Flatwoods emerged from the elevator along side Griffith who was holding her hand. Griffith's goofy "I'm about to get laid grin" was quickly replaced by a look of sheer terror as Ann jumped up out of her chair and headed straight toward the pair from the private lounge stopping just short of them.

Thompson tried to grab his wife, but she spun away from his grasp. The blond ducked behind her date, as if somehow no one would have really noticed she was there.

"So, Griff, who's your date?" she said in a measured tone. Ann's eyes seemed to change colors as they fixed on the young blond hiding behind the trio of Griff, the ball cap and the sunglasses.

"Christ, Annie," said Griffith. "I just met her in the bar. Give me a break. What are you doing?"

"Introduce me to your date Griff," she said changing the request into a demand.

"Well…okay…Ann…this is Amber. Miss Amber Burn," Griffith said as he swept the blond out from behind his back in one quick motion in order to introduce her to his friend's wife.

"Amber Burn. Amber Burn. Sounds like a stripper name to me. Doesn't it sound like a stripper name to you, Richard?" When Ann looked at her husband, he looked like one of those deer stuck in the headlights of an oncoming coal truck on the Double A Highway.

"Jesus Ann," said Griffith. "It's really none of your business who I bring up here after hours. And I'm not sure which one of us you owe an apology to first—Amber or me."

"Sure," she said sarcastically. "I'll give you both a big apology just as soon as your date here takes off her wig and sunglasses."

"Aw, come on Ann, we go back a long ways, but you're way the hell out of line now," said Griffith.

For a moment, there was an uncomfortable silent stand off. Then Thompson said, "Tammy…come on, go ahead, take off the wig and shades."

She looked at Griffith and slowly removed the sunglasses with her right hand and the wig and ball cap with her left revealing red hair and a black eye was so swollen that it was nearly shut.

Griffith could not have looked any more startled or confused as he looked rapidly back and forth between Thompson, Ann and the girl he knew as Amber.

"You all know each other?" Griffith asked. "What the hell happened to your eye, honey?"

Griffith's date began to cry softly.

Even more confused, Griffith turned to Ann and demanded, "Annie, you didn't give her the shiner did you?"

At that, Tammy burst into tears, and to everyone's surprise, perhaps even her own, she pushed Griffith aside and approached Ann. She put her arms around Ann, tentatively at first, and then in another instant collapsed around her like a falling parachute hitting the ground. Ann had looked away momentarily to say something to Thompson and hadn't seen Tammy coming. If she had, her anger might well have caused her to greet the oncoming redhead with a slap across the mouth. As it was, before Ann knew what was happening, Tammy was already huddled around her and leaning against her as if seeking forgiveness, comfort and protection all at the same time.

"I am so sorry. Oh God, please forgive me. I know, I've never even met you and you have no reason to…but please, forgive me. I'm so very sorry," she sobbed repeatedly to Ann.

Ann made eye contact with the three men, their collective mouths agape staring at her in disbelief of the scene before them. She firmly grabbed the young woman's forearms and slowly removed them from around her neck. "Come on, honey. Let's go sit down. You look like you could use a drink and we definitely need to talk."

Thompson started to follow them. "Not yet," Ann commanded at her regular volume. "She and I have a couple of matters to work out first."

"Would somebody like to tell me what the hell is going on?" Griffith pleaded. Extending a handshake to The Fat Man, he said "Oh, hi, Joe" in a tone indicating he hadn't seen him before this point in the drama playing out before him. "Wait a minute. Joe? Where the hell did you come from? What the heck are you doing here?"

"Joey, would you do me a favor and take Griff back to your room and tell him what's going on," asked Thompson.

"All of it?" asked The Fat Man.

"All of it!" demanded Thompson.

"I'll need the cookies," he said.

"I wouldn't go in there right now, if I were you," said Griffith as he nodded in the direction of two women now sitting side-by-side on a couch in the lounge with fresh drinks.

The Fat Man followed Thompson's nod toward the two women. "Good call."

The Fat Man beckoned to Griffith, and the two of them headed down the hall and into The Fat Man's room.

Thompson, now alone, stood by the elevators feeling very vulnerable.

On one side of him, his two best friends were in a room talking about the mess he had gotten them all into. There was danger there. On the other side of him, his wife was in the lounge consoling a young, weeping stripper whom he had seen naked only a week earlier when she tried to set him up and seduce him. There was definitely danger there. And while he couldn't hear what Ann and Tammy were saying to each other, he could certainly hear when Griffith began shouting obscenities as The Fat Man revealed fact after fact to him behind closed doors.

Every time Thompson started to make any movement toward the two women, Ann would shoot him a look of "not yet."

So, he just stood there. He didn't want to go into The Fat Man's room for fear Griff might punch him. And he damned sure didn't want to get near the women for fear either one of them might kill him…literally.

So, he just stood there, appropriately, with his back against the wall.

Chapter 22

"All right," said Ann sternly. "It's not that I don't care about what happened to your eye, but I've got to know why you're doing this to us."

"I'm so sorry. I'm so sorry. I'm so sorry," said Tammy in a rhythm between metered sobs. "I fucked this all up. I know I shouldn't be here, but I'm not the one doing this to you."

"I think I've seen pictures that say otherwise," said a stone-faced Ann.

"You know what I mean," replied Tammy.

"No, quite frankly, I don't know what you mean. I don't have any idea who you really are or why you're here." Ann's anger started to rise.

"I don't blame you if you want to hit me because of what happened to your husband," said Tammy. "But I didn't come here to cause you any trouble."

"Good, because you've caused enough trouble already. So tell me, then, exactly why are you here?" Ann asked.

Tammy paused. "I'm scared."

"You're the blackmailer setting us up and you're scared?" asked Ann. "I don't buy any more than I'm buying your crocodile tears and pleas for forgiveness."

Tammy paused and looked to the floor. "He tried to rape me."

"Richard? Now, you're telling me my husband Richard tried to rape you. Is this your latest blackmail scheme?" This time Ann really was fighting back the urge to strike the young woman.

"Oh, God, no. The guy who followed your husband into the club the other night was the one who tried to rape me. Your husband said his name was Lawson. He was the one," she said, visibly shaking as she spoke.

Remembering she was the one who had sent her husband to D.C. to find Tammy in the first place, Ann suddenly felt a sharp pang of guilt at the new claim being leveled by the girl. Letting go of her own intent to control the conversation, Ann leaned forward and, gently placing a hand on Tammy's shoulder, asked, "What happened?"

Ann probably shouldn't have shown much sympathy or empathy, because her touch was more than enough to open another flood gate of conversation which Ann truly wasn't expecting.

"This guy…Lawson…followed your husband to the club that night. Your husband made me point him out. Anyway, after your husband left to come back here, Lawson came up to me a few minutes after my set and showed me he had a gun in his waist band," she said as she lit up a cigarette. "He told me to just walk outside and get in the back of a black Town Car parked outside. All I had on was my robe, a bra and my g-string. But I did what he said. He made me get in the back seat with him, and he had the driver just start driving around. Once the car got moving, he kept asking me questions about what we had talked about when I was with your husband at the club."

"All of a sudden, I looked down and he's pulling out his dick. He's stroking his cock in one hand and grabbing my neck with the other. The fucker wanted me to give him a blow job. He grabbed my tit, so I slapped him. That's when he punched me in the eye."

She started to cry again. "He got real mad. He pushed me down on the seat and started pulling at my g-string. He kept hitting me and slapping me. Then he got on top of me and…" She paused.

"Did he…?" asked Ann.

"No. The driver, this big black dude, I think Lawson called him Bobby or something, stopped the car and pulled him off me. That's when I opened the door and ran. I ran as fast and as long as I could. The car kept driving around the neighborhood looking for me. So, I just kept running. And I've been running ever since."

She paused long enough to take a drag off her cigarette. "Look, I'm sorry I showed up here and laid this all on you. It's just that I didn't know what else to do. I don't want to go back to D.C.—I don't think that's safe. And, I've got no family to speak of."

"No family?" asked Ann.

"Yeah. I'm an only child. My real dad took off before I was born. Mom died when I was 12 and, her second husband, my step-dad, was in the military out of Quantico in Virginia." She let out a slight laugh in mock reflection. "That's how I started stripping. He'd go on tour for months at a time. When I was 16, I scored a fake ID and started stripping in bars around the base. I've always looked a lot older than I am."

"How old are you?"

"I'm twenty-six."

Ann noted to herself Tammy was young enough to be her daughter. "So, how did you know to find us…and here in Ashland, Kentucky?"

"I didn't even know your husband's name, but one of the girls at the club, my room mate, recognized him."

"One of the girls at the club?" asked Ann.

"Yeah. Suzi Q—she's a political science major at Georgetown," Tammy replied. "She recognized him in the club from a picture she'd seen in one of the D.C. newspapers. She remembered he was running for Congress in Kentucky."

"Suzi Q the stripping poly-sci major?" said Ann, slowly shaking her head from side to side in disbelief at what she was hearing.

"Ann…do you mind if I call you Ann?" asked Tammy as she took another draw on her cigarette.

"Oh, at this point, why the hell not," said Ann, trying to figure out at what particular moment she had lost control of the conversation.

"Anyhow, Ann," said Tammy, uttering her name with a familiarity reserved for long time friends, "most of the girls in the clubs are in college, making some money while they're in school. They're smart, pretty and most of them are probably making more a year than the guys who are teaching them."

Ann sat back in her chair. This is not how she had expected to spend the evening.

In The Fat Man's room the conversation was more confrontational.

"Okay, this isn't going to be easy to explain," said The Fat Man, trying to figure out how to tell Griffith the whole story.

"Why," barked Griffith. "Because you somehow perceive that I'm not as smart as you?" The way the night was going, Griffith was quick to take offense.

"No. I don't think that in the least."

"Good. Because, let me tell you something, my little round friend, I may not know all the words to one of your stupid movies, but I'm quite capable of understanding whatever in the hell is going on here."

"Noooo. That's not what I meant," said The Fat Man. "It's not going to be easy for me to explain, because I'm not sure I understand it all myself."

"Stop pissing me off. If you're half as smart as Rick's always saying you are, you probably do have it all figured out. Stop patronizing me and tell me what the hell is going on here."

"Fine," said The Fat Man in a matter-of-fact tone. "The girl you picked up downstairs in the bar is a D.C. stripper who tried to frame our friend, Rick Thompson, by taking pictures of the two of them in bed naked so he'd back off 936. There's dirty money in the campaign fund. But don't worry it's the Ranking Member of the House Rules Committee who's really the target of the F.B.I. investigation."

There was a pause as the two stared at each other nose to nose.

"I don't understand," said Griffith as he broke the stare and sat down on the bed.

"I told you so," The Fat Man gloated.

Back in the lounge, Tammy hadn't missed a beat. "So anyhow," she continued, "I woke up Suzi when I finally made it home from the club. She found your husband's campaign web site and we saw that he had this bus tour thingie going on this week. So Suzi gave me her tip money for the night, and let me borrow her car." She paused to take a breath. "And here I am."

"Yes, here you are," sighed Ann. Somehow she wished she hadn't started the whole conversation.

Tammy suddenly slowed down her pace and lowered her tone.

"When you saw me earlier, when you were getting off the bus, I saw the way you looked at me. I don't know how, but you knew who I was."

"Trust me," Ann said. "When you're in your forties, if someone gives you a bunch of pictures of your husband with some girl half your age, you'll have her face and body etched in your memory, too."

"I guess," Tammy responded. "I figured if you recognized me it must have been because your husband had shown you the pictures. I was afraid you were going to go all Springer on me or something. So, I just got out of there."

"Then, why did you follow us here?"

"I needed to talk to your husband," Tammy said. "That's why I was sneaking up here with your friend. I couldn't get onto this floor without a special key. So, I spotted one of the guys from the bus in the bar downstairs—what's his name, uh, Mike?—and I figured if I spent the night with him, he would introduce me to his celebrity boss in the morning."

"Knowing Griff, that would not have worked. He doesn't let karma he gets from young girls go to his head," Ann said quoting from the original *Godfather* movie.

"Huh?" said Tammy in a puzzled tone.

"Griff doesn't mix business and pleasure. You're lucky we were all sitting here when the elevator doors opened up." She didn't have the time or the patience to explain the *Godfather* rules to Tammy the Stripper.

"Well, that didn't turn out at all like I expected. I'm not sure what exactly I've gotten myself into, but I figured your husband did. After Lawson smacked me around, I didn't know what to do or where to turn. And your husband just seemed like the kind of guy who would help someone when they don't know where else to turn."

"Yup, that's my husband, the great stripper savior from Ludlow, Kentucky."

"No, seriously, the way he looked at me when we talked backstage at my club, it wasn't a sexual thing. He just looked like, if I asked, I could probably trust him to tell me what I should do next."

"Since you brought up the sexual thing, we've got a few things to set straight," said Ann, remembering why she wanted to talk in private in the first place.

"Look, nothing happened. And, believe me I tried to make it happen. I let him get a real good look at my…"

"Stop right there. That's the thing. I really don't want to know what you tried to show him or what you tried to do. I don't think I could handle that tonight, without beating the living crap out of you. But for the future, let me be very clear and precise," Ann said in a slow and deliberate cadence, her eyes turning steely in their gaze. "If you ever try to seduce my husband again, I will hunt you down to the ends of the earth and rip your fake tits off. Do you understand me?"

"Yes m'aam," said Tammy, looking away from Ann.

"Good. Now look at me and repeat it to me," demanded Ann.

"What?" asked Tammy.

"I want to make sure you understood," Ann said. "Now, repeat it."

"If I try to seduce your husband again, you'll rip…"

"No," corrected Ann, "I'll hunt you down."

"You'll hunt me down…"

"To where?" asked Ann.

"…the ends of the earth…"

"And what will I do to you?"

"You'll rip my tits off."

"Good. I think we understand each other. Now," she said glancing over at Thompson, "should we let Richard come over and join us, or should we let him sweat a little longer?"

CHAPTER 23

"Tammy, this is Joe, Richard's law partner," said Ann, as she started introducing Tammy to the trio of men entering the lounge.

"My pleasure," he said shaking her hand while admiring her face, her body and her black eye all at the same time. He was awestruck by her natural beauty and aghast at how someone could have struck such a gorgeous creature.

"We all call him The Fat Man," said Griffith. Bradley winced at hearing his nickname uttered in front of the first honest-to-God, stripper he'd ever met.

"And this gentleman, the one you used in the bar to get to us, is Michael Griffith," said Ann, insuring Griffith knew Tammy wasn't interested in him in the least.

"I thought you said your name was Amber," said Griffith.

"I hope I didn't hurt your feelings, but I really needed to get up to this floor to see your boss and you had a security key," said Tammy, sincerely hoping Griffith would accept her apology.

"And, as he has seen you naked on apparently more than one occasion, I think you'll remember my husband, Richard."

"I'd like to say nice to see you again, but I'd be lying. I just can't seem to get rid of you, can I?" Thompson asked rhetorically.

"Sorry."

"Well, that uncomfortable exchange is out of the way," said Ann.

"Tammy, how about you go downstairs and get the two of us a table at the restaurant, and I'll come down and join you in a few minutes. Okay?"

As they stood waiting for the elevator, Ann couldn't help but notice The Fat Man staring at Tammy's tight ass like he had never seen anything like it before in his life. He probably hadn't, she thought. She was embarrassed for him when they made eye contact, his face immediately turning a deep shade of red.

When the elevator had carried Tammy safely back to the first floor, the remaining four shifted their feet and relaxed their postures in a way suggesting they each knew they were now more at liberty to speak.

"First things first," said Griffith. He turned to Thompson, stared at him for a moment and then slapped him hard across the top of the head.

Thompson recoiled, stunned.

"How dare you not tell me you had your dick in a ringer like this! After all we've been through together over the years," Griffith said. He raised his hand again, unsure himself if he was actually about to slap Thompson again or if it was just a threat.

"We're not going to lose, Griff," said Thompson, instinctively raising his forearm to thwart the next possible blow.

"Is that what you think? You think I give a shit about winning and losing right now. This doesn't have a god damn thing to do with me winning or losing a campaign."

"It's' embarrassing, Griff, and scary as hell. I didn't know who to tell."

"You know, for as fucking smart as you claim to be, you're pretty stupid."

"Why, because I let these guys set me up?"

"No! Because you haven't figured out when somebody does something like this to you, they're doing it to me, too!"

"You were so focused on the campaign…"

"Fuck the campaign, man," shot back Griffith. "This is The Family Business. It involves both of us."

The two paused.

"Do you know why I want to win this campaign so badly?" asked Griffith. "Do you? It has nothing to do with my won-loss record. Man, it doesn't matter if I win this one or lose. I'm still the Golden Boy of D.C. I'll still have my spot on the talk shows and the next guy is going to hire me no matter what happens in the Fourth District of Kentucky on Tuesday."

Griffith began to pace. "All those people I've gotten elected over the years are clients. That's all they are to me, a faceless name on some forgotten ballot. The ones who lost are memories and the ones who won…hell…half of them are ideologues who think wrestling is real and the moon landing was fake. I don't respect those bastards who need a pin on their lapel to affirm their own self-importance to the world. They're retainer checks and victory bonuses to me and that's all.

"But this race is different. I've spent my whole career doing things for other people. But, you and me, we're one and the same. If you win on Tuesday, it will be like a little part of me is going to the United States House of Representatives. It sounds weird, but I'm doing this one for me."

He stopped and looked directly at Thompson. "Man, you're my family. You're the only brother I've got. Think of how many times you've gotten me out of a jam. This is for my own personal satisfaction of doing something right for you."

"You're right," said Thompson as he crossed over to Griffith and embraced him. "I'm sorry."

After a very brief pause, Ann resumed the conversation.

"About an hour ago, before I was so rudely interrupted, I was asking what we should do now. So, I reiterate, what should we do now?"

"We let the F.B.I. call the shots," said The Fat Man.

"And what shots would those be?" asked Ann.

"Well, apparently Congressman Lackner and his anti-Castro supporters are supposed to close on some sort of business deal on Monday. The F.B.I. wants to get Lackner on tape before the deal closes."

"And, as we were discussing before Griff arrived, I'm the lucky guy who gets to wear the wire," Thompson declared.

"Yup," said The Fat Man, "they want you to go to Key West on Friday evening, wire up and confront Lackner. Key West is in Lackner's District and he's hosting a breakfast on Saturday morning at the V.F.W. hall. You confront Lackner about the pressure being put on you about Section 936. He says whatever he says, which we hope is nice and incriminating. They fly you back to Kentucky and you close out the campaign over the weekend. Then, on Monday, when the deal closes, and the money starts flowing, they'll have all they need to start making arrests. If you cooperate, I've gotten them to agree to hold off on any announcement of arrests until after the election on Tuesday. And they're willing to try to avoid any mention of you at all if there's a plea. And, my guess is there will be a plea."

"I thought you were one of those black helicopters, 'don't trust the government' types, Joe. Aren't you the commandant of the Edgewood Militia or something?" Griffith said mockingly, in reference to The Fat Man's home town and libertarian tendencies. "You're the last person I thought would want to have the F.B.I. calling the shots when our collective asses are on the line."

"Well, then what do you suggest?" asked The Fat Man.

"I'm not sure," said Griffith, "but we've got an election on Tuesday, and I've been around Washington long enough to know the F.B.I. really doesn't give a big hairy rat's ass about how it turns out. We're winning right now, but if our boy's picture pops up on the Monday night national news in a story about Washington corruption, that will have the blog sites making up stories in minutes. It could be enough to make us lose."

"I thought you said this wasn't about winning or losing?" asked The Fat Man.

"It's not about winning and losing for me, man, but it sure as hell is for Rick and Ann," said Griffith. "They could do the right thing here and end up as a footnote in the written history of failed political campaigns. That's one helluva legacy to live with for the rest of your life. We don't have many options here, so we may have to roll with them, but we just need to be careful."

Thompson looked pensive, taking it all in.

"Plus, remember, if anything goes wrong, we've got a secret weapon waiting for Ann down in the restaurant," Griffith continued.

"What?" asked The Fat Man.

"Amber, Tammy, whatever the hell her name is. If what Joe told me is true, she can identify the players in a line up, she's the one in the pictures and the F.B.I. apparently doesn't even know she exists," Griffith said.

"You're right. They don't know she exists, and they don't know about the pictures or the blackmail," said The Fat Man. "They're focused on whatever role Lackner has in this Cuba and Puerto Rico thing. They seem to have no idea Rick's being blackmailed over this whole thing. So, do we tell them?"

"Hell, no," hissed Griffith. "That's just asking for a leak. And when we win on Tuesday, our new Congressman sure as hell doesn't need those photos showing up in his F.B.I. file."

"So, until something better comes along, we just prepare to combat the story in the event someone gives copies to the press?" The Fat Man asked.

"Right," said Griffith. "And for that, we need her, so we could trot her out in front of the press to tell her story that it was all a set up. And, unless she's here tonight as a spy, she's decided to take her cues from the blackmailee rather than the blackmailers."

"And one of them tried to rape her," Ann interjected.

All three turned to Ann, wide-eyed and incredulous. "What?" Thompson exclaimed.

"The guy who followed you to the bar in D.C. tried to rape her." Ann said. "That's why she's here. She's not a spy. She's scared shitless."

"I don't care why she's here. I just know I may need her to stand up in D.C. at a press conference and tearfully tell the world she was paid by someone to set up a good and honest man. Hell, people might just think Pope's behind the whole thing."

"I'm not sure he isn't," replied Ann.

"I know one thing," said Griffith. "We've got to get her ass out of Kentucky. Photos in bed at a hotel in D.C. I can explain at a press conference. Photos of her hanging around a hotel in Ashland, Kentucky, and we're screwed."

"Great plan," said The Fat Man. "But can we trust Tammy?"

"What's the consensus?" Thompson asked. "Can we trust her?"

The lounge went silent for a full 30 seconds.

"Yes," said Ann.

One hour and two pieces of cheesecake later, Ann brought Tammy back up to the secure floor to talk with her and Thompson about what they needed her to do.

"No way, Jose," she shot back. "I'm not getting in the middle of this."

"Not getting in the middle of this?" asked Thompson. "You've got to be shitting me. The pictures of our naked sexless romp could have cost me my family and career. Now, your sorry ass follows me to Kentucky and you're not getting in the middle of this?"

Ann jumped in. "Look, Tammy, you said you came here because you didn't know where else to turn and you want a fresh start, right? If we don't get the bastards who are behind all of this and do it on our terms, you'll never be free of it. Even if everyone, including the guy who tried to rape you, goes to jail, if my husband loses, you'll regret what you did to us for the rest of your life. You know that's true, too.

"My husband is going to win his election. And when he does, he'll be in an even better position to help you out. This could be your chance to do the right thing, protect yourself and move on to a new phase in your life. You can right all the wrongs you've done in this whole story. It could be your fresh start."

"And you'll help me through it," she asked Ann, as a daughter would of her parent.

"I must be nuts to say this, but, yes, I'll help you through it," Ann said.

Tammy looked around the room at each of the faces looking to her for a response. "All right, I'm in."

"Good," said Griffith. "It's time to put the Rules of Battle to their ultimate test. From this moment forward, we trust only each other. Don't let anyone outside The Family know what you're thinking."

"Personally, the only thing I'm thinking about is a shower and some quality sack time," said Tammy as she momentarily closed her eyes and stretched to the ceiling. As she did so, her t-shirt rose up and exposing her pierced belly button and a very shapely torso. The other four just looked at her in disbelief. When she opened her eyes she noticed all four were staring at her. "Sleep…by myself…okay. It's been a long couple of days."

"Yes, it has," said Ann. "Joe, will you go downstairs and get Tammy a room, preferably on the other end of the hall from Griff?"

"Very funny," said Griffith. "And make it quick, Joe, we've got a lot of planning to do tonight. Are you ready to become a war time consigliore?"

"I'll make Genko proud," said The Fat Man, impressing Griffith with his knowledge of *Godfather* characters.

"You two better get some sleep as well," Griffith said to Ann. "The next couple of days are going to be the longest of your life."

CHAPTER 24

As the campaign tour bus pulled out of the parking lot of the Ashland Plaza for the two and a half hour trip on Interstate 64 westward towards Oldham County, Ann looked out the window of the bus to see The Fat Man loading gear into the car Tammy had borrowed from her political science stripper roomie, Suzi Q.

Ann wanted to make sure someone was there to get Tammy on her way back to D.C. She was motivated in part by concerns for Tammy's safety, but also by a personal fear over the impact Tammy could have on their lives over the next couple of days if she hung around. Whether Ann's motives were pure or not, it was best if someone made sure Tammy started out her journey back to Washington as quickly as possible. The Fat Man would catch up with the bus tour later.

More importantly, she is east bound and we're west bound, thought Ann smiling at the very idea of their opposite direction movement as she snuggled up next to her husband for the long ride.

Ever since Richard had first shown her the pictures of their faux-tryst in D.C., Ann had been curious about the woman who had tried to set up her husband. Although Tammy was a real person to her now, Ann still wasn't sure the actual meeting had left her feeling any better than before.

Am I really going to play mentor to a young girl who tried to screw my husband? She clearly needs some motherly...okay sisterly...advice. So, why the hell does it have to be me? Oh well, hopefully it's only a couple of days. We do what the F.B.I. says and we're all in the clear. Joe's going to get Tammy to hole up with one of Griffith's old girlfriends in Northern Virginia and head home. Richard stings Lackner. We win. People get arrested. Richard helps Tammy get a job as a receptionist somewhere and I never have to see Tammy the stripper again as long as I live.

Ann watched the side of the road pass by as the bus pulled out on to the interstate. She felt a sense of satisfaction knowing her trust in her husband was justified and as strong as it had ever been. But the meeting with Tammy Stewart had left Ann with emotions she wasn't sure she was ready to deal with at this exact moment in her life.

Thompson had his laptop out and was connected by an air card to the Bus Tour page on the campaign website. He was going over the notes Josh had made for him about each stop for the day.

He's busy right now. I really shouldn't bother him with this stuff while he's getting ready for the day's schedule. There will be plenty of time to talk after the election.

Ann smiled as she looked around to the rear of the bus. There was the typical steady buzz going on as the morning tour started. Griffith was on the phone with the pollster talking about last minute tweaks to the campaign message which would be implemented via press interviews and radio talk show call-ins. Josh was on the phone as well, confirming the line up of morning talk shows which Thompson would call into from the bus. Four volunteers were laughing over a euchre game in the back.

To someone who had never been involved in politics, this might have all seemed like barely organized chaos. To someone from inside, it was remarkably peaceful.

Griffith always said one of the reasons he adopted *The Godfather* trilogy as his political bible was that politics, like organized crime, attracted misfits. They are smart, inspired people who don't always fit in with normal society. They'd rather sit around a tavern and talk about poll numbers than watch a football game on the television behind the bar.

The one characteristic which held all the misfits together was loyalty to their candidate. And they were loyal to a fault...loyal misfits, but misfits just the same. As Ann thought about the cast of characters helping in the campaign, she finally understood Griffith's statement.

She looked at her husband, typing away on his laptop computer and viewing web pages about some policy debate or another. He was geeky and committed to a fault. She loved him dearly, but recognized at this moment she was married to a misfit.

The Fat Man was a misfit...always quoting from movies and looking for a cause to support. Griffith was certainly a misfit...a middle-aged man with no chance at a normal life who traveled from campaign to campaign like a political nomad.

And Josh, God love him, was a misfit, or at least a misfit in training under the instructive eye of Michael Griffith. Yesterday, Josh had cracked everyone up on the bus by doing his impersonation of Fredo Corleone being confronted for double-crossing his brother in *Godfather II*. "I'm smart. Not dumb like everyone says. I'm smart and I demand respect!" he yelled to everyone's amusement. Ann had laughed until she had tears in her eyes, in part because she couldn't help but remember how her husband and Michael Griffith had done the same damned impersonations in their younger days.

Oh God, we've created another Michael Griffith, she thought to herself.

Everyone around her on the bus was a misfit. Who else would take a week out of their life to ride along on an uncomfortable bus and sleep on hard unfamiliar mattresses just to help someone else win an election? If her husband told any one of them to run through a wall, she believed they just might try to deliver.

The four young kids in the back playing cards were perfect examples. They were along for the ride with no hopes of a job or future glory. All they wanted was a campaign to belong to and a story to tell when it was all over.

It was the "loyalty thing" that Griffith spoke about so often which seemed to bond all of the Thompson clan together as a tight band of misfits. These folks really didn't feel comfortable outside the presence of other political junkies, so they found value in being the person on the bus tour whose job it was to walk up and down the aisle and squirt anti-bacterial sanitizer into everyone's hands after a rally stop of hand-shaking.

Maybe that was what had attracted Tammy Stewart to follow us to Kentucky, she thought quietly to herself. *She certainly fits into the misfit category. No family. No direction. Maybe she's just looking for something or someone to be loyal to . Great, she's Luca Brasi with tits. Why in the hell did she have to pick my husband as her Godfather?*

Thoughts of Tammy Stewart brought back that uneasy feeling which had been bothering Ann since she had met Tammy the night before. There was no good time to bring it up, but her thoughts of Tammy's motivation made now better than never. *Take a deep breath and ask him now .*

"Why'd you do it?" she asked her husband.

"Why'd I do what?' replied Richard, more intent on his web notes than the actual question being posed to him by his wife.

"Tammy. Why'd you kick her out of the room?"

"Oh, come on, hon, let's not go there right now. This is not the place."

"No, I'm curious. I promise I won't get mad."

"This conversation can't lead to anything good," replied Richard as he shut off his laptop and folded down its screen.

"Richard, I looked at myself in the mirror this morning. I've weathered the storm better than most women my age, but I can't compete with a 20-something stripper."

"Stop it," insisted Richard. "Remember, I'm the insecure one in this relationship."

But Ann pressed on with the impromptu deposition of her husband. "She's drop dead gorgeous. Admit it, counselor, she's pretty."

"Yes, she is pretty," he said. He knew he couldn't avoid the "yes/no" approach of her questions; it was a technique she had learned over the years from being married to a lawyer. "She's also the girl John Prine wrote about when he recorded *Barbra Lewis Hare Krisna Beauregard*. That girl's a shut-in without a home."

"Isn't she every man's dream?"

"I don't know about every man." He dodged a bullet with that answer and silently congratulated himself on his own dexterity.

"Well, she sure as hell set Joe and Michael on their ears last night. At least she's their dream."

"I suppose so," he gave in.

"And on two separate occasions, she wanted to have sex with you."

"Yes, she did."

"And you turned her down."

"Yes."

"Well, that's what I'm curious about," Ann said. "I want to know why. Last time I looked, your dick still worked. You proved that last night," she said looking back over her shoulder to make sure no one saw her grab at her husband's crotch.

"You're prettier than she is."

"Now you're just teasing me," insisted Ann. "Come on. Tell me. Why didn't you screw her?"

"I'm serious, babe. I admit a few of the parts may have sagged over the years," he said grabbing playfully at the nipple hidden beneath her polo shirt, "but still, you're prettier than she is."

Ann snapped her shoulder away from Richard, sat angrily back in her chair and stared straight ahead.

"I told you this conversation would go nowhere fast," he said with true exasperation in his voice. "You asked me a question and when I told you the answer, you got pissed off at me."

"Because your answer is bullshit. That girl is so pretty, even I wanted to sleep with her."

"Well, hell, why didn't you say so last night? I could have sent out for some cheap wine…" He hoped the joke would break the tension. It didn't.

Ann slapped his arm. "You know what I mean." Even in arguments, Thompson could make her laugh. "As I talked to her last night, I just couldn't get over how really pretty she was in person. I couldn't have blamed you if you had slept with her. I would have left you, and taken half of everything you have, but I would have understood why you were tempted."

"Do you know why I listen to the song writers I do?" he asked.

"Don't change the subject on me, Richard Thompson," said Ann.

"I'm not," he replied. "Do you know why I listen to guys like John Prine?"

"No, why?" she snapped.

"Because," he said, "over the years, they've changed with me. Or, I've changed with them. I'm not really sure which."

"So?"

"So, that's why you're prettier than her."

"I'm prettier than Tammy the stripper because you like John Prine?"

"Kind of. Let me try this again," said Thompson. "I've been

listening to John Prine ever since I was buying albums in junior high school. When a new CD comes out, I'm the first guy in line at the store on release day."

"Right." Ann was not quite sure where this whole conversation was heading.

"Why do you think that is?" he asked.

"I have no earthly idea. I just assumed it was one more of your geek obsessions," she replied.

"I don't want the new release because I liked the last one. I want the new one because I want to see where he goes next. I don't listen to the new music with any expectation based upon the past. I want to hear what's now. That's the beauty of the performers I've followed over the years. They've gotten older with me. I don't have any great expectations of them, because they've been there for me in the past and they'll be there for me in the future. I've not had to change for them because they've changed with me."

Ann suddenly saw where he was heading, and began to blink back tears.

"I don't care that as they get older their voices change an octave or two, or they're a little slower on the neck of a guitar. Those things are all superficial. Fact is, the older they get, the better their music becomes.

"That's why you're prettier. We're getting older together. Yeah, some of our standard equipment is starting to sag a little. Heck, I get up in the morning and look around to make sure everything is still attached. But, at the end of the day, that kind of beauty is all superficial.

"The beauty I'm looking for has less to do with firm tits and a tight ass than it does with the inner stuff we've shared over the years. You're right. Tammy's nice to look at...really, really nice to look at...really, really, really..."

"You've made your point," interjected Ann, "move on."

"...but she's not prettier than you."

There was a long silence as the two looked at each other, before Griffith plopped down in the seat on the aisle across from the pair. "You two all right?" asked Griffith.

"Never been better," said Ann as she snuggled back up against Richard's arm. She started singing a John Prine tune to herself, "In spite of ourselves, we're gonna' end up sitting on a rainbow..."

CHAPTER 25

The top of the steps outside the Boone County, Kentucky Courthouse felt like the top of the world to Richard Thompson. His wife, children and family were standing proudly on one side of him. His campaign staff, volunteers and close friends were to the other. As he wrapped up the bus tour to the applause and cheers of about 400 of Boone County's Republican faithful, he couldn't help but pause to take in the moment. It had been a difficult week, but he wanted to take time and remember what he had just accomplished.

This was the final stop of the bus tour.

For the candidate, the final stop of the bus tour marks the emotional end of the campaign. Sure, there is still the weekend, get-out-the-vote activities for the campaign. But, for the most part, those run by themselves. The candidate shows up to provide moral support to the volunteers, but the end of the bus tour is the end of the road in more ways than one.

On one hand, it's a welcome relief. No more grinding out mile after mile going from one stop to the next. The thought of finally getting a good night's sleep in your own bed is almost enough, in and of itself, to make one cheer the end of the tour.

But, on the other hand, there is also a degree of sadness that it's over. Bus tours are tiring and exhilarating all at the same time. Political hacks, professionals and volunteers are all in their element on the tour. Everything that happens along the way in a bus tour is the most important thing in the world at that moment. It's high octane politics.

There is a comradery that forms among those on the bus. There are stories that arise from the hustle and bustle of the tour which will be told for years to come. John had to run to Wal-Mart at 2:00 a.m. to find a toothbrush for the candidate. Dru had to run out of the hotel one night to chase away kids who were going to toilet paper the campaign bus.

Friendships form on the tour that will last a lifetime. But, at the end of the tour, it's over and everyone goes back to their normal routine.

Thompson knew all of this, so he paused for just a moment to take it all in before he shut it down for good.

"Once again, Ann and I want to thank everyone who made this bus tour and campaign happen. Over the past six weeks, all y'all have taken us into your homes and given us your hearts. For that alone, Ann and our family will be eternally grateful."

"And I've asked so much of you I'm almost embarrassed to ask each of you for just one more little, small favor," he asked in mock shyness.

"Anything, Richard," yelled Debbie, an old friend who had worked campaigns in the area since she had been in her teens. The good political veterans always know when to yell and make it sound spontaneous.

"Can you give me one more weekend?" he shouted.

The crowd started to applaud to the challenge.

"Can you give me one more weekend of knocking on doors?" he asked as the applause and cheers increased. "Can you give me one more weekend of calling your neighbors and asking for their vote? Can you put door hangers on one more street? Can you get one more voter to the polls? Then on Tuesday night can all y'all join Ann and me in celebrating Garrett Jackson's legacy of conservative leadership will be continued in the United States House of Representatives?"

He was shouting over the whoops and hollers of the crowd now. Josh couldn't help but think how cool this was all going to look on the television news that night.

"God bless you. God bless the United States of America. And we'll see all y'all at the victory party on Tuesday night."

Thompson shot a "thumbs up" to the crowd and then grabbed Ann and hugged her so tight it nearly took her breath away.

"I'm proud of you," she whispered in his ear.

Richard grabbed Ann's hand and walked her to the front of the small stage. As the crowd began to chant "Thompson, Thompson, Thompson," he smiled from ear-to-ear and thrust Ann's hand into the air, the confident movement of a soon-to-be victor.

Thompson turned and began to shake the hands of the campaign staff and volunteers. When Thompson reached his young press secretary, Josh was beaming. "I hope all those days of listening to my crappy music were worth it?"

"You better believe it, Boss," laughed Josh. "I may even buy my own John Prine CDs come Wednesday."

"How about Meat Loaf?" asked Thompson.

"I think I'll have to work up to that one," he replied.

Griffith approached Thompson, grabbed his hand and pulled him close. "It's all on auto pilot from here, pal."

Thompson whispered to Griffith, "I need the truth, Griff. Do we win on Tuesday or was this my last public speech?"

"You've got a lifetime of public appearances left, my friend. Now mingle with your folks. The Fat Man is waiting for you on a plane at the airport."

Thompson, Ann and the kids, who had joined their Mom and Dad for the last leg of the bus tour, walked through the crowd taking in the well wishes and shouts of support like a congregation taking in a sermon. Each passing word of hope and faith gave them a new spirit and a fresh spring in their collective step.

These people believe in me. I can't let them down on Tuesday. I won't let them down on Tuesday.

Thompson approached the car Griffith had pulled ino the parking lot to drive the two of them to the airport. Before he got in, Ann squeezed his hand tight, adding, "I love you. Be careful."

"I'll be home in time to welcome back the door-to-door walkers at headquarters at 3:00. If any one asks, tell them I'm in Ashland for the morning."

"Just be careful," she said as her eyes began to well up.

"Everything is going to be fine. Okay? I love you, too," Thompson said as he slowly got into the car. He looked in the side view mirror as the car pulled away and saw Ann crying. He wished he could go back and comfort her, but he knew he had to get to the airport and the crew waiting for him on the private jet which had been discreetly chartered by the F.B.I.

"It's just you and me now, Griff. What's bothering you? Are we going to lose on Tuesday? Give it to me straight," asked Thompson.

"It's not Tuesday I'm worried about," replied Griffith. "I've got that under control. At this point, I'm just like Willie Chi Chi. I can push a button and make anything happen. There isn't much else you or I can do. But if I were a betting man, I like our chances on Tuesday night."

"Then why are you so damn squirrelly?"

"Because when I drop you off at the airport, I lose all control over what happens to you," said Griffith. "You're about to wire up the Ranking Member of the House Rules Committee and I can't be there to help walk you through it."

"You know you've got to be here. The staff will notice if we both disappear two days before the election," said Thompson. "Anyway, I'll have The Fat Man with me. He'll be within earshot of me the entire time. Literally. He's going to be in the sound truck. He'll let you know immediately if I get shot or something."

"Don't even joke about that, man," said Griffith. "Here, I even picked up the new Warren Zevon tribute CD for you to listen to on the way to the airport," he said as he popped it into the CD player.

Great. Splendid Isolation. Who didn't see that one coming?

CHAPTER 26

During the bus tour, Ann Thompson had been quietly conducting a little investigation of her own.

The blog entries from the anonymous woman warning about the evils of the color red (whatever the hell that meant) had continued and the warnings themselves had become increasingly dire. So, from the bus tour, and away from her husband's sight, Ann had decided to make a call to the webmaster for the campaign's web site, David Ellis, to see if he could have any success at running down where the entries were coming from.

David Ellis was a campaign volunteer who, in his real life, ran a local computer technology company. Like most loyal volunteers, he was someone who was eaten up with Republican politics. Richard and Ann were elated when he called to volunteer for the campaign. Not only would his volunteer efforts save the campaign a lot of money on technology, but they would probably have the most advanced campaign web site in the country.

After Ann had sent Griffith and Thompson on their way to the airport, she turned her attention to Ellis, who had come to the Boone County Courthouse at Ann's request to celebrate the end of the bus tour.

"Your eyes are red. Have you been crying?" asked David's wife Leslee, as Ann approached the couple.

"Tears of joy," said Ann, firming up her shoulders and putting on the best political face she could muster. "If I had to sit on that bus one more day, I'd have to get butt replacement surgery."

"I love the new ads," said David. "Who says the camera adds 10 pounds?"

"David," said his wife. "Don't tell her about the camera adding 10 pounds."

"Well, that's what I mean," said David, awkwardly defending his previous statement. "Ann and the kids look great in them."

"Thanks," said Ann graciously. "I know what you're trying to say."

"Well, if you need anything, just let us know. We started this thing with you and we're going to see it through to the very end," replied Leslee.

"No. You guys have gone above and beyond the call of duty. David has done so much work on the campaign I'm beginning to wonder if he has any real clients at his business. And, speaking of free work, did you find out anything about those blog entries?"

"Well, Ann, it's like I told you it would be. I can't tell you the exact person who has been sending the blogs, but I am beginning to be able to figure out the server they come from."

"And?"

"And," said Ellis, "it's pretty interesting. They're coming from a server at the Library of Congress."

"The Library of Congress?" said Ann in a tone indicating she had been caught totally off guard.

"Yup, and I called the webmaster for their web site. It turns out this server is reserved exclusively for remote access by former Members of Congress."

With more than a woman's intuition, Ann immediately knew who was sending the increasingly ominous blogs.

CHAPTER 27

The allure of Key West had captured Richard Thompson from the first time his grandfather had taken him there as a child for an overnight adventure.

Thompson's grandparents had lived in Ft. Lauderdale for years before he was born. When he was a kid, his parents spent every vacation at their home on the inter-coastal waterway, just a couple of blocks east of A1A. When he was old enough to travel by himself, Thompson's parents would send him down on a plane a couple of weeks early.

Those weeks were the most special of times for little Ricky Thompson and his grandfather. Grandpa would plan adventures for the pair that had to be kept secret from all in the family except Grandma. The young boy thought the secrecy was due to the pirate-like nature of the trips. It was only as he got older he realized the secrecy was due to the fact Grandpa was taking him to places of which mom and dad would not have approved. "Kitty Hawking" they called it. Even after Grandpa died, there were trips he never told his parents about.

The drive to Key West was one of those trips, and its details were etched in Thompson's memory as if it they had just happened yesterday. The drive down US 1, which included a bridge that went seven miles over water, took nearly the entire day. So, when the two Kitty Hawkers got to Key West, Grandpa wanted a quick dinner and sleep. But for the young boy, sleep was nearly impossible. He laid awake in a bed at the Southern Cross Hotel on Duvall Street listening to the noises coming from the street. Once Grandpa was asleep, he crept to the window and gazed for hours at the festival of sights and sounds taking place just outside their hotel window.

The next morning the pair went to the diner where Harry Truman occasionally went for breakfast, hoping to catch a glimpse of the former President. Looking back on it, Thompson wasn't even sure if Truman was alive at that point in time. But, it really didn't matter. Grandpa had sworn he saw Truman walking past the store front. Years later, Thompson realized he had only said it to heighten the thrill of the adventure for the young boy.

They stood at the southernmost point in the United States. They got their picture taken at U.S. 1, Mile Marker 0. Grandpa even gave the youngster his first sip of beer from a table at Sloppy Joe's (the original one where Captain Tony's stands today).

From that day forward, there had always been something about the small island which could put Richard Thompson at ease. It was where he and Griffith had gone on spring break each of their years in college. And it was where he and Ann had gone for their honeymoon and almost annually for a getaway by themselves.

Thompson loved to walk the streets of Key West. He would spend hours just going from store to store and tavern to tavern to discover the city. Once, he stumbled across Jerry Jeff Walker playing guitar in a bar off the beaten path where the urn on the counter by the cash register was purported to hold the ashes of the drug runner Jimmy Buffett sang about in *A Pirate Looks at Forty*.

Maybe it was the briny smell of salt in the air. Or maybe it was the fact that Key West was the one place in the world where Richard Thompson could let his guard down and just be that kid again looking for another adventure. Whatever it was, when the wheels of the small jet touched down on the dark runway, Thompson literally felt the tension of the campaign and the bus tour melt away from his body.

In order to avoid raising any suspicions, the pilot had first landed at the airport on Marathon Key to drop off The Fat Man and F.B.I. Agent Leo Argo, a strapping Hispanic man with arms as big around as tree trunks, where they boarded an awaiting van. And that was just as well, from Thompson's standpoint. The endless coaching from Agent Argo about Saturday's sting was about to send Thompson out the door of the plane without a parachute. He knew the details were important, but if he heard them one more time…

I've got it already. Tonight I'll check into Ambrosia II under the name of Nathan Wallace. A credit card and identification provided by the F.B.I are in my wallet. Agent Argo and The Fat Man will be checking in later to an adjoining room. In the morning, they'll wire me for sound and then send me on my way to the VFW breakfast meeting where Congressman Lackner will be mingling with his constituents and homeless veterans while turning flap jacks. The agents will be a half-block away in a Federal Express van listening. If I get in trouble, use the words "Harry Truman" and they'll rush the place. I'll leave the meeting and a cab driven by an agent will take me an hour up the road to Marathon where a different plane will be waiting to take me home.

But all of that was tomorrow. Tonight, he needed to decompress. So, before dinner he just walked. And walking Key West did decompress Thompson, because the slow pace brought back a flood of childhood memories from a more innocent time in Thompson's youth. Not that the world was more innocent during his youth, mind you. Naval ships once blockaded Cuba just a few miles to the south of the Keys. But the walk allowed Thompson to evoke a more idyllic view of his own nature and being.

As Thompson walked he noted the old bars along the main drag, Duvall Street, had over the years been replaced one-by-one, with neon-lighted national chains. But one block away was a world where banty hens rush out between your legs and an occasional scorpion still causes neighborhood havoc. It's a world being changed by the constant buzz of electric tools rehabbing old houses, but still a place where old guys like Crazy Larry paint pictures of post-modern cats on sea shells and coconut husks (although it's not at all clear that Larry realizes his art has such a snooty classification as "post-modern").

In Key West, life can be put into its proper perspective in a 10 minute walk from the Atlantic Ocean to the Gulf of Mexico. And as Thompson passed alleys containing entire communities, he couldn't help but ponder his current situation in a melancholy way. Was he suddenly troubled by memories of a changed Key West or by the memories of a changed Richard Thompson?

Am I longing for the old Key West or the old me?

The pondering didn't last too long. On their honeymoon, Ann had befriended the local Episcopal priest who had introduced them to a restaurant which was a favorite of the locals. Pepe's was known, not only for its fresh fish, but for a menu item called "steak smothered in pork chops." Just as it's described, it's a big cut of steak, covered in pork chops and surrounded by mashed potatoes and gravy. Thompson couldn't shake the thought of Judas having a last meal before betraying Jesus. But he was no Judas and Marcus Lackner was certainly no Jesus of Nazareth.

So Thompson sat in the pleasant solitude of Pepe's enjoying a meal so heavy in cholesterol he could almost hear his veins slamming shut with each bite.

The next morning, the big meal and the three Manhattans he had used to wash it down felt like a pleasant lump in his stomach when The Fat Man and Agent Argo entered the room.

"Up and at 'em, Mr. Wallace," said The Fat Man, "you've got pancakes to eat."

"Did you enjoy your meal at Pepe's last night, Mr. Thompson?" asked Agent Argo.

"Yes," replied Thompson. "And how did you know where I ate?"

"I had you followed after you landed," said the agent.

"Great. Did I have fun?"

"No," laughed Argo. "Apparently, you're a pretty boring guy. I just wanted to make sure no one else was following you around down here. I don't think these guys know we're on to them, but I wanted to make sure for your safety. So I had someone on your tail at all times."

"I sure hope when Mr. Wallace gets his credit card bill next month, he doesn't mind I ordered an entire key lime pie for dessert," said Thompson to Agent Argo. "It's over in the fridge, Joey. You guys can take it with you in the van this morning."

"Thanks," said The Fat Man as he pulled the pie from the refrigerator by the mini-bar. "It's a wild place down here. I don't know that I've ever seen anything like it, but I now understand why this place relaxes you so much."

"Joey, you're going to see everything down here today," said Thompson. "Old hippies stoned in alleys, drunken college girls throwing their sexuality around like a captain throwing a chum line and old fogies on the Old Towne Trolley. If you see a store advertising 'water sports' make sure it's for sporting gear before you go in."

There was an uncomfortable silence.

"Are you ready for this?" asked The Fat Man.

"Wire me up, boys," Thompson replied as he spread his arms.

"Okay, this is your main wire," said Argo as he went to work taping a small fiber to Thompson's chest and running it down his right arm to a point just above his sleeve line. "It runs down to the transmitter we've built into this belt. In case it gets disconnected somehow, I'm taping a second one to your other arm. I like to run it just shy of the end of your sleeve. We usually get really good reception out of putting them on the arm, although I'm using a second one as a backup today, because you're wearing short sleeves. Long sleeves are better, but you'd stick out with long sleeves in this weather."

"I thought they'd be bigger," said The Fat Man.

"Yeah," replied Argo as he worked on wiring up Thompson. "It looks cooler in the movies to have small microphones taped to your nipples, but actually the technology is way beyond that. In fact, you can buy all the stuff to put this together at Radio Shack: the fiber, the transmitter, the receiver, the whole works. Put your shirt on and see if your range of motion is okay."

Thompson twisted from side to side. "It feels normal to me."

"Now, let's try to get some audio. Joe, look out the window. Guys, flash the lights on the truck if you're picking this up."

"They got it," said The Fat Man as soon as he saw the flashing headlights from the van.

"Mr. Thompson, why don't you say something so they can get a sound check," instructed the burly Hispanic agent.

Feeling somewhat embarrassed as to what to say, Thompson began reciting the introduction to an old Meat Loaf song. "On a hot summer night would you offer your throat to the wolf with the red rose." The Fat Man started laughing and Argo looked at the pair like they were from another planet.

"I think it's time to go," said Argo. "You know where the VFW Hall is, don't you? It's about a block down from Pepe's. Walk down to Sloppy Joes. That will give us a chance to check the range of the equipment. Wait for a pink cab to drive by and honk his horn three times. That's how you know the equipment is working and Congressman Lackner is at the pancake breakfast. When you get there, remember we're looking for statements to prove he's in a conspiracy with this guy Guidos and all your pals from Miami."

"They're not my pals." Thompson interjected with a glare. "I've never even met them."

Argo continued, "Okay, okay, okay. Whatever. Actually I think I believe you. In any event, after you have taken your best shot at Lackner, get the hell out. And no drinks at Sloppy's. If you end up having to testify, it looks bad if you have a drink before the sting."

"Let's get this over with," said Thompson looking directly at his law partner. "I'm doing the right thing, right?"

"Actually, you're doing the only thing you can do under the circumstances," The Fat Man responded. "If the F.B.I. ain't happy, ain't nobody happy."

The Fat Man glared at Agent Argo with a smile. Argo did not reciprocate, instead giving Bradley a look that suggested any further quips about the Bureau would not be appreciated.

Seeing his own misstep, The Fat Man continued, "All right, then. Wow, tough audience." Turning back to face Thompson, he said, "Go get 'em. I'll be listening the whole time and only a couple of seconds away. If all goes well, I'll see you in Marathon in about an hour."

It's about a six block walk to Sloppy Joes from the hotel. Thompson was trying hard to look natural as he made his way down the street. But, on a Saturday morning in Key West, he stood out like a sore thumb. There aren't many people on the street at 9:00 am. Most tourists are sleeping off the Friday night party and trying to ignore the crowing roosters in the trees. The locals were just opening up their shops and cleaning up the palm leaves which had fallen during the thunderstorm that had passed through the night before. The only other folks on the street at that hour were the homeless, many of whom hadn't yet vacated the spots in which they had slept.

In spite of the reason for his current visit, the stroll down Duvall Street under the shade of the banyan trees still brought back all the pleasant memories of Thompson's prior trips there. He wondered what the guys in the van thought when he laughed out loud as he walked in front of the Southern Cross Hotel. He stopped, looked up at the window he had gazed out of as a child and pulled a freshly rolled Rodriguez cigar from his pocket. As he fired up the Churchill stogie, he continued to look at the window, then tipped his hand to the heavens.

Thanks, Grandpa. Keep an eye on me for a little while here. I'm going to need it.

As he walked further down Duvall, the majority of the bars he passed were closed. There was one where the smell of the bartender freshly squeezing a glass of orange juice for some reason seemed to put him at ease, if only for a moment.

But when he got to the corner of Duvall and Caroline Streets, Sloppy Joes was open. Sloppy's is always open. It probably closes at some point each night but if it does, it's long after Thompson's bedtime. He could never remember walking past it when its doors were closed. The one-time haven of writers like Ernest Hemingway and Shel Silverstein had a certain ambiance about it that was traditional to Key West and couldn't be replaced by the national chains. The walls are covered with photos of Hemingway and his fishing trophies. As you sip a beer at the bar, you can almost hear Papa's voice from a nearby table bragging about the fight the catch of the day had just given him.

And, as usual, Sloppy's already had a couple of patrons sitting around the bar sipping on beers when Thompson arrived.

Thompson sat down at the bar on the side with the open door to Caroline Street, and he ordered a cup of coffee. After about 20 minutes, a pink cab pulled up to the corner of Caroline and Duvall Streets and honked its horn three times in rapid succession. Thompson put a $5 bill on the bar and headed up Caroline Street to the Key West V.F.W. hall.

The V.F.W hall is classic Key West…a white stucco building with a mural of a sailor painted on the outside by the door. The inscription below it read: REMEMBER THE MAINE—VFW POST 3911—FEBRUARY 15, 1893. There were old bikes parked out front and a patio surrounded by life preservers from many of the ships which, at one time or another, had been docked at the Naval Station on the northeast side of the island. To the left of the door was an old artillery gun painted in green and black camouflage. Faded red, white and blue bunting hung over the door.

When Thompson walked through the front door, the building was packed with vets and the pancake breakfast was in full swing. Thompson bought a ticket and headed to the line where Congressman Marcus Lackner was serving up stacks and political stories all at the same time.

"So this guy is in bed at two in the morning when the phone rings. 'How should I know? That's two blocks away,' he says and slams down the receiver. 'Who was that?' asks his wife. 'Oh, I don't know,' the guy says, 'some idiot who wants to know if the coast is clear.'"

As always, everyone was laughing at the Congressman's joke. Lackner froze in an expression, part confusion and part anger, when he saw Richard Thompson sticking out a plate and asking for a short stack.

"Thompson? What the hell are you doing in Key West? Don't you have an election to win on Tuesday?" asked the Congressman.

"I do, Congressman, and quite honestly, right now I'd rather be in Kentucky walking door-to-door than here eating pancakes with you. But I need to speak with you on a matter that can't wait until after the election," Thompson replied hoping Lackner didn't notice the nervousness in his voice.

"Herb, take over my spot on the line for a minute. I need to talk with an old friend of mine from Kentucky," said Lackner as he grabbed a cup of coffee and went with Thompson to sit down at a table in the far corner of the room.

"What are you doing here in Key West? You need to be home getting the vote out. The party leadership is counting on you to win this race. We need you to keep our numbers steady," said Lackner. "I'm very disappointed you're not taking it seriously."

"I'm taking it very seriously, Congressman, but I wish I could believe you really want me to win," Thompson replied.

"Hell, son, of course I want you to win," said Lackner.

"I don't think you do, Congressman," replied Thompson. He leaned forward and said, in a tone both confidential and accusatory, "If you wanted me to win, why would you send your goons to Kentucky to have me back off Section 936?"

"Send my goons?" replied Lackner in a low voice. "What the hell are you talking about?"

"With all due respect, Congressman," Thompson replied, "you know exactly what I'm talking about."

"Son, I don't have the first clue what you're talking about," said an agitated Lackner as he stood up from the table to leave. "And I'm not going to listen to you making wild and irresponsible allegations. Now, just run on back to Kentucky and win your little race up there."

"Cut the crap, Lackner," interjected Thompson, afraid the Congressman would leave, "and sit your ass back down. If you don't, maybe I'll just go ahead and call the Chairman of the Ethics Committee right now and tell him all about your involvement in union politics in Puerto Rico."

"I don't know what you're talking about, son," said Lackner with a tone expressing something far short of sincerity. He sat back down.

Thompson sensed his momentary advantage and pressed it. "Please don't play games with me, Congressman. After what you did to me, I'm really not in the mood for games.

"That night we had dinner in D.C. You wanted me to back off 936 reforms. Don't deny you and your union goons are pushing me on this."

Lackner could see he wasn't going to get rid of the young man from Kentucky easily. "Look, son, be pissed at me if you want, but I had nothing to do with whatever he did to you."

"You tried to get me to back off the 936 issue," pressed Thompson.

"You're right. He asked me to intercede on the 936 issue, but after you said no to me that night at the Palm, it was out of my hands. I've got my own problems with 936 and those boys. I wish you would have listened to reason and just backed off. I've got some constituents with a lot riding on something, and your fucking campaign ads were getting in the way. Yes, I said I'd try to talk you out of it. Yes, there are people who asked me to do it. But when you told me no, he took over from there. I had no say in whatever happened after that."

Thompson was stunned. *"He?" Who the fuck is "he?" Holy shit. Lackner wasn't behind all of this. It's not the union. Someone else is involved.* Thompson tried to regain his composure.

"Hell, I'm sorry, son," Lackner said, now attempting to convey a paternal tone. "But, believe me, cozying up with him wouldn't be the worst thing that could happen to you in this business. He didn't release it to the press, did he?"

"No. I backed off. Who is he?" asked Thompson.

"None of your god damn business," Lackner said, suddenly realizing Thompson probably knew less than his earlier comments might have indicated. "And if you know what's good for you you'll walk out that door and make believe you were never here. Personally, I'm going to consider your little visit here a 'rookie mistake' and pretend it never happened."

Lackner stood up again, but this time he turned and started to walk back to the pancake line. After two steps or so, he looked back at the young candidate hoping to offer some guidance. "Take my advice, now. Just go home to Kentucky and win your race. In a couple of days this will all just be a bad memory. By the time you're sworn in next Thursday, none of this will matter. Now get out of here and don't ask me any more questions."

Thompson walked out of the air conditioned hall and took a deep breath as the hot Key West summer air hit him in the face. Right on cue, the pink cab pulled around the corner. Thompson hailed the cab and jumped in the back seat.

"Great, we got it all," said the driver. "You did a good job, Mr. Thompson. Now, let's get you up to Marathon so we can get you home to win your race."

"Can I take this stuff off now?" asked Thompson, as he started to unbutton his shirt. "It's starting to itch."

"Sure. Your days as a 'double ought' spy are over and done with," the nameless agent replied.

Thompson looked over his shoulder and saw a Federal Express truck turning the corner and following them up U.S. 1. for the sixty mile trip to Marathon. He and the agent exchanged small-talk along the way, but Thompson couldn't get his mind off the conversation with Lackner.

Who the hell is HE?

When they finally arrived at the airport, the agents exchanged pleasantries with Thompson and The Fat Man. Agent Argo thanked them both—with apparent sincerity—for their cooperation.

"We'll try to let you know when all of this is going to hit," said

Argo. "It'll probably be sometime next week. And after Tuesday. Our hope is that Lackner will know he's screwed and cop a plea. As I explained to your friend here," he said gesturing to The Fat Man, "in that case, he pleads guilty, there's no trial and you're off the hook. No one ever knows about your involvement."

"And if he doesn't?" asked The Fat Man.

"Then we'll need your client to testify and, obviously, we'll need you to go public. But, trust me," he added, "he'll plead. They all do. A guy like that will never even entertain the scenarios that would involve a risk of doing hard time."

The agent who had driven the cab chimed in. "A powerful guy like him will shiver at the thought of sharing a slow dance in a cell with some big guy named Bubba. We'll cut a deal with him. You watch. In return for his guilty plea, resignation and future cooperation, he gets a couple of months in a half-way house and probation. We'll get all the information we need, and he doesn't have to face the thought of having to be someone's boyfriend in federal prison."

"Good luck on Tuesday. I'll be watching CNN," said Agent Argo as he directed the two to the plane that would take them home. "Speaking for myself rather than the Bureau, I hope you win."

"So I guess it's probably not the time to hit you up for a campaign contribution, is it?" asked Thompson.

"No," laughed Argo. "But seriously, good luck."

As the pair sat down in the facing overstuffed leather seats of the private jet, Thompson looked at The Fat Man and put his fingers to his lips as if to silence any real talk for the moment.

A few seconds later, the loud piercing whine of the jet engine began. The Fat Man struggled to lean forward toward Thompson as if to say something confidentially. But Thompson gestured for him to sit back, and then said in a half-shout that was clearly audible over the sound of the engine, "How did it go in the van?" As he did Thompson scribbled something on a legal pad.

WE COULD BE BUGGED.

"Good. You came through loud and clear," replied The Fat Man looking somewhat puzzled as Thompson held up the pad a second time.

LACKNER ISN'T CALLING THE SHOTS.

With a nod of understanding, The Fat Man waved for Thompson to hand him the legal pad and the pen.

"Did they think they got enough to convict Lackner on conspiracy charges?" asked Thompson, while reading the response The Fat Man was writing back to him.

I KNOW—THEY THINK IT'S THE UNION GUY.

"Yeah," replied The Fat Man. "Lackner probably gave them enough to prove that he's in on it. If it does make it to a jury, they shouldn't have any problem at all proving a conspiracy charge."

NO—IT'S SOMEONE ELSE.

"Did you get a chance to call the headquarters like I asked?" Thompson asked The Fat Man. "How's Ann holding up?"

HOW DO YOU KNOW?

"I called," replied The Fat Man. "But I don't know about Ann. She didn't come into the campaign office today. She was pretty scared about this whole trip. She just wants you back safe and sound. We'll call her on her cell phone as soon as we're wheels down at Lunken."

HIS EYES. LACKNER WAS SCARED.

HE'LL NEVER GIVE UP WHO'S BEHIND THIS.

"Who did you speak to—Josh?"

The Fat Man nodded affirmatively as he scribbled on the pad.

"Did he say how the 'get-out-the-vote walking' went this morning? Did we get a big crew out on the street?" asked Thompson, now struggling for topics to discuss while they continued to write back and forth.

WHO IS IT THEN?

"Josh said we had a great crew out on the streets. He said even Griff was impressed at the ground game you had out today," replied The Fat Man.

DON'T KNOW.

CLEAR THAT IT'S NOT THE UNION GUY.

BUT WE'VE ONLY GOT 24-48 HOURS TO FIGURE IT OUT!

AFTER THAT, TRAIL GOES COLD—

PICTURES OF YOU OUT THERE FOREVER.

"I'll just be glad when this whole election and F.B.I. sting crap are both all behind me," said Thompson.

How?

"You and me both, pal. Our partners are beginning to wonder if I'm ever going to work again. You're going to D.C., but I've got to start practicing law again sometime soon."

Tammy?

"If I win on Tuesday, do you have my partnership resignation for me to sign? They might want to swear me in as early as Thursday, you know." Thompson was starting to run low on both energy and phony conversation.

Why didn't you tell Argo about Tammy and the pictures?

"Yeah. It's all together. I've got a special partners' meeting set up for Wednesday to say goodbye and sign all the papers."

Don't let anyone outside the family know what you are thinking.

"I'm going to get some shut eye before we land. I'm beat and I get the feeling I'm not going to get much sleep in the next couple of days."

It was the first honest line of conversation Thompson had spoken since they had taken off.

In any election, after all the votes are tallied, only one person can be declared the winner.

Not that a victory or loss should come as surprise to any candidate. Both sides have pollsters making calls to the same demographic of people, asking the same basic questions. The pollsters have been asking questions the entire campaign seeing what issues will move voters to their candidate's camp. As the campaign nears an end, a candidate almost always knows where he or she stands with the electorate.

It was no different in the special election for Congress in Kentucky's Fourth Congressional District. Thompson knew from his polling he was winning. Pope knew from his polling he was losing. The strategy for the final weekend, thus, was set.

Thompson's team had to keep their voters energized about turning out to vote on election day. Volunteers were out on the streets knocking on doors of voters who had been identified as supporting Thompson. Pre-recorded voice messages from Garrett Jackson's widow, Eunice were being made to all female voters. The message on Thompson's television ads were changed from discussions of issues to quotes from newspaper endorsements being voiced over warm shots of Thompson and Ann sipping coffee at their breakfast table.

Pope's strategy was one of near desperation. He had to find some knock-out wedge issue that would demoralize Thompson's base of supporters and keep them home on election day. It's hard to convert voters on a final weekend, but there are a lot of tactics to try and motivate your opponent's voters to stay at home on election day. For Pope that meant also using the phones to call Republicans. But instead of having Eunice Garrett's kind voice endorse, it had a husky male voice, which sounded like a conservative radio personality, blast Thompson as a "Washington insider" who cared much more about power than the folks back home. They chose a similar message for their closer television ad.

Griffith loved their choice of weekend message. "I'll take a call from Eunice over their message any day of the week," he told Josh when they got hold of a recording of the call from a supporter's telephone answering machine.

Each candidate's headquarters was a flurry of activity. Neither let their volunteers know what the polls were saying. Thompson didn't want his folks to get cocky and quit short of the finish line and Pope didn't want bad news to do the same to his.

However, there was one thing that was puzzling to William Pope's campaign team. Where was Richard Thompson? A Pope mole masquerading as a Thompson volunteer had reported Thompson was reportedly campaigning in Ashland on Saturday, but so far as Pope's supporters in that area could tell, Thompson was nowhere to be found.

"That sonofabitch has done it again," shouted Pope at his hired gun consultant. "Griffith figured out who your mole was and gave him misdirection on Thompson's whereabouts just to throw you off his trail. Jesus, maybe I should have hired Michael Griffith to run my campaign. You guys suck!"

Losing candidates always reserve the right to blame bad campaigns on their campaign consultants.

But Pope had raised a good question that was also being asked by Thompson's paid staffers as well, "Where the hell are the Boss and his wife?"

CHAPTER 28

As she sat in a booth at the truck stop diner, over runny eggs and strong coffee, Tammy pondered the mess she had gotten herself into. Since leaving her home years ago, her life had been a slow spiral downward, culminating in the various blackmail schemes that now were ruining her life.

It hadn't always been this way.

She sipped her morning coffee and silently swore to herself that when she returned Suzi's car, she would turn around and get the hell out of D.C. forever. *Maybe Richard and Ann Thompson are right. If I play along with them, maybe I'll get a second chance. I'll get out of the tits and ass business and move to a town where no one has ever heard of Amber Burn. Wow, I've been a stripper so long I'm even calling myself by my stripper name. I could move out west. People mind their own business out there. No one would know or care that, in another life, I was a bi-sexual blackmailing stripper.*

Tammy smiled openly at the prospects of a new life. It was quite possibly the first genuine smile she had had in months. She sipped her coffee and gazed out the window of the truck-stop diner, content to be thinking pleasant thoughts about her unpleasant life.

She was so deep in her own thoughts she didn't notice the build-up of police cars across the street at the small hotel where she had stayed the night before and where Suzi's borrowed car was still parked. The deep voice of an older police officer ordering take-out coffee at the cash register caught her attention

"What's up across the street, Max?" asked the hostess.

"There's an APB out on some young broad who killed a stripper down in D.C. Apparently some kind of lesbian lovers quarrel," said the officer. "One stripper stabbed the other and killed her. Then the killer takes off in the dead girl's car. Sad case—dead girl was a college student and the killer's some kind of a drifter. That blue Honda Accord across the street belongs to the dead one. We think the killer is somewhere in the hotel."

Tammy slowly put on her shades to cover her black eye and pulled her cap down low.

"We've got the hotel locked down until the local D.C. police can send us a photo of the killer. We should have it in about 15 minutes and then we'll start a room-by-room search. So, I thought I'd grab a cup of Joe while we wait. It's a weird world we live in, Betty," said the cop as he put a buck on the counter and left the restaurant.

Tammy was struggling to catch her breath and trying to keep from shaking at the same time. *Jesus Christ. Suzi is dead and the cops think I'm to blame.*

She didn't know what to do, but she knew whatever she did, she had less than 15 minutes to do it.

As calmly as she could under the circumstances, Tammy paid her bill and slowly walked out the door of the restaurant. To her left was Interstate 64. Across the street there was an ever growing number of police. To her right were a group of truckers. She opted for her right.

"Any of you guys headed west towards Kentucky?" she asked in as sexy a voice as she could muster with her chest rattling so badly.

"I am," said a short overweight man in a "West Virginia is for Lover's" t-shirt.

"Lookin' for company?" said Tammy, as she grabbed the man by the arm in an attempt to look like a girlfriend to anyone watching from across the street.

"Sure. We don't get many girls out here as pretty as you," said the man as they reached his rig. "How much you chargin'?"

"I'm not a whore," replied Tammy in a voice showing her confidence in the situation was waning. "But take me west on 64 and I'll take care of you. I promise. Please."

The trucker looked across the street at the police cars and back again at Tammy. "Are you carrying a gun?" he asked.

"No," she said handing him her purse to prove her statement.

"Hop in," he said handing her back her purse. "And duck down so your friends across the street don't see you."

CHAPTER 29

Ann sat in the mini-van in front of the spacious ranch home in a quiet suburb of Dayton, Ohio. She was uncharacteristically nervous about the meeting that was about to take place.

She had been unable to think of anything else but the coming encounter ever since she had made the call to set up the appointment the evening before. She had lain awake in bed for hours playing out different scenarios in her head, between her frequent glances at the ever advancing alarm clock on the table by her bed.

Now, after a short 45 minute drive from her home in Northern Kentucky, Ann sat in front of the comfortable home with a southern-style porch, questioning whether she had made the right decision in making the call in the first place. She was about ready to put the car in gear to drive away, when a slightly overweight brunette woman in her late-forties emerged from the front door in smart business attire carrying a coffee tray and smiled sincerely in her direction.

Too late to turn back now. Ann turned off the ignition, exited the car and walked toward the house.

The woman put the tray on a table next to two wicker chairs on the spacious front porch and stuck out her hand to greet Ann.

"Hi," she said as the two shook hands. "You must be Ann Thompson. I'm Congresswoman Debbie North. Well, officially I guess I'm now 'former

Congresswoman.' And, yes, to save you asking. I'm your campaign's anonymous blogger. Have a seat."

"Thanks."

"I have to ask, though, how did you figure out it was me?"she inquired as she poured Ann a cup of coffee.

"One of our campaign volunteers traced your entries back to a server at the Library of Congress used exclusively by former Members. The blogger, you, said you had known Garrett, and I remembered he had been a featured guest at one of your fundraisers when you had run last year. Then, I read about your health problems and the resignation. I put two and two together and here I am."

"Good. I'm glad you were paying attention. I was aiming those blogs more at you than your husband."

"I got that feeling," said Ann. "Why?"

"Well, I've had a lot of time on my hands since I resigned." She looked away. "I've had too much time to think and reflect on my, uh, very short career in the United States Congress."

"Oh, I'm sorry," said Ann suddenly remembering North had recently resigned for health reasons. "We jumped in so fast, I forgot to ask. How is your health?"

"My health is fine, thanks for asking."

"What are the doctors saying about your," Ann paused briefly not really knowing what was wrong with her, "condition."

"Unfortunately, for my sorry self, I have no 'condition'…"

Ann looked at her puzzled. "I don't understand."

"My only health condition was a one night fever for a young redhead named Amber."

North looked directly into Ann's eyes for a reaction and, as hard as she tried to show a poker face, Ann's reaction was obvious.

"I see you know of her. I was afraid of that. That's why I started sending the blogs. Young Miss Amber is the terminal illness which caused the death of my political career."

Ann collapsed backwards in her neatly appointed wicker chair. *Tammy said she had set up several men and one woman. Congresswoman Debbie North was that one woman.*

"I'm sorry you know her, because that means my early hunch was right," said North. "I don't know how you handled it, but my husband went ballistic when I told him. I suspect we'll be getting divorced over it some day soon.

But, for now, we're keeping up appearances for the sake of the party and the special next month to replace me. Public life first, you know."

"Then, I guess I'm sorry, too," replied Ann.

"Don't be. I'm paying for my own lust for power. Miss Amber sought me out, but I went to her room quite willingly. Look at me. I don't have your looks and body. A young woman approaches me and starts a conversation which eventually turns to sex. I was more than turned-on by being sought out by someone like her. I nearly had an orgasm on my bar stool from the power of it all. I never considered myself anything but straight, but that night my badge went to my head. And, other places, I guess."

"Why?" asked Ann. "Why did she go after you?"

"Well, I was the freshman Member on the House Select Committee on Intelligence."

"With Garrett," interrupted Ann, remembering that one blog entry had mentioned her friendship with the late Congressman Garrett Jackson.

"Yes," she smiled weakly as she looked at the polished wood on the porch floor, "with my dear friend Garrett Jackson." North struggled to say his name. "The Select Committee is a great committee to be on, because we get to ask questions to the executive branch about any topic and they're required to answer us. While the Committee was doing some investigation into anti-Castro activities, I discovered one of our Members from Florida, Marcus Lackner, was tied up with some union guy from Puerto Rico who was running guns into Cuba. I went to Garrett and asked him if I should turn it over to the House Committee on Standards and Conduct—you know, the ethics committee. He encouraged me to do so, but he said that, out of professional courtesy, I should tell Lackner about it first."

"So did you?" asked Ann.

"Yes, I did."

"And how'd Lackner take it?"

"Remarkably calmly," said North. "Upon reflection, which as I said I'm doing a lot of lately, he was too calm. That was the morning of the night I ended up as Amber's one night love affair."

Damn. How many lives is this little girl going to ruin, thought Ann.

"The photos were personally delivered to me the next day by a lobbyist for some drug company. Virgil Lawson was his name. The message was pretty clear. Shut up about Lackner or they'd release the photos to the press."

"So you shut up?"

"Not before going back to Garrett. He told me to stand up and fight. He told me Lackner was one of the worst Members in our party and should be called to answer for this. He was going to go to Leadership with me, but…," her voice trailed off.

"But, what?" Ann asked.

"But Garrett was all about protocol and professional courtesy. He wanted to confront Lackner himself."

Ann continued the questions, not at all liking the direction the answers were leading. "And did he?"

"Yes. And that's why they killed him."

"What," said Ann, her voice rising so loud that a neighbor across the street looked over in their direction. She regained her composure and spoke in precise words. "He wasn't killed. Garrett died of a heart attack."

"Yes. It was a heart attack, but Garrett was in great shape. He worked out in the House gym every day. He was a health nut. And they killed him."

"Who is 'they'?"

"Minutes after his death was announced on the floor, Virgil Lawson came to my office. He told me someone had broken into Garrett's office the night before and replaced his vitamin pills with pills laced with a drug which causes instant heart failure. He did die of a heart attack. But, Virgil Lawson killed Garrett Jackson—or had him killed—and he wanted me to know he could do the same to me."

Ann sat in stunned silence upon learning her husband's mentor and surrogate father had been killed. She fought back tears.

"So, I resigned. I told my husband about the affair, resigned for 'health reasons' and moved my stuff home to the relative obscurity of Dayton, Ohio. I was happy when I read your husband was chosen by the party to replace Garrett. Garrett told me about him once. I started following the special. Then I saw your husband talking about 936, and was afraid he had somehow stumbled onto what I knew about Lackner. So, I found your web site and started blogging. If I was wrong, no harm would come from a few crazy blogs on some web site. But, if I was right, someone would search me out." She paused and looked sincerely at Ann. "And you did."

"Yes," said Ann. "And I'm not sure if I'm glad about it or not."

"Glad or not, you're playing in the big leagues against pros. And the pros are playing for keeps."

CHAPTER 30

"How was Ashland today?" asked one of the volunteers when candidate Richard Thompson stepped through the doors of the campaign headquarters, early in the afternoon. "I bet they didn't get as many folks out on the street as we did."

Thompson paused. He had forgotten momentarily Griffith had told everyone he had been in Ashland all morning. "They're doing great down there," he said with little conviction in his voice.

Ann walked up to her husband, and as discreetly as she could in front of the unknowing volunteers, hugged her husband like she had never hugged him before. She kissed him gently on the neck and then placed her head on his shoulder. "I'm so glad you're home. Where's Joe?"

"He went home," said Thompson. "Where have you been all morning?"

"Can we step back into Griff's office?" asked Ann calmly. "I need to talk to both of you alone."

Behind the closed shelter of Michael Griffith's doors, the trio began to discuss what had happened that morning. The candidate and the spouse took turns describing the events in Key West, Florida, and Dayton, Ohio.

When they had both finished relating their respective encounters, Thompson sat stone-faced as the reality of his situation sank in. He was outraged about Garrett Jackson. He was scared for himself. But he was absolutely terrified that Lawson, or whoever was behind him, would try to do something to Ann and the kids, especially if they learned Ann had met with North at the very same time he was meeting with Lackner.

Unfortunately, they had probably given a strong impression they knew far more than they had actually known. Therein, lay the true danger.

Ann put her head in her hands, and asked, "This isn't over yet, is it?"

"If your new friend in Dayton is right, it's not over by a long shot," said Griffith.

"Well, this explains why Lackner was scared this morning. He's afraid for his own life, and he'll never cop a plea," said Thompson. "I'm telling you, Griff, something, or more appropriately, somebody has him spooked."

"You say Lackner kept talking about 'him' in the conversation. Surely the F.B.I. picked up on that. Who do they think it is?" asked Ann. "Is it this Virgil Lawson guy?"

"Joe was in the van listening with them the whole time," said Thompson. "The F.B.I. thinks it's Guidos who's trying to become the union head at some drug company in San Juan."

"So, how do you know they're not right?" asked Ann. "Maybe this is all just your imagination running wild."

"It just doesn't make sense," replied Thompson to his wife. "Why would a powerful Congressman in Washington be afraid of a guy who doesn't have any power yet?"

"The boy is right," said Griffith, "slightly neurotic, but right. If there is one thing Richard knows, it's people's eyes. He made the biggest decision in his life based on eyes, didn't he, Ann? No, there's somebody else out there we don't know about yet. Somebody behind Lawson, Alley or Guidos. Somebody big enough and with enough power or money for a senior Congressman like Lackner to be afraid of them. We've got to figure out who that is and turn them over to the F.B.I."

Griffith leaned back in his chair and looked at Thompson. "If you're right, Lackner has probably already called this mystery guy, and he's ready to run to the press like a sprinter with your photos and we're toast by the 6:00 news on Monday."

"If that happens, how bad will it hurt us Griff?" asked Ann.

"Baby," said Griffith, "by Tuesday morning, our high hopes of a 10 point victory will be old news and we'll be lucky to finish the day in double digits."

"Shit. I really hate these people," said Ann.

"Don't hate your enemy. It affects your judgment," said Griffith, reciting from *Godfather III.*

"So what do we do now?" asked Ann. "I know I need to call your mother and have her pick up the kids and take them someplace safe. I've been thinking, how about if she takes them down to your sister's house in Lexington for a couple of days. It's a gated community and she's got a different last name. The kids can spend some time with their cousins. Make sense?"

"Yeah," Thompson said with conviction. "If you can arrange that, that'll take a load off my mind."

"Consider it done," Ann said. "What's next?"

"Right now, well—I've got a plan, but you two aren't going to like it," said Thompson.

They both looked at Thompson expectantly.

"Griff, I've got to drop everything and go with The Fat Man to D.C. Joey's already at home packing right now, and based on everything I know now, I probably should go with him."

"Junior, I know I told you I needed you going 24/7, but, frankly, in reality, it doesn't matter much now if you're here or not. We've got just a little more than 48 hours until the polls open. Like I told you yesterday, this fuckin' thing is on auto-pilot. The only thing left to do is count the votes on Tuesday night. Right now we have to get our priorities straight."

"What do you mean?" asked Ann.

"Remember in *The Godfather* when, right after they had picked up a box of cannoli at the bakery, Fat Clemenza killed Don Vito's driver for setting up the old man?"

"Another rule is on the way, isn't it?" asked Ann.

"When Clemenza killed Paulie the driver, what did he tell the trigger man as they looked over the dead body in the car? Remember? 'Leave the gun. Take the cannoli.' There was a man who had his priorities straight."

"So what's my priority here?" asked Thompson.

"Winning," said Griffith. "And without some level of comfort on what this other guy is going to do, that's up in the air right now."

"Seriously, can we afford another day away?" asked the candidate.

"I have you scheduled to walk door-to-door tomorrow just to keep you from getting too antsy," Griffith told his friend. "Go do what you have to do. Ann and I will just tell everyone you've got food poisoning and you'll be in bed all day tomorrow."

"And why won't *I* like your plan?" Ann asked her husband, almost knowing what the answer would be.

"Well, hon, you aren't going to like it because it involves Tammy Stewart," replied Thompson.

"Oh, this ought to be good," said Griffith, leaning back in his chair with a laugh.

"I thought I was paying you to *help* me," said Thompson to Griffith.

"Hey, man, I only do campaigns," said Griffith. "You should have figured out an ex-wife and a dozen wasted relationships ago that I'm not the guy to rely on for advice about how to deal with women. Anyway, I'd give some of your money back right now just to see how you're going to explain this one."

"But," Griffith said as he stood up from his chair and walked to the door, "I'm a compassionate conservative and I think you and your wife need some time alone right now." He opened the door , as he walked out, he began to sing out loud, "me and, me and Mrs. Jones. Mrs. Jones. Mrs. Jones. Mrs. Jones. We got a thing goin' on."

Yes. That's the guy in whose hands I've put my future.

"Look babe, I'm not very excited about this either," Thompson began to explain to his wife. "But I've got a plan and she's the only one who really knows much of anything about these guys in D.C. The F.B.I is focused on Lackner and Guidos. It's pretty clear they don't know anything about Tammy or Lawson or the pictures or the blackmail."

"We could tell them," said Ann.

"Yeah, we could. But it would mean them knowing about the pictures, and, once we start down that path, I'm not sure where it ends. And if those pictures end up as evidence at a criminal trial someday, my political career is over, just like former-Congresswoman North's. So, I don't want to tell them unless I have to. And, even then, I still don't want to unless I've got living proof with me to swear to the F.B.I. and everybody else it was a setup by somebody I can actually point to. Otherwise, it just looks like a lover's triangle story. And to get the one setting me up, we need Tammy. She can probably lead us to them."

"And you've already called her, and she said yes?" asked Ann.

"Actually, no," he said. "I was kind of hoping you'd call her for me."

"You've got to be shitting me?" Ann replied.

"She trusts you," he continued. "And besides, you promised her you'd help her through it, if we needed her. You're like a mother to..."

"Watch it, bud," interrupted Ann.

"...older sister...you're like an older sister to her," he said. "Come on, Annie. You know it's true and, as sad as it may seem, that girl may be our only shot at proving whether or not there's someone else out there."

"And besides," Thompson added, "if we figure that out, we probably are also going to find out who was behind the killing of Garrett."

There was a pause before Thompson handed his cell phone to his wife and, pointing to the touch pad, said, "It's speed dial #7."

She shot him "the look," that universal piercing glance which wives give when their husbands are about to step over the line, indicating no further talk is really necessary, or for that matter, even permissible. "I'm going to run home and pack. I'll ask The Fat Man to pick me up in an hour so we can get to D.C. by dinner time."

"I've got to be nuts," mumbled Ann. "I'm actually calling my husband's stripper."

CHAPTER 31

Griffith came back into the office after Ann had made her call to Tammy Stewart.

"You know he loves you, don't you? He wouldn't have asked you to make the call unless it was really important."

"I know, Griff," said Ann, staring at her cell phone and mustering up all her strength to talk to him after the call which had just taken place with Tammy. "She's here in town. I need you to pick her up and bring her to the house."

"Who's here? Tammy? I thought we sent her home to D.C.?"

"We did, but she got detoured and she hitched a ride back here. She just got in, and she's in room 123 of the Days Inn on Dixie Highway in Ft. Mitchell, hiding out."

"Hiding out? From who?"

"Well, apparently, our friends have struck again. Tammy's roommate is dead and Tammy's wanted in her murder. We're her alibi. It happened while we were all sitting around the top floor of the Ashland Plaza."

"Shit the bed," mumbled Griffith. "If we're her alibi for a murder, we're sunk. A Congressman can't be an alibi for a stripper with a dead roommate. If that happens, we lose anyway. If not this time, we'll lose in the next cycle."

"Griff, this whole thing has gone to hell in a hand basket so quickly. It's not just about winning and losing anymore. Now, it's about life and death. And quite honestly, I'm scared Richard won't live to see the next election cycle."

"Annie," Griffith responded, "I swear I'll deny it if you ever tell anybody I said this, but some things are more important than winning and losing an election. As much as I hate to say it, you may need to work on Rick to get him to rethink things here. I think it may be time to go to the F.B.I. and tell them the parts of the story they don't already know."

"It's too late for that now," said Ann. "You should know by now that once Richard has made up his mind on something like this, there is no turning back."

CHAPTER 32

"They've got any kind of beer you want here," said Thompson to his two companions, "just as long as what you want is either Schaffer or Schaffer Light." He looked at the slightly puzzled faces of The Fat Man and Tammy, waiting for a response before he told the waiter, "Well, then, I guess that's three Schaeffer Lights."

The Fish Market was an institution in Old Towne Alexandria, Virginia. Thompson, Ann and Griffith had spent nearly every Friday night of their lives there when they were younger. Griffith's political shop was only a couple of blocks away. It was a fun place to eat and drink, but they had no worry about being discovered there. It certainly wasn't the kind of place where Members of Congress hung out. It was not only a younger crowd than Thompson remembered, but a louder crowd as well.

Then again, maybe I'm just older and quieter than I used to be, he thought to himself.

Saturday nights were still pretty wild in the place. The Fabulous Trotta Brothers from Middletown, Ohio, Ron and Mark, were on stage doing their dueling rag time piano routine to the cheers of the crowd, when a young 20-somethingish black man approached the corner table where the three of them were seated.

"Are you the folks who called me?" asked the young man. When Thompson stood up, the man smiled. "So, you're the cracker that has them so pissed off," he laughed. "Mister, let me shake your hand."

"Yeah. I guess I'm the guy," Thompson said as he shook the man's hand. "Richard Thompson. This is my law partner, Joe Bradley. And I think you've already met Tammy Stewart."

"Bobby. Bobby Richmond. Pardon my saying so, lady, but your eye looks like hell," he said, looking at her from one side and then the other. "Is that what that sonofabitch Lawson did to you?"

"It would have been a lot worse if it hadn't been for you," said Tammy. "God only knows what he would have done to me. I owe you one, Mr. Bobby Richmond." She smiled a seductive smile his way.

"That's no problem," he laughed. "I was a little scared at first. You know all those cowboys I drive around pack guns. But once I saw he had his pants down and the gun was on the floor, I was so pissed, I really didn't care. I smacked him right in the mouth."

"No shit?" said Tammy.

"Yeah. It nearly cost me my job," said Bobby. "My boss was mad as hell at me for messin' with somebody he had me drivin' around. But I threatened a discrimination suit. The Ranking Member of the House Rules Committee can't have his 'colored driver' suing him for discrimination, now, can he?"

"Wait a minute," said The Fat Man. "You mean to tell me you work for the top Republican on the House Rules Committee, Marcus Lackner of Florida?"

"You bet. I work for old Elmer Fudd himself. Actually, since I was driving somebody other than the Congressman that night, I was working off-line for his Leadership PAC." Richmond looked at Thompson with a half smile. "You don't remember me, do you, sir?" he asked of Thompson.

"I'm sorry, son. I really can't place you," Thompson replied.

"I was driving for the Congressman that night he met you at The Palm for dinner," he informed Thompson. "I thought that was probably how you found me."

"No, Joe here found you online at the web site for the District of Columbia Department of Motor Vehicles. It wasn't too hard. All chauffeurs have to register with the department. Tammy remembered the guy who attacked her yelling your name when she was running from the car."

"I recognized you from your picture on the registration page," she added. "You were cute."

"Your cuteness aside, when Tammy recognized you, that's when I called you and asked that you meet us here," said Thompson.

"Tammy, I'm really sorry about what happened to you that night. I did the best I could do, but Lawson is a fucking psycho! I thought that he was going to kill me. Hell, I'm still not sure he isn't going to try someday," he said. "Anyway, I dropped Lawson off after about an hour of searching for you. Then, Lackner called me on my cell and ordered me to come back to his condo. Damn, that man was pissed off."

"That's when he tried to fire you?" asked The Fat Man.

"Yeah. I was just makin' shit up on the fly, but I told him I'd go to the D.C. Human Rights Commission with a discrimination charge. When he realized he couldn't fire me, he demoted me to answering constituent mail as a Rules Committee staffer. Do you know what a Legislative Correspondent is, Mr. Thompson?"

Thompson sat up proudly in his chair. "As a matter of fact, I do," he said, proudly thinking back to his entry position on the Hill.

"He's only the lowest mother fucker in the Congressional Staff food chain," he replied, entirely deflating Thompson's ego.

"Ouch," said The Fat Man.

"I was once a Legislative Correspondent," said Thompson with a somewhat pitiful tone in his voice.

"Oh, no disrespect, sir," Bobby recoiled. "I'm sure that being an LC was a lot more important back when you were young."

"Double Ouch," said The Fat Man.

"I'm not helping myself here any, am I?" asked Bobby, with a laugh. "Well, in any event, I'd rather be using my political science degree to be answering constituent mail than acting like Stepn' Fetchit for Lackner and his wacko pals like Lawrence Carpenter and those guys."

"Who's that?" asked Thompson.

"Lawrence Carpenter—he's the Chief Financial Officer for Livius Drugs in D.C.," The Fat Man interjected.

"Yes, sir. Exactly right." Richmond laughed and pointed at The Fat Man. "Damn, this boy ought to be on *Jeopardy*, or something."

"Carpenter's in the binder I gave you, Rick. But how do Lackner and Carpenter know each other?" The Fat Man asked.

"I really don't know for sure. But I know Lackner has me pick Carpenter up every day and drive his ass around town. As best I can make out, Carpenter raises big money for the PAC, so he thinks he owns the Congressman. Hell, maybe he does. Personally, I think Lackner is scared of him. He probably should be, I think that smug sonofabitch Carpenter and his whole crew are crazy. Do you know Carpenter?"

"No," said The Fat Man eagerly, "but I know of him. Rick, do you remember when I made that call to the President of Livius Drugs and you got all pissed off?" The Fat Man was so excited he kept going before Thompson could even answer. "The President of the company, Carl Bontiff, tried to refer me to his CFO, Lawrence Carpenter. He said Carpenter was in charge of all Caribbean Basin investments."

"So, let me get this straight," said Thompson. "You've been working for Marcus Lackner's Leadership PAC as a driver, but you've spent most of your time driving around some guy named Lawrence Carpenter?"

"Yes, sir," replied Bobby.

"And you know where he lives and his movements?"

"I've picked him up just about every day for nearly two years, until a couple of days ago. I know what he does every day better than he does."

"Well fuck-a-doodle-doo," said Thompson. "We've just found our missing link."

CHAPTER 33

The only time when there is very little hustle and bustle in the Greater D.C. area is Sunday morning. The only people on the streets are those going to church and, well, those going to church. Those who really should be going to church are at home, leaving few cars on the main roads. No one is traveling into the business district to go to work. And, unless it's the end of a session when Members are working weekends in order to get home, the Hill is virtually dead. Even the tourists don't really start appearing from their hotel rooms until about noon.

The same generally holds true for the Northern Virginia suburbs just south of the District of Columbia. On Sunday morning, if you time the lights just right, you can drive down the George Washington Parkway through Old Towne Alexandria without even hitting the brakes.

It was that sleepy kind of morning in Northern Virginia on the Sunday morning before the special Congressional election in Kentucky's Fourth District. And, when Lawrence Carpenter exited the Christ Episcopal Church in Old Town Alexandria into that uncommon calm, he seemed to have an extra spring in his step.

Soon, his days of sweltering in the summer heat along with the rest of Washington D.C.'s business elite would be replaced by relaxation in the constant summer breezes that blow across the white sand beaches of Belize.

He would miss church services at this old church and its historical lore. It was the church George Washington and Robert E. Lee had attended. The inside of the church didn't have pews; it had family boxes, square cubicles with benches around the interior perimeter on which to sit. You had to enter each box via a swinging gate. If you didn't get to a box early, you might be forced to sit in the portion of the box with your back to the priest.

From Lawrence Carpenter's viewpoint, the historical ruggedness of worshiping in a George Washington pew would soon be replaced by the beauty of white sand. His devotion to the Church was in his own mind somehow cleansing his soul of the crimes he was committing. If God could be found in this old building, he could certainly also be found on a sunny beach in Latin America.

Carpenter exited the church and took a deep breath as he made a right down the tree lined sidewalk of the G.W. Parkway. His stride was hitched, however, when he was approached by a man in a sharp blue business suit.

"Lawrence Carpenter?"

"Yes. And who are you?"

"Richard Thompson...from Kentucky."

Carpenter stopped and looked Thompson in the eye for at least ten seconds. The length of the stare, in and of itself, was unnerving to Thompson.

If nothing more than to break the uncomfortable silence, he spoke again. "Did you hear me? My name is Richard Thompson. I'm running for the United States Congress in Kentucky."

Carpenter smiled. It was a sly smile, but a smile nonetheless. "I can assume you're not here to ask me for my vote."

"Let's not bullshit each other, Mr. Carpenter," said Thompson. "I think you know exactly why I'm here. And you're correct in your assumption it's not to ask for your vote."

"So, what **do** you want, candidate Richard Thompson?" asked Carpenter.

"For starters, a cup of coffee and some answers," replied Thompson. "I saw a Starbucks a block down the street on the corner. We can figure out what else I want as we go along."

"Shouldn't you be in Kentucky campaigning right now?" asked Carpenter as they walked.

"I should be," replied Thompson, "but your pals Lawson and Alley didn't just come to Kentucky to work on my 72 hour get-out-the-vote drive, did they?"

"I should have known those photos wouldn't be enough to stop you," said Carpenter as the well-dressed pair walked down the street to the corner Starbucks. "You're in on it aren't you?"

"No, I'm really not," said Thompson not knowing what Carpenter was referring to. "I only want what I work for and what I am entitled to. I've earned my shot at this seat, Mr. Carpenter. And, neither you nor Lawson nor Alley are going to take that shot from me. In fact, even Congressman Marcus Lackner is not going to take my shot away from me."

"So your bosses, whoever they are, told you about my connection to Elmer Fudd?" asked Carpenter.

"No one told me. It wasn't really all that difficult. Any high school kid with a basic knowledge of how to use Google could have made the connection." Thompson was lying on this one, knowing The Fat Man had connected the dots with the precision of a drafting engineer.

"If you're not in on it," said Carpenter, "then why did you come here today, 48 hours before your big shot, to find me?"

"Three reasons really. First, I wanted you to know that I know who you are."

"So, now you know who I am."

"Yes, now I know who you are. And now that we've met, you need to realize I've got as much on you as you have on me." Carpenter opened the door to the Starbucks and, when they reached the overly friendly man at the counter, he ordered two cups of coffee before he sat down with his newly established foe. The place was empty except for a man in a Washington Redskins hat who was sitting in a leather chair in the corner with the Sunday *Washington Times* up in front of his face.

"Okay," said Carpenter as he took his first sip of coffee, "so now what?"

"Well, your identity leads me to the second reason I'm here," said Thompson. "I know who you are and you know who I am. But I also know things about you. I know you and Marcus Lackner had Garrett Jackson killed, and I suspect that if he's dug up and tested for certain chemicals, I can confirm you killed him. I've got something on you about Caribbean Drugs and a dead Congressman, and you've got photos of me with a redhead who's wanted for a murder that I suspect your pal Lawson probably also committed."

"Then it's an interesting position we find ourselves in, isn't it Mr. Thompson?" said Carpenter calmly.

"Yes, it is, and my proposition is quite simple. You stay the fuck out of my life and I'll stay the fuck out of yours."

"That's it? Fine," agreed Carpenter.

"And, it's not that I don't trust you, but I've established a little insurance policy at my law firm."

"What's that?"

"Well, they know everything about you and your role in the Livius acquisition of Caribbean Drugs. Now, they're my lawyers and everything I told them is protected by attorney-client privilege. But, if something should happen to me while I'm in public life—say I get mugged and killed by some unknown assailant on the mean streets of D.C.—the attorney-client privilege dies with me. When I die, it dies and they go straight to the feds." Thompson paused. "Understood?"

"Understood," replied Carpenter as he calmly continued to sip his coffee. "What's the third thing?"

"I want my cut," said Thompson boldly.

"You want what?" laughed Carpenter.

"You heard me, dick head, I want my cut," Thompson repeated, hoping to find out who else was in on the deal. "I'm not sure what you're getting out of this, but it's enough to be paying off Congressmen, lobbyists and union reps. You've caused me a lot of heart ache. You owe me just as much as you owe them."

"Go fuck yourself."

"Oh, now don't be that way," said Thompson, almost mocking Carpenter now. "You're taking this very personal. This isn't personal. It's strictly business."

"I guess my boys were wrong when they told me you were one of those true believer types," said Carpenter.

"We're both businessmen here, Mr. Carpenter," said Thompson, "and you've got a business decision to make. A simple decision really. Do you want another business partner in your Caribbean Drugs deal, or do you want to go to jail for arranging the murder of a Congressman and a stripper?"

Carpenter sat in stunned, angry silence for a moment and then gave Thompson his decision. "Fine. What do I care? Guidos will just have to up the union dues to cover your portion. By the time the money is flowing to you, I'll be far away from here." Carpenter paused, stuck out his hand and in disgust said, "Congratulations, Mr. Thompson, you're going to fit in well in this town."

When Thompson reached across the table to shake Carpenter's hand, his shirt sleeve rode up his arm just enough to reveal a thin micro fiber attached to his forearm by tape.

"You sonofabitch," snarled Carpenter as his eyes took on a wild look. "I knew you were one of them. You're wearing a wire."

People tell stories about how, when they're in an accident, everything seems to happen in slow motion. This was that moment for Richard Thompson. The next several seconds seemed to take hours.

Lawrence Carpenter stood up from his chair and pushed the table back towards Thompson, spilling both cups of coffee over the table and into Thompson's lap. Carpenter then reached into his suit coat and pulled a 9mm pistol from a shoulder holster. Two shots split the Sunday morning silence of Old Towne Alexandria in quick succession. The first one seemed to come from Thompson's left side. The second one followed nearly simultaneously from only a few feet in front of him.

As Thompson fell back over the table behind him, he could see blood spraying in every direction. The table flip landed him face first against the full length glass window facing the street.

In a haze, he looked out the window and saw that The Fat Man had jumped out of the panel van they had rented to monitor the sound equipment he had taped to Thompson earlier in the morning and was running, as best he could, toward the door of the Starbucks.

The pain was intense. As Thompson bounced off the glass window, his momentum spun him around and he saw Carpenter spinning in the opposite direction, as the gun fell from his hand. A large portion of his head was missing.

As he lay there in pain, unlike any pain he had ever felt before, Thompson glanced back over his shoulder and saw the man in the Redskins cap methodically pacing one-half step at a time towards Carpenter, his gun aimed with both hands at his lifeless body, as if another shot might be necessary. With surprising athleticism, the clerk behind the register had jumped over the counter gun in hand and was likewise moving toward Carpenter's prone body.

The Fat Man threw open the door and rushed to kneel at Thompson's right side. He was frantically trying to get Thompson into a more comfortable position, all the while repeating, "Oh, my God! Oh, my God! Oh, my God!"

"Are you okay Mr. Thompson?" asked Agent Leo Argo, as he removed his Redskins ball cap. The agent dressed as the Starbucks cashier checked the limp body of Lawrence Carpenter. Argo put his gun back into its holster and knelt beside Thompson on his other side, opposite The Fat Man.

"Jesus, it really hurts. Where the hell did you come from?" replied Thompson.

"Did you really think we'd quit following you after Key West? One of my people was sitting at the table next to you at the Fish Market last night. We heard your whole plan about today. And what we didn't hear directly from you, that kid Bobby Richmond called and told us."

The other agent was now saying something about an ambulance, but he appeared to be talking into his fist.

As Argo flopped Thompson's tie out of the way and started to open up his shirt, he kept talking in a very conversational tone. "We thought we'd stick close to you two in case you tried to be junior F.B.I. agents on your own. And sure enough, we followed you out to Radio Shack last night."

Having finally located what he was looking for, Argo pulled a .9mm slug from the Kevlar vest covering Thompson's chest. "You know, when you figured out who Carpenter was, you really should have called us. We would have handled it. Nice vest."

"Thanks. We represent a company that makes them. I told them we wanted the best they had," said The Fat Man who was still trying to catch his breath.

Thompson looked at the grotesque figure lying across from him on the floor, a pool of blood gathering around his head. "I think I broke a rib." He winced as he tried to sit up.

"If you want to be an agent, you can't act like a pussy now," Argo said with at least a touch of anger in his voice. But he quickly reverted back to a more sympathetic tone when he remembered the trauma Thompson had just undergone. "Actually, Mr. Thompson, it's probably just a real bad bruise. You're lucky he was only carrying a 9mm. Anything larger would have penetrated the vest from that close a range. Help me get Mr. Thompson the hell out of here and into our van," Argo instructed the other agent dressed as a Starbucks cashier. "I want him out of here when the local cops arrive. I've got enough explaining to do about an on-going F.B.I. investigation, without trying to explain why some geek candidate from Kentucky needs medical attention."

"Thanks," Thompson said to Agent Argo, the extreme pain still radiating from the spot under the vest where he had been hit. Thompson looked over at The Fat Man, who was white as a ghost and visibly shaking. He knew he better change the mood of the conversation before his friend literally had a heart attack. "Where did you learn how to wire someone up?" Thompson asked The Fat Man, "The Wyle E. Coyote School of Electronics?"

"When we were in Key West, he said to tape it just above the sleeve line," The Fat Man said motioning to Argo, as he and the other agent helped Thompson off the floor.

"Just above the sleeve line for a short sleeve shirt," said Argo. "It has to be higher for a long-sleeved shirt. If you two hadn't tried to be cowboys, we could have told you that long sleeved shirts ride up on the arm. What the fuck were you two thinking?"

As they piled into another F.B.I. van, this one disquised as a delivery vehicle of a local dry cleaner, they could hear the sounds of approaching sirens. Thompson and The Fat Man both recognized the driver as a Fish Market patron who had sat at the table next to them the night before.

"I really think it's probably just a really bad bruise, Mr. Thompson, but you ought to have it checked out. Do you want to get that x-rayed here or at home?" asked the driver.

"I just want to go," said Thompson.

"I'll take you directly to the executive aviation hanger at Reagan," the driver said. "We have one of our planes waiting to take you back home to Kentucky and your election."

As Agent Argo prepared to close the door he leaned in and said to Thompson, "I'm sorry we let you take it this far."

"You're right about that," said Thompson. Then, with a puzzled expression on his face, he asked, "Wait a minute. You were at the Fish Market last night. Then, you know about Tammy?"

Argo grinned. "Well, we've had her in protective custody since just after you and Mr. Bradley said good night to her. She confirmed that everything we heard at dinner was real. But we've been keeping an eye on her for quite some time. Long before you ever met her. I'm really not at liberty to say exactly how long—let's just say that it's all part of an ongoing investigation."

"Then you knew about her and the pictures all along?" Thompson asked.

Argo looked at Thompson with a coy expression on his face. "Pictures? What pictures?" he said with a tone of exaggerated innocence. Argo locked his eyes on Thompson's, smiled and closed the van door.

EPILOGUE

During the administration of President Ronald Reagan, in protest against military action in Grenada and Lebanon, a domestic terrorist group calling themselves the Armed Resistance Unit placed a bomb just outside the front doorway of the United States Senate. The Senate was supposed to be in session late that night, but for some reason they adjourned around dinner-time instead. When the bomb detonated at 10:58 p.m., just outside the world's greatest deliberative body, there was no one in the chambers except for two staffers working late in the Republican cloak room.

The bombers had placed the brief case bomb next to one of the stone podiums holding a bust of some former Vice President, commemorating his term as President of the Senate. The bomb shattered windows and chandeliers and ripped the portrait of Daniel Webster to shreds. However, the barrier of the stone podium helped shield the blast from doing even more damage.

Security around the House and Senate was really tightened after that explosion. For the first time, staffers were required to carry identification cards and the corridors immediately around the House and Senate were closed to the general public. Today, tourists visiting the Capitol get to go within about fifty feet or so of the entrances to each Chamber, but no closer.

The sections of the United States Capitol marked off by uniformed police standing in front of purple velvet ropes hold some of our nation's greatest treasures. Original paintings and ornate sculptures are hidden in these back corridors. The reconstructed portrait of Daniel Webster, retrieved by some custodian from a garbage can following the 1983 bombing is an example of such a masterpiece.

Hidden just past the velvet ropes on the Senate side are the busts of all the Vice Presidents who have served as President of the Senate. On the rare occasions when House staffer Richard Thompson could get his friends past the ropes, he loved showing them these busts and telling stories about how these men served the Senate. "That's Hubert Humphrey, Vice President under Lyndon Johnson," Thompson would say. "Barry Goldwater said that Vice President Humphrey spoke so fast that listening to him was like trying to read Playboy magazine with your wife turning the pages. And over there is one of the greatest orators from Kentucky, Alben Barkley, the guy who got the funding to locate the Greater Cincinnati Airport in Boone County, Kentucky. In 1956, he was giving a speech at Washington and Lee College when he was asked a question about having gone from Vice President to junior Senator. He responded by saying that he'd rather be a servant in the House of the Lord than to sit in the seats of the mighty. Then he fell over dead from a heart attack. Now that's a movie script ending for any politician."

At the other end of the building, the shiny and porous marble steps just past the side door of the House Chambers held Thompson's favorite Capitol story. Those stairs are stained with the blood of Congressman William Preston Taulbee. Congressman Taulbee was a Methodist preacher from Salyersville, Kentucky who was shot outside the chambers by Charles Kincaid, a reporter for the *Louisville Times*, who had just reported the Congressman's affair with a young woman who was described by the journalist as "petite of figure, but plump as a partridge." The day prior to the shooting, the two had physically struggled over the article, and the larger Congressman had pinched the reporter's ear and told him that if he ever returned to the Capitol, he had better come back armed. The reporter did return and shot the Congressman in the head. As the Congressman fell, he tumbled down the stairs. The porous marble used in the construction of the stairs allowed his blood to penetrate. To this day, a 21ˢᵗ century visitor can still follow the stains from the droplets of blood in a path down the stairs where a pool of blood formed at the spot where he died. "They never even suspended Kincaid's press credentials," Thompson would laugh as he told visitors the story.

Just outside the front doors of the House is a small brass plaque on hinges. It covers a spot on a window frame where Representative Will Rogers once signed his name.

It was these little tidbits about the world's most important office building which Richard Thompson loved to tell visitors. When they were dating, he and Ann used to wander around the corridors until they were completely lost. They'd find a Capitol Hill Police officer to point them in a familiar direction. Then they'd do it all over again.

As a staffer for Congressman Garrett Jackson, Thompson had always liked volunteering to take tourists visiting from Kentucky who came by Congressman Jackson's office over to the Capitol for a tour. In the beginning, he'd always be sure to latch on to a tour guide, but after a year or so, he was better at conducting a tour than almost anyone hired to do so. The late Congressman always joked with his young staffer that if the "law thing" fell through, Thompson would always have his career as a tour guide to fall back on.

So, when Richard Thompson was to be sworn in as a Member of the United States House of Representatives, somehow it just felt natural that he start the day by giving his friends and family a private tour of the Capitol. Now that he had a badge on his lapel, he could go behind those velvet ropes with whomever he pleased.

The final stop was Statuary Hall, the room which used to be home to the House of Representatives, before the Capitol was expanded in 1850.

As Thompson said his goodbyes to the well wishers who were about to head upstairs to the public gallery, he reminded them to look at him on the Floor after the swearing in. "I'll open the drawer on the desk where there's a bullet hole from the Puerto Rican nationals who shot up the House from the gallery you'll be sitting in." Earlier in the tour Thompson has told his friends the story of how terrorists had rained 30 rounds down on the House Floor during a session debate over immigration reform in 1954. In true bi-partisan fashion, five

Congressmen (three Democrats and two Republicans) were wounded. The assailants were sentenced to life terms, but released by President Jimmy Carter in 1979. The drawer in the desk from which the Majority Floor Leader had spoken still bears the battle scars of the attack as an eerie reminder of the security risks of serving in the United States House of Representatives.

As the group started to make their way to the galleries on the next floor, Thompson turned and rubbed the bronze boot of the statue of Henry Clay, "The Great Communicator" from Kentucky. "This will bring a Kentuckian good luck," he said instructing Jeff and Suzanne Himes to follow suit before going upstairs. It was obvious from the statue they were not the first to do so. The tip of the boot was shiny from the rubs tourists gave it for good luck. Thompson winced as he rubbed the boot. His chest still hurt from the incredible bruise which was emblazoned on his left side.

"Well, gang, it's about that time," he said looking at his watch as he led everyone past the purple velvet ropes outside the entrance to the United States House of Representatives.

The police officer guarding the entrance to the House Chambers noticed the lapel pin on Thompson's blue suit and stood straight to greet him. "Good morning, Congressman," he said with authority. "You must be the new Member from Kentucky. I see you have the whole family here for the occasion. Good looking family, sir."

"Thank you. I've got them all here today, officer," said Thompson with a smile as he squeezed Ann's hand. "Nobody wanted to miss this one."

"Why don't you all wait around the back in the Speaker's Lobby. The kids will be more comfortable there," said the officer. "I think they're about to ring 'three bells.'"

"That badge is starting to turn me on," whispered Ann in her husband's ear.

"Better watch out," Thompson whispered back as he kissed her on the cheek, "you'll get a reputation as a badge fucker."

"There's only one badge I want and you know whose lapel it's pinned on?"

"Ted Kennedy?" said Thompson as Ann punched him in the arm.

"Congressman Thompson, I presume," said the hispanic man in the sharp suit as he stood up from his chair in the Speaker's Lobby.

"Agent, you're the last guy I expected to see here today," said Thompson with a smile on his face, as he shook his hand and then embraced him as if he were his oldest friend in the world. He winced slightly as Argo hugged him back.

"Are your ribs a little sore from the other day?" asked Argo.

"Sore isn't the word for it," said Thompson.

"Better sore than the alternative," replied Argo as he straightened Thompson's jacket near the place where Carpenter's 9mm slug was stopped by the Kevlar vest on his left side.

Ann cleared her throat in the manner that a wife does when she's being excluded from a private conversation. "Oh, my gosh, I'm sorry, hon," said Thompson, "I need to make an introduction here. Ann, this is F.B.I. Agent Leo Argo," he paused as he looked into Argo's eyes, "the man who saved my life."

Not quite knowing how to react, Ann formally shook his hand. Then, with tears welling up in her eyes, she said "Oh, what the hell," as she leaned forward and gently kissed him on the cheek. "Thank you for what you did. I owe you more than I could ever repay."

Argo looked at The Fat Man. "Mr. Bradley, the Director wants your assurance that in the future, you're content at being a lawyer and not a Special Agent. Please save your trips to Radio Shack for batteries and such."

The Fat Man lowered his head and said quietly, "Please assure the Director that my days in law enforcement are over."

"Good choice. And as for repayment, Mrs. Thompson, the Director has already told me that I'm designated to lobby your husband the next time the F.B.I. appropriation bill is up in the House. Don't worry." Argo smiled, "I'll get repayment." He turned again to Thompson. "Seriously, Congressman, I wanted to be here to wish you the best of luck. You're not like a lot of the other people out there on the Floor. Try to stay that way."

"If he changes," said Ann, as she wiped her eyes to dry away the roller coastering emotions of the day, "you have my permission to follow him again, except this time just shoot to wound."

"Whose side are you on?" Thompson asked his wife. "Neither of you have to worry," said Thompson reassuringly. "I'll never forget that I'm just a boy from Ludlow, Kentucky."

Everything on the Hill revolves around the bells that ring throughout the Capitol and the adjoining office buildings, signifying that something is about to take place on the House or Senate floor. When three bells ring, it means that Members have 15 minutes to make their way to the floor for a quorum call or some other vote.

When Thompson had been a staffer, on one occasion he was standing in the cafeteria food line with an old and colorful Congressman from Florida who was half-deaf. As they made their way down the food-line, the old man paused and grabbed Thompson's arm. Shaking it vigorously, he asked, "Young man, young man. How many bells? How many bells?" When Thompson told him that no bells had rung, the old guy shrugged his shoulders and grumbled as he turned, "Well then, I don't have to be anywhere then, do I?"

As the reunion between Argo and Thompson concluded, the three successive tones of the House bells sounded, signifying a vote on the Floor. Thompson reached for his newly acquired, government issued pager to listen to the announcement from the cloakroom.

"Three bells at 11:00 a.m. signifying that Members have 15 minutes to make their way to The Floor for a quorum call, after which the oath of office will be administered to the Gentleman from Kentucky," came the anonymous voice over the pager.

"Well, boy, I'm sure proud of you," said Griffith fighting back tears.

"Griff," said Thompson as he looked deep into Griffith's eyes. There was a moment of awkward silence. "This is the first moment in my life that I don't know exactly what to say to you...other than 'Thanks.'"

"Someday, your *Godfather* will ask a favor..." Griffith tried to start into a rant from *The Godfather*, but his emotions were getting the best of him.

"Michael Griffith, are you getting choked up?" Ann asked with fake incredulity. "See, Richard, I told you that somewhere in that crusty exterior, he had a heart."

"Griffith has a heart," said a jovial Thompson.

"Yeah. He keeps it in a jar by his desk," laughed The Fat Man. "I'm going to miss you at the firm, but you're destined for great things up here, Rick," said The Fat Man, beaming with as much pride as if it were him being sworn in instead of his best friend.

"Thanks, buddy. You went way above and beyond the call," said Thompson. "I don't know if I could have pulled this off without you by my side."

"Have fun storming the castle!" replied The Fat Man.

"You boys have got to get out and see a different movie," said Griffith in mock disgust.

They all stood around in awe of the ornate room as the bells continued to go off, indicating that Thompson's time was getting closer and closer. Members started arriving in waves, with many dropping by the small gathering to shake Thompson's hand and offer congratulations to Griffith for another brilliant victory.

Josh walked up looking more than a little excited.

"Boss! Boss! Congressman Lackner's holding a press conference at noon announcing that he's resigning his seat effective immediately. I just got a call from the Minority Leader's office. Somebody from the Judiciary Committee is getting Lackner's seat on the Rules Committee. You're getting the open spot on Judiciary. You'll be on just in time for the steroid hearings."

Thompson looked blankly at Griffith, Argo and The Fat Man and smiled. "Any idea what it's about?" he asked Josh.

"Word is that he got caught up in an F.B.I. sting and his resignation is part of the deal he cut with the U.S. Attorney in South Florida," he replied.

"Well, get a press statement ready. I'll look it over when I get back to the office," he said. "Oh, and Josh, call over to the Rules Committee. Lackner had some kid working for him as a Legislative Correspondent named Bobby Richmond. I got a good recommendation on him from the guy who was driving me around D.C. last week. Tell him I'd like to talk to him about joining our staff as our Legislative Director."

The Fat Man and Griffith laughed out loud at the reference to Thompson's driver. "What?" he said back to them, "Don't you guys think that we could use a little diversity on our staff?"

Thompson noticed Ann had been speaking to a Member from Wyoming who had sought her out. "What was that about?" asked Thompson.

"He just wanted to thank me for recommending that new case worker to his District office staff in Jackson Hole. He said he was surprised that a smart, beautiful redhead wanted to relocate her life to the mountains, but he liked her in the interview this morning and was going to offer her the job. He said you're definitely going places up here if you keep doing favors like that for other Members."

"Wyoming? You got Tammy a job in Wyoming?" asked Thompson with a laugh.

"I'm happy she's getting her life together, Rick, I really am. She just doesn't have to get it together around us."

"Tammy's going to work for a Congressman in Wyoming? Did she blow him?" asked The Fat Man.

"Maybe," said Ann. "I did tell her to be sure to impress him in the interview."

"Jackson Hole, huh?" said Griffith jokingly at Ann. "I was thinkin' of taking a couple of weeks off after this one. Maybe a fishing trip to Jackson Hole is just want I need."

"Back off, horn dog," replied Ann. "Don't think for a minute that next year you're showing up for Thanksgiving dinner at my house with her on your arm."

The White House Congressional liaison, Rob Duncan, approached Thompson with a cell phone in his hand. "Congratulations, Congressman Thompson. I've got someone here who wants to speak to you."

"Richard Thompson!" the new Member said forcefully into the receiver. As he listened, his eyes got wider than Ann had ever seen before. He stood straight up.

"Thank you, Mr. President. We'll do our best."

There was another pause as the small crowd around him pressed to listen. "I will tell her you send your best," he said as he winked at Ann.

Just then the House Doorkeeper turned around and said. "It's time, Congressman Thompson."

"I don't mean to rush, Mr. President, but I think they're ready for me now. Yes, sir. Good bye… Oh, my God, I just hung up on the

President of the United States," he laughed as he handed the phone back to Duncan.

"Well at least you didn't tell him that *Lost in Yonkers* was filmed across the street from your boyhood home," said Griffith.

"Congressman Thompson," the Doorkeeper's body language seemed to push the couple to the door.

Congressman Thompson. Wow, that sounded good.

Thompson had waited for this moment for a long time, but even so he still was not prepared for the continuum of emotions which shot through him as the door to the House was thrown open to the thunderous applause of those assembled. Well, at least one side of the room, where the Republicans sat, was thunderous. The other side, where the Democrats sat, was polite, but they were applauding nonetheless. Thompson gripped Ann's hand tightly as the family made its way to the special seats designated for them to sit in before the swearing in itself.

So many thoughts were rushing through Thompson's head. His emotions were running in 15 different directions at the same time. He was trying hard not to cry himself when he looked up into the gallery and spotted his mother standing at her seat in the Members' Family Gallery. She was not crying, but standing straight and proud and applauding along with those assembled. She blew her son a kiss and then gently pointed upward, indicating that Thompson's, dad, too was proudly looking down from his perch in Heaven. Suddenly, a wave of calm came over Thompson; he felt an inner peace of belonging. Thompson truly felt that being a Member of the "People's Chamber" was his destiny in life.

"Mr. Speaker," said the Majority Floor Leader, "It gives me great pleasure to introduce to this august body the distinguished gentleman from Kentucky's Fourth Congressional District...Congressman Richard Thompson..."

As the applause started again, Richard Thompson thought to himself:

"If Meat Loaf, John Prine and Warren Zevon could just see me now..."

Acknowledgments

Lawyers live under the mistaken impression that we can write. We're wrong. We can't. We scribe. It's good editors who help us turn our legalese ramblings into print quality fiction. Jeff and Penny Landen were constantly there to make sure that my writing didn't lapse into a brief to the Kentucky Supreme Court. Any resemblance between Jeff and The Fat Man is purely coincidental.

Likewise, Vicki Prichard was more gentle in her coach-like editing style, but she pushed me just as hard to finish. She never flinched when I told her I had a deadline and needed her help. She did actually write the AP article which appears early in the book.

In the spring of 1977, I picked up the telephone and called some guy named Barry Caldwell and volunteered to help on his campaign for the Kentucky General Assembly. Thus began my thirty plus years in politics. Barry and his wife Trina taught me basics of campaigns which could never be taught in a college political science class.

More importantly, Barry introduced me to three people: my first boss (and Barry's successor in the General Assembly whose campaign I also ran) Lawson Walker; my running mate and closest confidant in politics for the last thirty years, Debbie McKinney; and my eventual political mentor Senator Jim Bunning.

I spent six years in D.C. as Jim Bunning's Legislative Director. He hired me to that position despite the fact that I had absolutely no Hill experience on my resume. He and his wife Mary have been an important part of my family's life since that time. As Luca Brasi would say, for that I pledge my never ending loyalty.

If I owe my life in politics to Jim Bunning, I owe a lot of what is contained in the pages of this book to the Bunning family of staff who served from 1987 to present...Dave York, Jon Deuser, David Young, Blake Brickman and everyone who served under them in Kentucky or Washington or staffed a Bunning campaign over the years.

Over the years, I ran many campaigns and worked on countless others. If I had to list all of the candidates I've worked for over the years, ranging from city council candidates to those running for President, it would take a separate book. However, I've learned something from each of those campaigns which is more than a part of this book; it's a part of my internal make up. Special thanks in that regard to: Senators Bob and Elizabeth Dole, Congressman Geoff Davis, Congressman Gene Snyder, Secretary of Public Instruction Raymond Barber, Judge Executive Ralph Drees, State Representative Adam Koenig, State Representative Sal Santora, Commissioner Dave Otto, Judge Chris Mehling, Judge Patsy Summe, Mayor Ron Turner, Kevin Murphy, County Attorney Garry Edmondson, Marcus Carey, State Senator Damon Thayer, Glenn Gunning, Judge Executive Clyde Middleton, Judge Executive Dick Murgatroyd, Gordon Wade and Ken Upchurch.

Many of the places mentioned in this book are real. If you're traveling on the AA Highway anytime soon, stop in the General Store in Tollesboro, Kentucky, and say hello to Jeff and Suzanne Himes. And, at Chez Nora in Covington, Jimmy and Pati Gilliece really do prepare the best pork chops I've ever tasted.

I ran for Congress in 1998 and a lot of the people who helped me in that race will certainly find some of their own characteristics in the people who are wandering through these pages. All my county chairs and volunteers are somewhere in this book—if not in a specific character, then in the passion which caused me to write it. And I did appreciate those who drove me around the Fourth District. In particular, thanks to my campaign chairman, Fred Wolf, Mike Daley, GOP National Chairman Mike Duncan, Chief Ray Murphy, Lt. Col. Bob 'Scooter' McCray, the late Paul Proctor, Doug Morgan, Shelley and Ed Stewart, Jay Townsend, Hayes Robertson, Dave and Leslie Hatter, Jack Graham, Debbie Shannon, Bob Rusbuldt, Tony Valanzano, John Cooper, and Bill Schilling for their assistance in 1998 and their inspiration in writing this book.

The fundraisers described in this book may seem to my contributors strikingly similar to those that I held at the homes of Tim and Teresa Ann Matthews and Brian and Vicky Collins. Thanks for the use of your home and thanks to all who contributed to my efforts. Special thanks to my fundraising guests at a couple of events, Governor Carroll Campbell and P.J. O'Rourke.

While writing this book, I bugged the living hell out of a bunch of people to read, re-read and re-re-read my manuscript for their thoughts. Debbie Strietelmeier, Jeff Rohr, Amy Tolnitch, Jeff Eger, Robin DeHate, Aref Bsisu, John Carey, Mike and Debbie Edwards, Bob Schrage, Jim Lawson, Tom Saelinger (who actually gave me the idea for this book), Pat Crowley, Jim Brewer, Joe Lacy, Mike Murphy and Scott Kimmich should all be given a medal for putting up with my calls asking, "Well, what do ya think?"

Thanks to my "special research" assistants Dr. Lee Carter, Dru Ellis, and Sue Palmer-McVey. Thanks also to Kevin Kelly and Denny Landwehr for their help with the cover. And to Paul Alley who now knows all about the Fair Use Doctrine.

A lot of folks smoke in politics and I was not going to ignore that fact simply because I am an officer in the American Cancer Society. However, for programs to quit smoking, please go to www.cancer.org or call 1-800-ACS-2345.

To Mom and Dad for always wondering why I was getting mixed up with these political types, but never questioning me as to why.

Lastly, and certainly not least, thanks to my wife Linda and our three children Joshua, Zachary and MacKenzie. Over the past twenty-six years, they have put up with more missed dinners and late night phone calls from frantic candidates than they should ever have had to endure. Linda seems to read just about every book that comes out and, when I was satisfied with my book, she wasn't. There are about 10,000 plus additional words in this book because she kept telling me I wasn't done yet. I love you.

Sniper Bid

By Rick Robinson
(available in Fall 2008)

After winning a special election to the United States House of Representatives, Congressman Richard Thompson is settling into life as a new Member on Capitol Hill. The death of a fellow Congressman thrusts him center stage into the ongoing debate on steroid use in professional sports. As he pushes for answers into a southern California steroid distribution ring, someone wants him and anyone associated with the investigation, silenced.

The only question is 'who'?

While Robinson's first book, *The Maxium Contribution* takes the reader into the day-to-day operations of a modern day political campaign, *Sniper Bid* gives an insider's look into life on Capitol Hill.

For more information on Rick Robinson and *The Maximum Contribution* visit:
www.richardthompsonforcongress.com